Naomi Rose

Naomi Rose

Kirsten Esden

Matador
9 Priory Business Park,
Wistow Road, Kibworth Beauchamp,
Leicestershire. LE8 0RX
Tel: 0116 279 2299
Email: books@troubador.co.uk
Web: www.troubador.co.uk/matador
Twitter: @matadorbooks

ISBN 978 1838592 530

British Library Cataloguing in Publication Data.
A catalogue record for this book is available from the British Library.

Printed and bound in Great Britain by 4edge Limited
Typeset in 11pt Minion Pro by Troubador Publishing Ltd, Leicester, UK

Matador is an imprint of Troubador Publishing Ltd

For Tim

Preface

ALTHOUGH THE EVENTS IN THIS BOOK ARE fictitious, the character of Naomi grew from the impression left behind by a girl I knew for just six days, or at least the version of herself that she wanted me to know.

A few years back, I found myself sitting on a jury listening as a young girl gave evidence. The details of the trial have faded and, in any case, are not mine to share, but the girl's unusual character, her striking ability to perform so eloquently in such daunting circumstances, plus her father's behaviour in response to the whole spectacle, remain with me.

I came away with many unanswered questions. I also came away with a fierce reminder that without trust in our own judgement, we are always at the mercy of the storyteller.

AT THE TIME, MY ACTIONS WERE ATTRIBUTED TO the death of my mother. Naturally. Because people like to have explanation and reason and cause at their disposal so that they can understand and make sense of everything; after all, the alternative is to accept that someone may behave in a despicable manner for no other reason than to please themselves and that would never do – much better to have an explanation.

What would they say about my behaviour now, if they knew? Would my poor mother still be blamed for the decisions I make in adulthood or is there a cut-off point when grief becomes an excuse rather than a justification? Not that I've ever much cared what people think, nor given time over to questioning the past; it's the present which interests me and I was taught early on that analysing behaviour does little more than shift blame around.

God, it's hot today. I push back from my desk and head over to the window, opening it out as wide as the safety catch will allow in the hope that the air will move, even just a little. The office was chosen solely for the view with no *thought to it being west facing and on sunny afternoons the room becomes a furnace. Occasionally, it becomes too much and I close the windows and succumb to the annoying hum from the air conditioning unit; but not today, today I want to hear myself think.*

I had my pick of office spaces because, at the time, the building had been largely empty. Now, it is full of PR firms and marketing companies and solicitors, with Esme and me sandwiched neatly between them all on the fourth floor. I could have gone higher (a status thing – the higher the floor, the higher the rent), but I didn't want Esme to feel uncomfortable. Besides, I had no need for status, just a need for the view out onto the immaculately kept grounds of the clinic opposite. I like to keep an eye.

He's returned from his three o'clock tea break and I see he's decided to wear a wide, floppy hat to keep the sun off. Sensible, even if he does now resemble a cricket umpire. He works methodically, pulling at the leaves with his rake and shaking them into a growing pile. The grounds offer no shade and despite the hat, he stops frequently to run a shirt sleeve across his brow. Still wearing well-cut shirts, I note, though there is no expectation for him to do so. None of the staff wear uniform and so long as they avoid jeans, they have freedom to wear what they like. The one common accessory is the identification cards which swing about their necks on blue ribbon, something they really should change, I think; the shade is too similar to that of those worn by NHS staff, and the Wellbridge Substance Abuse Clinic is most certainly not part of the NHS – the dent in my bank balance is proof of that.

"Naomi, are you still with me?"

The rake falls to the ground and he wanders off towards the open shed beside the main building. He must be exhausted, poor thing.

"Still with you," I say, keeping my gaze fixed on the man's frame as he returns with a wheelbarrow. Is he starting to hunch over, or is it just the effort of pushing the barrow over the grass?

"So, I'll schedule the interview for ten-ish tomorrow? You have Kat's sports day and they want to start at twelve-thirty sharp before the kids get tired… you don't want to cut it too fine."

Sports day, for five-year-olds, whatever next? But the mention of my daughter is enough to pull me away from the window, and I turn to face Esme with a smile. "That sounds perfect; what would I do without you?"

She doesn't miss a beat. "You would become a sad, lonely woman. Your daughter would disown you for missing all of her important events and your books would only be read after your death because no one would know they'd been written until they were found gathering dust next to your body."

"That's cheery."

Esme grins, showing off neat dimples either side of her mouth. She is sickeningly beautiful. The colour of her smooth brown skin has been deepened a little by the recent spell of good weather and her hazel eyes – green in certain lights – are framed by long, dark lashes. It's usually her hair you notice first but today she has it scraped up into a tight, high bun. I like it best when it's left to spiral out from her *head in a cushion of caramel curls, then it reminds me of how she'd looked when I'd first met her. She's always been beautiful, but adulthood has seen her develop a certain polish. As a child, her eyebrows were little fuzzy thatches which she would wiggle proudly, one at a time; now, they are teased and plucked and arranged into neat, symmetrical arches using the mirror which sits unashamedly on her cluttered desk. Esme is proud of her appearance and makes no apologies for it. I like that about her. In fact, she makes no apologies for anything and says exactly what she's thinking and asks every question she wants an answer to with a blatant refusal to acknowledge anyone's privacy. If I'm ever vague, she'll look at me so intensely, one sculpted eyebrow raised up high, that I feel uneasy even if I'm telling the truth. Feeling uneasy is not something I am particularly familiar with; I can only liken it to going through customs at the airport and questioning whether I really do know the contents of my own luggage.*

"Okay, cool," she says, rising from the chair and scrolling through her phone. "Oh, one more thing," she looks up to catch my expression, "Kat's dad... should he meet you at the school or do you want him to pick you up?"

I sigh. "Call and say I'll pick him up, that way I won't get there smelling of kebab meat."

Esme rolls her eyes. She likes Katerina's father and thinks I'm too hard on him.

I return to the window. The sun is lower now and shadows are beginning to form across the lawn. The gardener is talking to a member of staff, the leaves all tidied away. Perhaps the older lady is his mentor. Does he even still have a mentor? It's been a year since he was taken on under the rehabilitation scheme so perhaps he no longer qualifies. Patient to apprentice to member of staff – quite the success story. Good man; it takes courage to come back fighting.

"Right, I'm off." Esme throws her phone into her enormous handbag. "I've got the release date to get out which I'll do from home tonight... unless you want to do it yourself?" But she's grinning; she knows better and doesn't bother to wait for my reply. "How's your dad doing, by the way?"

"Much better," I nod, but I'm not thinking about my father, "things are going in the right direction."

"That's good... really good. Right, see you in the morning and don't forget they'll want new photos so wear your hair down."

I poke my tongue out at her reference to my ears and she laughs her way out of the office taking the last of the sunshine with her.

A few years back, I'd plucked a teenage Esme out of a hole of impending depression and forced her to knuckle down and help me. She might have been a strange mix of glitter and gloom and "Whatevers" at the time but I had been determined to root out the clever, motivated girl who I knew was lurking inside. Now, at twenty-one, Esme is confident, bright and, despite being several years my junior, wholly indispensable.

The lady is laughing at something the gardener has said as they make their way across the lawn. They enter the clinic and out of sight for the day, and my thoughts turn to Katerina and the promise I'd made to spend the evening *going over her lines for the end of term assembly. "I've got to learn twenty-two words, Mummy," she'd said at the weekend with a huge sigh. "I really don't want to get them wrong, everyone will laugh." Katerina is five and likes to be dramatic. I don't discourage her for there's nothing wrong with a little drama. By the time she's ten years old, Kat will be playing the lead in the school productions and I'll be there to cheer her on amongst all the eye-rollers and the not-so-hushed whispers of "No prizes for guessing where she gets THAT from…"*

When I was ten years old, my mother died.

chapter one

I HADN'T BEEN TEN THAT LONG, JUST A FEW short weeks, but I already had the maturity (*everybody* said so) that accompanies double-digit status. I knew, without a shadow of a doubt, that I could cope and, more importantly, I knew I could help Dad through it. Two life-changing events in one year and it wasn't even the end of spring. The first, the significant birthday, had passed with limited fuss due to the imminence of the second, and the second, due to my father's insistence that we remain "dignified at all times", was passing now with, again, limited fuss.

It was wrong to be bored at my own mother's funeral, I knew that. But I sat picking at the pearl beading on the hem of my flouncy dress wishing that the slopey-eyed vicar would speed up his dreary voice. I was bored, not because I didn't care but because I had already said my goodbyes and had no intention of letting my father down by sharing my grief publicly. He was sitting next to me, poker-straight as always, his face arranged so that everything pointed downwards – the corners of his lips, his eyelids; even the troublesome cow's lick which lifted in the slightest breeze today played by the rules and pointed down in a gentle arc. Every now and then, his expression changed a little, as though he were contemplating the best way to appear mournful. His grief was genuine (I'd heard him crying at least twice) but if no one else knew, did it really count? Appearances were everything, after all.

"Sit still and leave your dress alone."

I flinched and stared hard at the photo propped up on the coffin. It was a beautiful black and white shot; Mum looked like a model from a magazine, all shiny, with laughing eyes and big, breeze-whipped hair. And so *young*! It had definitely been taken long before she had me.

Dad thought I was coping "admirably" with my mother's death. Miserable Joyce from next door disagreed; she felt it had not affected me the way it was supposed to; *she* thought that I wasn't sad "*enough*". I wanted to tell her that my eyes watered at the drop of a hat, making my eyelashes stick together, but of course I didn't because emotions are a private matter. I'd heard her telling Dad last week, whilst dropping off yet another disgusting quiche, that he should watch me carefully as I was behaving as though nothing had happened which "really wasn't right at all". I had wondered a lot about the correct way to behave but found it all rather confusing because on the one hand, it was odd to carry on as though everything was normal but on the other, it was what Dad wanted. In the end, it seemed easiest to stay quiet and commit to neither avenue.

The church was cold despite the sun attempting to pierce the high stained-glass windows and I wished that I had listened when Dad suggested I wear tights. He was wearing his best grey suit and yellow tie and was rigid, straight-backed and focused. I suspected he was concentrating on being dignified because when he'd been adjusting his tie this morning he'd said, "It's okay to be sad, Naomi, but sadness should be dignified. Mum wouldn't have wanted a fuss." I had loved my mother and I missed her presence and her flowery, clean scent, but I did not miss her company. She had always been sad, even when there was nothing to be sad about, and sometimes when I'd spoken she had transferred her gaze to a window and made no secret of the fact that she was thinking about something else altogether.

To stop myself pulling at a loose thread that had caught my eye on the skirt of my dress, I copied my father's pose and placed my hands in my lap. When that didn't work, I sat on them. For a moment I was still, but when a mobile phone beeped behind us, I turned with interest. A frantic rustling followed and I felt Dad's elbow nudge my hip. The vicar frowned. Dad lifted his chin.

Today was Friday. I hadn't been to school for a total of three weeks and I knew I'd have my work cut out with the girls when I returned; Imogen might be missing me but Molly and the others would definitely be preparing

3

to give me a hard time. Once, in Year 3, I had been off with a serious bout of tonsillitis and when I returned, the girls had changed the rules for all the games we played. It was only after I'd ruined our dance routine for the third time that Imogen had taken pity on me and explained that the cartwheel after the second spin was now a flip. I had nodded but I couldn't perform a flip so Molly said I shouldn't be in the dance anymore and the others had agreed, even Imogen, although she did at least have the grace to shrug and mouth "sorry".

Fridays used to be good days because Mum would pick me up from school herself rather than sending me off to one of the many after school clubs that Dad felt I should attend. We would go the long way home and stop at a café where I would have hot chocolate with marshmallows and a slice of cake without talk of it ruining my appetite. I would eat and drink happily while Mum stared out of the window. It was our secret treat, a poking-out of tongues at Dad who said that a healthy body maintained a healthy mind and the mind was very important. He was an English professor at the university and his mind was full of opinions and essays and journals and *critical thinking*. Mum's mind was full of stuff that nobody really understood. Mine was full of stories. Right now, my favourite character in the whole world was Jem Finch and even though I knew I should have been thinking about my mother, I couldn't help thinking instead of how different my life would be if I had a brother like Jem Finch. Lucky, lucky Scout. I stared at my mother's name on the order of service and tried to focus but still Jem Finch lingered.

4

Maybe Mum wouldn't mind. After all, I pilfered the book from the shelf next to her bed.

When Mum and I had last sat in that café together, I'd given myself hiccups and she'd turned from the window to laugh softly at my chocolate moustache. She was thin by then, her former softness replaced by angles and shadows, and I remember thinking her collar bone absolutely fascinating the way it jutted and moved when she yawned. I knew she was ill long before that day. Dad thought it would be easier for me to process the situation if I were to be given plenty of time, so they had me sit down one Sunday afternoon while Dad explained what had already happened, what was happening now, and then, in a strange voice which didn't really sound like his, what was most likely to happen. Mum held my hand the whole time he was speaking but when he got to that bit, she took his hand too and we sat in a sad little triangle while the sun pushed through the living room window and created a cloud of dust fairies. I don't remember crying but I do recall Mum wiping my face with a tissue and telling me to blow my nose so I suppose I must have. In the weeks that followed, I was given several opportunities to discuss my worries but I could never think of anything to say so the opportunities took the form of the three of us sitting awkwardly together at the kitchen table and not saying very much at all. Being an only child was hard work and during those awkward silences, I would wish very much that I "had a Jem" because a brother like Jem would think of something to say.

Today was not about talking. Dad had given strict instructions to keep quiet; he said that church was a place to show respect and not somewhere to have a conversation, and I had to take his word for it because the only time I had been to church in the last five years was with my class to sing carols on the last day of the autumn term. Dad said I wasn't allowed to slouch, and I should sit still and upright as though I were balancing a book on my head. Showing respect was not about feeling comfortable.

I wondered how long the service would last and whether there would be doughnuts at the wake. The chocolate I'd been given earlier had long ago melted between my tongue and the roof of my mouth and I looked down to see traces of it on my fingers. I considered licking it off but caught Joyce staring at me from the other side of the aisle and kept my hands where they were.

If I looked beyond Joyce and her grey birds' nest hair, I could see Violet's ginger head nestled between the broad shoulders of Uncle Robert and Aunt Chrissy's rounded back. I tried to catch Violet's eye but she refused to look up. I could see the cream card in her hands on which the hymn lyrics and prayers for my mother's life were printed – simple and tasteful, no fuss. Uncle Rob glanced over and caught me staring. His lips were closed and pointing downwards like Dad's, as though he were smiling upside down. In the pews behind him people were crying; a few openly, others doing that weird thing of sniffing and swallowing a lot whilst dabbing the corner of their eyes with a tissue. No one seemed particularly bothered about appearing dignified. I edged a little closer to Dad. He placed a hand on my knee and gave it a little tap before removing it again.

A few weeks ago, on one of Mum's better days, I had curled into the crook of her arm as she lay on her bed and listened as she told me about the wonderful place waiting for everyone after the moment of death had passed. I'd heard it before but I liked those rare moments when she wanted to talk so I left it a good while before I interjected with what I hoped was an intelligent, considered question: "But how is that actually possible? Mrs Palmer says that the world was created by a huge explosion and not by G…"

But Mum hadn't liked my question. She had placed her finger under my chin and tilted my face up to hers. "Mimi, surely you know better than to believe everything you hear? Mrs Palmer has to say that because there are children in your class who are from different backgrounds… different cultures and with different beliefs… it wouldn't be PC to talk about *our* God, it might be deemed *offensive…*"

PC was a term used a lot in our house and I knew what it meant. When Alfie Richards called Josh Adams "a fucking faggot" for missing an open goal at lunchtime, I'd marched over immediately to explain that it wasn't acceptable to use that sort of language and Alfie had bounced the ball on the ground between us and sneered, "*Everyone* swears."

"No, not the swearing, *the faggot bit.*"

Alfie had crinkled his nose and called me a weirdo.

"… but isn't it nicer to believe we ascend into Heaven rather than a hole in the ground?" Mum had continued. "It's like that Toploader song, darling, 'Dancing in the Moonlight', you know the one … that's kind of how I see it." She'd dragged herself into a sitting position and taken

7

my hands. "So, 'moonlight' because it's the end of the day and kind of the end of life, but 'dancing' with happiness because we know what's about to come... do you see?"

I hadn't seen at all, and now, in the church, it seemed as though no one else did either. There was not one person in the church who looked remotely happy at the thought of Katherine Rose leaving this world for the eternally flowering gardens and sunshine and laughter and love of Heaven. The only person in this church who believed things were better after death was my mother herself. And perhaps the vicar.

I leaned my head against the soft wool of Dad's jacket and slipped my hand into his pocket for warmth.

"Stop it," he hissed, "you've had all the chocolate."

I lifted my head. "But I—"

There was no time to clarify my intentions because at that moment the organ launched into a heavy hymn and the congregation shuffled to their feet. Retracting my hand as we both stood, I stared at the words on the order of service. Dad's voice was strong and low, and I tried to join in with the unfamiliar melody, every now and then glancing up to see if I could catch a reassuring wink or a smile, but Dad was still concentrating hard. It was such a miserable hymn and *so* slow; my heart sank when I realised there were two more verses on the next page.

After the service, everyone wanted to talk to Dad. I heard the same couple of sentences over and over: "Oliver, it was a lovely service", "I'm so sorry for your loss", and to me, lots of, "Your mother would have been so proud of you". I snuck under Dad's jacket but he kept pulling me out and making me stand tall. People were stroking my cheek and ruffling my hair, making it even more tangled than it was already. Combing after bath time was going to *kill*.

"... and you, my darling, are quite simply the bravest little girl I have ever met..."

I crushed my head into Dad's waist and peered at a short, fat woman in a black and yellow jumper. She looked like a bumblebee.

"I'm Genevieve," she said, "I used to work with Mummy in the bookshop, she was *such* a lovely lady." The bumblebee was now holding my hand, and I could feel the pressure of Dad's hand on my back so I knew he wanted me to come out from under his jacket. I stepped forwards reluctantly. "You look so much like her... same dark eyes, same blonde hair... such a wonderful combination... dark and fair... I used to say to Mummy she had hair like the 'Timotei' girl." Genevieve stopped and chuckled which made her chest jiggle beneath her jumper. "Of course you won't know those ads, will you? It's all 'L'Oréal' and *because I'm worth it*, now." She leaned over and kissed my cheek and I disappeared back under Dad's jacket.

"Now, Oliver," I heard her say with a voice suddenly low and serious, "Kathy was a good friend to me when I started working at the shop. She made me welcome and helped me feel right at home..."

I was used to people speaking about my mother like this – "so sweet, so full of love". Odd when I remembered her mostly as sad.

"... even though I was always struggling with the guilt of leaving the kids... and then of course she was always rearranging her shifts to help me out when I couldn't get childcare…"

I hadn't known this. I wondered whether Genevieve sometimes returned the favour so that Mum could leave work and pick me up on a Friday.

"… so look, if there's anything… anything at all I can do to help… if you ever need—"

"That's incredibly kind," Dad was saying now. "Katherine spoke very highly of you, Genevieve. I'll be sure to let you know if you can help."

"Can we *go* now, Dad?" I leaned heavily against his hip and he stumbled an inch to his left.

"Naomi, *please*."

"Oh dear, I cannot imagine how difficult this is for you, my darling…"

I fixed my gaze upon Genevieve's wide ankles and willed her to go away.

"She's coping very well," said Dad, "but I'm sure you appreciate it's a difficult time. In fact, we really should be making our way outside now; if you'll excuse us, Genevieve?"

As the bumblebee shook her head sadly at the tragedy of it all, I took Dad's hand and he led me down the aisle towards the light outside. It was only when we stepped into the glorious sunshine that I noticed the unmistakable trace of chocolate on his suit.

After a short ceremony in the grounds of the church where the long wooden casket containing my mother was lowered into a deep hole, I stood very still and looked up at the sky. All around me people were talking softly, murmuring words of condolence and love. I listened to the birds chattering in the nearby trees. They sounded happy. I had an urge to sit down on the grass and did so, just a foot or so from the grave. The grass was cool and tickled my bare legs. I leaned back on my hands so I could still look up at the sky.

"Oh, Oliver, look. Is she okay, do you think?"

It was Aunt Chrissy who I knew in a moment would want to sit and pull me into her warm squishy arms as she had done a million times. She would expect me to cry; everyone expected me to cry but I couldn't understand the obsession with it.

From inside that wooden box I hoped Mum would still be able to hear the birds, even though she had never liked birds because once, as a child, a baby herring gull had swooped on her chips and made her jump so badly she had fallen over. But these birds wouldn't hurt her, they were just starlings – small, chattery and happy.

"Naomi, stand up. It's time to go." Dad's hands appeared under my arms and lifted me gently. I rose to my feet, and immediately his hands were replaced by my aunt's as she turned me round to face her and pulled me into the anticipated embrace. She whispered soppy things into my ear that I didn't want to hear and I rested my head on her chest and focused on the birds. Small, chattery and happy... Small, chattery and happy. I could see people starting to move away from the graveside and I watched them as they linked arms, blew noses and smiled through their sadness.

chapter two

THE MERTON SUITE IN THE KING'S ARMS WAS CRAMMED
with people. Aunt Chrissy still had hold of my hand and was
asking me if I needed the toilet but I just wanted Dad, not
the loo. I stood on tiptoes to search for his grey suit amongst
the mostly black, eventually spotting him as he wove between
guests, nodding and shaking hands with all of those sad
grown-ups that I didn't know. When Dad smiled, even sadly,
his cheeks dented in the middle – "overgrown dimples", Mum
had called them – and his persistently furrowed brow opened
out flat. I thought he was very handsome.

"I want to go and stand with Dad."

My aunt looked down at me and put her head to one
side. There was only a year between her and Dad but

she looked much younger than him; her face was round like her body and her skin soft and smooth. I imagined she was wrinkle-free because she didn't worry as much as Dad did about the environment and the impact of technology on children and the plight of young factory workers in Bangladesh and *how on earth we were going to stop Tesco from taking over the world*. Dad was concerned about humanity; Aunt Christine was concerned about the football clashing with *EastEnders*. She wore too much eyeliner and it escaped into the corners of her eyes, like now. In a moment, she would raise her chubby little fingers and scoop out the excess.

"I think we need to let Daddy talk to people, Mimi. Why don't we go and get something to eat and then we can go and find out where Violet's got to?"

I watched Dad become swallowed up in hugs and handshakes and kisses to his dented cheeks. My face grew hot and I pulled my hand away, crossing my arms over my flouncy dress. My tummy hurt. A woman with a loud voice came over to talk to Aunt Chrissy and I took the chance to slip off into the throng of people, ducking under arms and narrowly avoiding waiters with trays of drinks until I reached Dad and snaked my arms around his waist.

"Nah nah *naah*… I don't believe it! Who is this little beauty, all grown up?"

A man with a bald head in the shape of a lightbulb was grinning down at me and whacking Dad hard on the shoulder. He had the brightest, whitest teeth I had ever seen.

"*Mate*, this *cannot* be your baby though, little Mimi?"

Dad manoeuvred me away from his body and held me straight. "Yes, this is Naomi. Say hello to Mo, Naomi. Mo is an old friend of mine."

"Hello, Mo," I said, looking directly at his teeth.

Dad nudged my arm and frowned. "Don't stare."

"Nah, mate, she's alright. She just lost her mum, innit?" Mo leaned in close to Dad before adding, "Anyway, she most likely thinks I look a bit strange – it's like spot the commoner round 'ere, know what I mean? You mixing with a *posh* crew now for definite!" He threw his shiny head back and laughed loudly, making other people in the room turn and stare too. I noticed that at least two of his teeth were coated shiny gold. His laugh ended in a long downwards arc and then stopped abruptly. "Oh, sorry, mate, not the time for jokes… just that, you know… kinda different *breed* in this room, know what I mean?" Mo placed his hands into the pockets of low-slung trousers and craned down to my level. He seemed huge but he was just tall. A long, spindly body in baggy clothes.

"So, Mimi, how old are you now? Last time I saw you I reckon you'd just been born," he said, turning to me.

"I'm ten."

"Ten? Naaaah, you're not ten! Can't be a decade since I see your dad…" He looked up at Dad. "Olly, mate, it's never a decade since I see you, is it?"

"Could well be," Dad said as he looked over Mo's shoulder and waved at a couple making their way across the room with food-laden plates. "Time flies, I'm afraid."

Mo lurched up and did his funny laugh again. "Ooh, get you with your accent – '*I'm afraid… Time flies*' – what happened, mate? I reckon you the only man who can leave London for Essex and manage to go *up* the social ladder!"

Dad smiled, but it was his fake smile again, the one he used at parents' evening when Mrs Palmer told him I was bright and he had to tell *her* that bright children needed pushing before they became bored. "It's North Essex. We live in *North* Essex, it's very nice."

Mo nodded his agreement but winked at me when he said, "Right…" Then he placed a hand on Dad's shoulder and his voice grew serious. "Anyway, as I said, it's not the time, is it? Don't matter where you live, no one should have to go through this shit…"

I gaped at Mo and then giggled. Dad frowned and did something weird with his head, trying to nod at me without me seeing him do it. I liked Mo and his gold teeth. I liked that he laughed at funerals even though you weren't supposed to, and I liked that he accidentally swore in front of me. I had never heard an adult swear. Alfie and Josh were always using the S-word, and I told them over and over that swearing shows a lack of available vocabulary, but they always answered with "Well, you're a fucking weirdo," before running off.

"… I mean, I couldn't believe it when I heard, mate. Devastated I was, fuming that life could be so shit as to take away one of the good ones, know what I mean? No one deserves to die young but 'specially not a good one, like Kath. Cancer's a shitter… really is." Mo's expression altered as he spoke, eyebrows reaching for the sky one moment and plummeting into a frown the next. I watched, fascinated.

"Naomi, why don't you go off and play with Violet?" Dad was doing that thing that he did when he wanted me to go away – hands on my shoulders, turning me physically. I could see Violet in the corner of the room sitting on a chair playing with a games console and swinging her legs. I didn't want to go over, I wanted to stay and listen to Mo and his terrible language. I stiffened and fought against Dad's fingers as they dug into my skin.

Although Violet was the same age as me, we had little in common. The last time we had seen each other was a week before Christmas during the small, sedate family get together, which came filled with the underlying sense that it would be the last we would ever have. We spent most of the day in Violet's bedroom while the adults talked about *how they would all cope afterwards*. After closing the bedroom door, Violet had dragged me over to look at her Barbie collection. I hated playing with dolls, not because I was too old (though I was), but because Violet was so bossy about what was allowed to happen. Now and then I had tried to vamp up the game with a more interesting storyline, but Violet always took umbrage with the idea of Barbie running off barefoot with the cool lifeguard and would promptly re-dress her in a floral skirt and black boots and send her on a date with Ken. It always had to be Ken.

Dad released my shoulders with a gentle shove and I mooched over to where my cousin sat. She was short like Aunt Chrissy and had a body like a little barrel and bare thighs which squidged out on the chair beneath her grey school skirt. Her ginger hair was tightly plaited in bunches with an enormous green bow on each side, but it wasn't a nice strawberry ginger like Imogen's, it was a proper *orange* ginger. Mum used to say the best hairstyle to protect against nits was plaits and I suspected Aunt Chrissy felt the same. I did not want to catch nits, mainly because of the *blatant embarrassment* but also because the thought of Dad reaching for that tiny metal comb made me shudder and want to gather all my hair inside a protective fist.

"Hi."

Violet was directing coloured blocks into various positions at the bottom of the screen and did not look up. "Hi. Sorry about your mum," she said.

I sat on the chair next to her and watched the coloured blocks disappear when they were placed into complete lines. "S'okay. Thanks. What you playing?"

"Do you want a go? Hold on, let me get you to the next level and I'll show you what to do."

I shrugged and crossed one leg over the other, but it was uncomfortable and I uncrossed it again. On the other side of the room Dad was gesturing a need to move away from an oblivious Mo who was still talking loudly. A red-headed woman approached from the other side of the room, touched Dad lightly on the arm and gave him a kiss on the cheek. Even then, Mo continued to talk. The woman looked across at me and smiled sadly like everyone else did then she patted Dad again and nodded in my direction. I edged closer to Violet and kept my head lowered.

"Hello, my darling, what are you watching?"

She smelt of shampoo, or fabric softener. "Just a game, it's my turn next."

The woman paused. "Well, I just wanted to say, your mother would have been so proud of you today. All these people, wanting to pay their respects and you, you've simply been a little star, haven't you?"

When people spoke to me, they changed their voices into something high and fluffy and called me "darling" or "sweetie" or "little star" instead of my actual name. And they felt the need to touch me – a pat on the head or a stroke of my cheek – like I was some sort of pet. It wasn't even because Mum was dead because they'd always done it. Mum said it was because I was so beautiful that they found me irresistible, but I knew this wasn't true because Aunt Chrissy said I had an interesting face – "a clever girl with an interesting face" – and I also knew I wasn't that pretty because my ears stuck out and Alfie Richards said my forehead was "massive". But I was definitely prettier than Suzy Longman because her new teeth were too big for her face and stuck out at weird angles and I blatantly had nicer hair than Imogen's because Imogen's hair, despite being strawberry ginger, was thin and wispy and never stayed in her ponytail whereas mine was long and thick.

"You probably don't remember me; I met you once when you came into work with Mummy. I'm Angela. Your mum and I worked together in the shop. She was a wonderful woman… and such a proud mum, she loved the bones of you, she really did."

I stared at the woman. Her nose had a bump on the bridge and there was a large red spot to the left of her nose which I couldn't take my eyes off; the redness matched the colour of her hair – fiery, angry. What a strange saying –

"loved the bones of you" – as though there was no flesh or features, just skeleton.

"Yes, I miss her very much," I said to the spot. That was the right thing to say, wasn't it? I wanted the woman to go away so that I could have a turn on the game that Violet was at last holding out for me.

"Yes, you must do. But, you know, you have a wonderful father over there and lots and lots of people around who care about you and want to do anything they can to help out. I've already offered to have you over if Daddy needs to work so maybe we'll get to know each other a little better in the future."

I very much hoped not. Angela flicked her hair away from her shoulders with an air of finality. "Anyway, lovely to see you, darling. I'll leave you to get on with your game."

I took the console from Violet and concentrated on the blocks while the woman walked away.

"People are weird, aren't they?" Violet whispered.

"Yeah, really weird," I said, thinking about the huge bows in Violet's hair.

A few weeks ago, when Mum knew she was going to die *imminently* (the word was bandied about the house a lot at the time just so as I was fully prepared), she called me into the bedroom and asked me to reach under the bed to fetch a large cardboard box. It was prettily decorated with blue and green flowers and had a matching lid. I'd seen such boxes in the stationery section at Tesco and was told they were for filing important papers. She'd seemed like her old self and I'd embraced the feeling of her being really *present,* curling up happily next to her on the bed. I'd opened the lid carefully, sensing I should conceal my excitement because it probably wasn't appropriate to be excited when Mum was dying. This box did not contain papers. Placing an arm around my waist and hugging me close, Mum had whispered, "Just a few essentials, sweetheart."

Inside was the most fascinating array of items and I'd lightly fingered each one in turn. First, a brush – circular and black, designed to work gently through even the most unruly hair. A diary – a bright marbled cover containing enough space on each page to write or draw whatever I was feeling on a particular day because "sometimes we work through emotions best by writing them out", and then a small cardboard box containing a leaflet and ten little tubes wrapped in green paper. I'd picked up the box and examined it carefully, pulling out a single tube and turning it in wonder and then quickly stuffing it back from where it had come.

"Come on now, no need to be embarrassed… you won't need these yet, but I want you to know that they are there for when the time comes. And when it does, you will tell Daddy and he will get them for you in future but the first time… I need you to understand what to do. This here," she said, unfolding the accompanying leaflet with a slight giggle, "will explain everything in more detail and look, it shows you exactly how to put it in!"

I giggled too then but I couldn't take my eyes off the diagram; what an extraordinarily odd-looking thing the vagina was; how strange that I would somehow have to place one of those paper-wrapped tubes up inside it. I was aware of Mum watching me and I turned to see her pale, hollow face twisted in a mixture of emotion and amusement. But it was the final item in the box that had been my favourite. Trying not to appear too keen, I had purposely left it until last to pull out the small white bra with the tiny pink bow in the centre. The material was soft and stretchy and really very pretty.

"Again, you won't need it yet but it's there for whenever you do. For now, you can keep on wearing your crop tops under your uniform but perhaps when you get to secondary school, you might want to try it out?"

But of course, there was no way I was going to wait that long and the very next morning, I'd tiptoed back into the room while my mother slept and removed the bra from the box and that same day, I'd called Imogen into the toilets at break time and lifted my shirt proudly.

"Wow, that is *really* cool," she'd said, her eyes wide.

I had barely made it through to the third level on Violet's game before Dad was calling me back over, saying it was time to have some food. Mo had moved away and was standing in the corner of the room speaking loudly into a mobile phone – I guessed, as he had a lot to say, he needed someone to talk to while Dad was busy with other people. The food on the buffet table looked unappealing and my reluctance to choose more than a sausage roll resulted in

Dad taking the paper plate from my hands and working his way down the table, piling it up with various beige foodstuffs.

"Daddy, I don't like those," I said, petulantly removing a chicken drumstick from the pile and dropping it back onto the platter from which it had come.

Dad sighed quietly but his shoulders drooped. "Fine, but you really shouldn't put food back once you've touched it."

"But I don't want it."

"No, but… oh, never mind."

Uncle Robert appeared over Dad's shoulder, his head to one side. "Oliver, how are you doing?"

Dad handed me the plate and turned with a shrug. "I just want this all to be over," he said quietly.

My uncle patted Dad's shoulder and nodded gently; he had a knack not only for smiling upside down but for showing his affection even when the words were missing. Dad leaned into him momentarily and then righted himself. I snuck a handful of Pringles onto my plate.

"Well, don't feel you need to stay longer than necessary. Chrissy's doing the rounds, playing hostess… people will understand…"

My aunt was at that moment being harangued by Joyce who had a bee in her bonnet about something. Mum used to say that Joyce always had a bee in her bonnet and that was why she was always twisting her head round, getting involved in everyone else's business; I thought she'd never get a bonnet to sit atop of all that wiry hair. I watched her dip her head towards a man helping himself to food at the table and then, with pursed lips, shake her head at Aunt Chrissy.

A piece of sausage flew out of the gap where I'd lost a tooth and landed on Uncle Robert's shiny black shoe.

"Naomi!" Dad's tone was sharp.

"Sorry, Uncle Rob," I said, "I just lost a tooth, see?" I opened my mouth wide to show off the gap on the bottom row. "And food keeps escaping."

He put an arm around my shoulders and laughed. "Don't you worry, Mimi, tooth loss creates all kinds of precarious predicaments."

"Like what?" I asked. "Other than flying food, I mean."

But before he could answer we were rejoined by Mo as he ended a call on his phone.

"Mate, I'm gonna have to shoot. I'm so sorry but Taylor's being a little shit again, and Esme is screaming blue murder."

"That's quite alright, Mo." Dad offered his hand which Mo pumped up and down vigorously. "It was good of you to come. Let's not leave it so long again." The fake smile was back, and I believed that Dad did not really mind leaving it so long.

"Right," Mo said, and then his voice went loud and high again. "Well, take care, mate, and you know… anytime you want to chat… goes without sayin', you know?" He splatted Dad on the back one last time and gave a final grin down at me. "See you soon, little lady," and he was gone.

"Maybe I'll have to get gold teeth if my gaps don't fill out," I said, but Dad was staring at Mo's retreating back. Eventually, people started to leave and Dad murmured that we were going home. As we made our way towards the exit I could feel the eyes of the last remaining mourners upon us. I felt their pity for the man who had lost his wife so tragically early, and for me, the little girl who would grow up without her mother. The sympathy ebbed around the room but I didn't know what to do with it, so I copied Dad and made my back straight and tall and kept my eyes forward. Uncle Rob and Aunt Chrissy walked with us and Violet trailed behind with her game until I heard her being told to "put the damn thing away". Outside, the sun had disappeared behind a thick wedge of cloud and I shivered my way across the car park to where a taxi waited with softly humming engine.

"Are you sure you don't want us to come back to yours tonight?" Uncle Rob asked, opening the back passenger door and gesturing for me to get in. His hair was slicked to one side but a few greying strands had made their escape across his forehead.

"No, honestly, I'm good. I want it to just be the two of us tonight."

"Okay, if you're sure? But—"

"I know, and I'll call you if I change my mind."

I watched from the back seat as my uncle pulled Dad into a tight embrace before moving to allow Aunt Chrissy to do the same. She was crying again and Dad kissed the top of his sister's head before gently pushing her away. Next to them, Violet stood and gave me a little wave. I lifted my hand and waved back. Dad slid into the seat next to me and closed the door. He sighed heavily and leaned his head on the back of the seat, gave our address to the driver and placed his arm around my shoulders, drawing me to him. "I'm proud of you, Naomi," he said into my hair as I wrapped my right arm around his waist and squeezed him tight.

Even though we'd already been alone for a couple of weeks, I hadn't noticed the quietness of the house until now. There had always been a phone ringing, or somebody popping in with flowers or a home-cooked meal or an offer to look after me if Dad needed a break. Now we were *really* alone, just Dad and me, and neither of us seemed to know what to do. He asked if I wanted something to eat; I said that I'd help myself and he looked incredibly relieved.

I left him slouched on the sofa with a glass of foul-smelling whisky and padded into the kitchen. When I returned a moment later with a glass of milk and a plate of leftover biscuits, Dad was lying on the sofa, legs tucked up under him like a child. He was crying into a cushion, weird little strangled sobs, and the whisky glass sat empty on the carpet. I stood motionless, mildly horrified, and then turned and left, pulling the door gently closed.

Upstairs, I tried to manoeuvre my bedroom door handle open without spilling milk and managed to catch the sleeve of my dress on the corner of my ballerina nameplate. I heard the rip of material. But who cared? I'd never wear this dress again.

Arthur was curled into a tight ball on my pillow and refused to move when I prodded him, so I lay down next to him, burying my cheek into his tabby fur. There was a long crack in my ceiling which Dad had promised to replaster several times. When I stared at something hard, I could blur my vision, and I tried this now, fixating on the widest area of the crack until the line became a foggy smudge. Arthur woke briefly, stood up and arched, then resettled himself in the opposite direction. I refocused and sat up. I reached for my new diary, located a biro from under the bed and wrote today's date, underlined it three times and stared at the blank page. After a moment, I wrote, "Today, the world was proud of me," then I closed the diary, retrieved *To Kill a Mockingbird* from the drawer of my bedside cabinet and curled up under the duvet.

chapter three

DESPITE MY FEARS, I RETURNED TO SCHOOL TO find that I had achieved a celebrity status of sorts. The boys continued to ignore me but the girls took it upon themselves to "look after" me and for the first time ever, Imogen and I did not have to ask to spend break time as part of a group. It was a revelation. We were used to circling the playground as a sad duo yet suddenly, Molly Smith and Nadia Begum were at our sides, linking arms and leading us towards the coveted picnic benches where Suzy and two other girls *moved over* to allow space for us to sit down. I tried catching Immy's eye as she sat but she was busy, already nudging up to Molly and giggling, her smile wide and toothy. Impossibly grateful.

"So, Naomi, what was it like, was it awful?"

All eyes fell in my direction. I looked around at the expectant faces of girls who had competently avoided more contact with me than was absolutely necessary for the best part of six years and tried to savour the moment. I wanted to resent their cruel laughter when Alfie tripped me up in PE last term, and when Josh stuck Blu Tack in my hair in singing assembly; I wanted to remind them of how they'd changed the rules of our games and their snide remarks about being "a *boring* walking dictionary"; I wanted to grab Imogen's hand and march her off and say, "Sorry girls, we don't need you actually..." and watch their stupid faces melt into open-mouthed incredulity. But I couldn't do it. My lips curled into a smile, and I pressed my hands together beneath the table as my entire body tingled with a sudden warmth and confidence; I was inexplicably giddy that these girls were asking *me* questions, looking at *me*, giving *me* the time of day.

"Well, it wasn't pleasant..." I began, "She was in a lot of pain." As I spoke, I played to their reactions. The wider their eyes, the worse I made it sound until I was no longer talking about my own mother but some distant fictional character.

Thankfully, Mum had spent her last few days dosed up in an unrecognisably dreamy state before succumbing peacefully in her sleep, just the way that Dad had hoped. But my audience did not want to hear such a tame tale and I owed it to the opportunity to make the most of it; I gauged their reactions and vamped up the death scene into an almighty torment simply *intolerable* to *witness*...

Mum doubled over in agony... nothing the doctor could give her... Aunt Chrissy sobbing... Dad beside himself with grief...

And I had their absolute attention, the whole table in the palm of my hand.

By the time I had finished speaking, Molly's blue eyes were huge and pooled with tears, and Nadia and Imogen were openly sobbing. I sat back with an immense feeling of satisfaction. But if I was glad to have made such an impact with my story, I was equally as cross with Imogen because she knew full well it hadn't happened like that and I certainly didn't want her tears diverting the attention from me when we went back to class.

The other girls at the table were silent but I could see that my words had affected them too. Maia, immediately to my right, placed a hand tentatively on my shoulder like an adult might. Suzy shook her curly head and said, "That's just awful, Nae, I'm really sorry." It was the first time anyone other than Imogen had abbreviated my name at school and I struggled greatly to maintain my mask of sadness.

The remainder of the week passed in a blur. At break and lunchtime, the girls swarmed and fought over who would sit next to me. During a practical lesson on the solar system, I was chosen to be the sun while the "planets" circled me adoringly, and for the first time ever, I was not the last to be picked for the hockey teams. Imogen fared equally well (as I suspected she might) achieving popularity by default, and her cheeks shone pink with happiness. The boys, though keeping their distance, could not help but notice the shift in classroom dynamics and on

Friday, Alfie Richards made his way over to the cloakroom where we were gathering our belongings and nudged me with his shoulder.

"Oh yeah," he muttered, "I meant to say before… sorry about your mum though."

And I stared open-mouthed at his skinny back as he sauntered off, shirt untucked; cool, too-long hair swept to the side. First time he had ever bothered to speak to me… unless you counted the time he called me a *weirdo*.

Dad and I settled into a routine of sorts. He went back to work but swapped some classes around so that he could be there for when I got home each day, and I would walk the short distance from school and open the front door to the sound of pots crashing about in the kitchen as he prepared dinner.

That Dad cooked was not unusual; for as long as I could remember, he had been the one to provide the evening meal while Mum lay on the sofa, exhausted, reading or watching television. I was never sure why she was so tired but if I ever asked Dad, he just said that she was going through a tough time and had a lot on her mind. It was Aunt Chrissy who first used the "D" word.

I had been six years old, colouring at the kitchen table one Sunday afternoon while Mum slept upstairs. Aunt Chrissy was standing near the sink and speaking to Dad in a funny hushed voice.

"She's not right, Oliver, surely you can see that?"

I dropped a crayon on the floor and slid off my chair to retrieve it.

"Leave it, Chrissy, please? I'm dealing with it."

"How? By letting her sleep all day?" She glanced in my direction and dropped her voice still further. "When's the last time she took that child out to the park, or walked her to school?"

My hearing was impeccable. Mrs Palmer said I had the ears of a bat.

"She picks her up every Friday."

"Once a week. Come on, she's depressed, she must be."

"For God's sake, she's holding down a job, how can she be depressed if she's managing to get to work every day?"

I picked up my crayon. I knew that Dad was lying because quite often he brought me back from a school club and Mum was already home and dressed in leggings and a jumper which I did not think were her work clothes.

"Just leave us be. Why are you always here anyway?"

And then my aunt had huffed and lifted her handbag from the side and walked away, ruffling my head on the way out. From then on, I had taken more notice of Mum's behaviour. Even at that young age, I was able to sense that certain things were not to be remarked upon but I began to notice the times when Mum cried over a ladder in her tights or ate nothing but bread, or when she stopped washing her luxuriant "Timotei" hair so that it became dull and stringy, and when she disappeared to make a cup of tea only to return from the kitchen empty-handed. I knew Mum was sad and that it made her forgetful, but I also knew better than to mention it. *Best just to get on with things.*

Since the funeral, people had gone back to living their lives, giving us space to *come to terms* with it all. I wasn't quite sure what it meant to come to terms with it all or really how to go about it, but I imagined that whatever it entailed would probably take a while. I expected Dad to mope and let things slide like a bereaved character in one of Mum's novels; I envisaged scratching around for something to eat amongst piles of dirty crockery, imagined searching through unlaundered clothes for a crumpled uniform and getting to school late in the mornings, but I was wrong. Dad became increasingly efficient; after sitting down to our evening meal, he would spend an hour going over my multiplication problems and spellings before sending me off for a bath while he made a start on looking through his students' work. Everything was ordered and neat and rigid. And I tried to be grateful that Dad was putting my needs, especially my academic needs, above everything else but just occasionally, I wanted to talk about non-serious stuff and it was a little hard to find the time because of all the order and neatness and rigidity.

The day that Alfie spoke to me in the cloakroom was monumental. Elated, I skipped home to find Dad at the dining room table surrounded by piles of typed pages all covered in his familiar inky scrawl. Before he could say a word, I climbed onto his knee and wrapped an arm around his neck. He made a sound somewhere between a grunt and a sigh and ushered me off. Undeterred, I clung to his arm and told him that the girls were really looking after me at school and that I felt I had some new friends. Still wearing his work attire – blue shirt, dark tie – Dad shuffled some papers to the side and gave a tiny nod of acknowledgment. His face had thinned, making his cheekbones sharper than ever.

"Dad?"

He glanced up briefly. "That's good news, Naomi. I'm glad."

But he didn't *seem* glad, so I tried again. "Really, up until now, I've only had Imogen but it's like, with Mum and everything…"

But he was already lost, fiddling with the damn papers on the table.

"Dad!"

"I'm listening…"

I stared at the smattering of grey on top of his head and grew cross. Then I remembered that I wasn't supposed to upset my father because he was grieving, so I let my shoulders sag and muttered that I was going upstairs to my room.

"Yes, fine. I'll get on with dinner in a bit and then we'll have some time to practise your maths, okay?"

I nodded, but he wasn't looking.

Someone must have had a word with him around that time. I guessed it was Aunt Chrissy because she asked *a lot* about how we were getting on and when I said sadly, "Dad cares more about his work than about me," she told me that I had to be very patient. Still, she must have mentioned something to him and whatever it was did have a brief effect because for a while afterwards, Dad made a real effort to look at me when he spoke, and he even remembered to ask after Molly and Nadia and Suzy.

"Do you remember my old school friend Mo?" he asked one evening, after I'd filled him in on the important facts about who sat where at lunch. "He was at the funeral, quite—"

"Yes! I remember him." How could I forget Mo, with his shiny bald head and magic gem teeth?

"He's coming over." Dad shrugged out of his jacket and loosened his tie. "Mo and I used to have a lot in common. If we had stayed in London, we… well, sometimes life gets in the way…"

"In the way of what?"

He was stacking plates now and paused to lick a dot of pasta sauce from his thumb. "Staying in touch. People take different paths. Your mother and I felt it best to move out and bring you up in quieter surroundings… we wanted to give you a safe environment with opportunities."

"Is London not safe?" For me, London was a magical place full of music and theatres and different sorts of people. Dad had taken me there twice, once to see *The Lion King* and once to see *Swan Lake* – I could not imagine how anywhere so lit up and vibrant could be dangerous.

"It is, for the most part, yes. But it is also overcrowded and expensive; your mother was uneasy there, and I wanted to be able to afford somewhere bigger to live, with a garden."

I liked it when he spoke to me as though I was an adult who understood things like house prices, so I collected cutlery and nodded enthusiastically. "I think London is amazing. But I really like it here too," I added, ever eager to please.

Mo arrived just as I was putting away the final plate. He was an amalgamation of grin, noise and colour; his dark jeans rolled up above the ankle revealing skinny legs and vast trainers, while on top he wore a black puffa jacket over a lurid pink T-shirt – most likely the *London look,* I concluded sagely. I stood at the open door and he flung his arms out to the sides expectantly. I smiled politely and offered my hand as Dad had taught me to do with people I didn't know well, but Mo laughed and playfully hit my outstretched palm with his hand.

"What's this all about, Dad bin teaching you social etiquette? No need for that with Mo, Mimi… now give me a proper welcome."

I stepped forward and put my arms tentatively around his waist. He smelt of aftershave and chewing gum.

"Dad's in the kitchen. Come through," I said, in my best adult voice.

"Aren't you just the little lady of the house!" Mo laughed again as he followed me down the hall. Dad was opening a bottle of wine in the kitchen but promptly put it down to shake Mo's hand.

"Good to see you, Mo. It really is."

And I saw that his smile was genuine this time, the kind I had not seen for a while.

"I need to finish my homework, Dad," I said, thinking that he probably wanted me out of the way so that it wouldn't matter if Mo dropped the F-word. Or the S-word. Or any other word that I wasn't supposed to hear at my age.

"Good idea, Naomi, you go on up. Oh, and on the way, could you move your shoes from the top of the stairs… accident waiting to happen."

I nodded. Before I could pull the door shut, Mo launched into a tirade of speech as though continuing a previous conversation and, enthralled by such energy and enthusiasm suddenly spilling into our quiet house, I left it ajar and loitered in the hall to listen for a moment.

"Man, I am proper knackered! So, I said to Benjamin only last week that he needs to be cleaning them machines *proper*, you know? Ain't no good jus' wiping round the edges, you gotta get right in there, right into the cracks 'cos that's where the germs breed, you know? He ain't got a clue though, just looks at me like he stoned or something and I say, 'c'mon, man, get with it, if you ain't awake, you're asleep, you know?' An' we can't be serving no food and drinks in a place with bare germs breeding 'cos we'll get shut the fuck down quicker than you can pour that wine, you know? Don't suppose you've got a beer, have you? Wine plays havoc with my brain, can't remember a damn thing the next day."

"Of course, yes, I should have offered…"

I heard the fridge being opened and shut and then the click of a ring-pull.

"Cheers, mate. See, it ain't all pie and gravy and fish and chips… there's a *lot* more to it… people expect the best now, they expect the same quality of food as they get in a fancy place, but they want it at half the price and you know what half the price means, right? Yep, half the wages and half the staff. They jus' don't get it, no one gets it, only ones that get it are the real people, the workers… hey, you okay, man?"

"I'm fine," Dad said. "Honestly, Mo. You know, you're like a breath of fresh air. I'm so fed up with hearing how sorry everyone is that it's refreshing to listen to the dramas of pub catering instead. Really, please go on."

"Uh-huh… but I know I have a tendency to talk too much so… only if you're sure? I dunno though, you seem a little… down to me. I'm thinking maybe you're a bit depressed or something… now don't get all defensive because there ain't no shame in it, no stigma at all… because for instance when my mate Phil was depressed a while back, he put the whole shenanigan on all this social media stuff – now, you *know* I don't use it 'cos I really got enough to deal with already without everyone knowing my business – but you know what I'm talking about, all the Facebook, the Twitter, the lot – said he wanted to 'get it out there', tell the world because he reckons it's all about, you know, *raising awareness*, creating *support networks*, getting people to fight the long battle with you… and all that shit, but also getting to the doctors to get some happy pills, jus' short term… and like… no one's judging, mate…"

"Oh, God, no. I'm not depressed."

"Nah, course not, mate. You're grieving. But still, no shame in any of it."

I tiptoed away from the kitchen door and crept up the stairs where I stopped to step neatly over a snoozing Arthur with one foot, and neatly over my white trainers with the other.

chapter four

"LOOK AT THAT." MO WAS POINTING AT A TODDLER sitting in a pram and gripping the sides of some sort of computer game. "What are they called again... tablets, ain't it? It's unnecessary, ain't it? Kid should be looking at his surroundings, not watching cartoons." He shook his head and emitted a low whistle. "Olly, remember back in the day when we had to wait around to use a phone box when we wanted to make a call?" There was no pause for Dad to respond. "Now the kids all got mobiles before they even at their fifth birthday! Where's all that innocence gone, man? We don't even know what they looking at half the time... YouTube and all dat sh... stuff."

We were sitting in a pub having "a quick pint" with Mo. We went for quite a lot of quick pints just recently, but I didn't mind; I liked the way that the awkward silences between Dad and I were obliterated by Mo's never-ending dialogue.

Mo had become a regular feature in our lives and I had come to realise that Dad liked him being around, perhaps for the same reason that I did, though I suspected it was more because of their shared history. Mo had known Mum when she had been younger and happier; Dad liked that.

They were a strange pairing: Mo with his loud, flowery language, his bright clothes and even brighter teeth, and Dad, with his neat hair and dull suit, whose every sentence was given full and reflective consideration. If we couldn't make it out for a "quick pint", Mo was in the habit of turning up on a Friday to spend the evening hunched on the sofa, arms resting on his gangly knees while he "contemplated life" over a few beers. I liked him being around because Dad would become a different person. More smiley. Perhaps it was the alcohol, or perhaps it was the fact that Mo laughed every time Dad got "so pretentious, man!" but either way, Dad was easier.

I was used to other adults bowing to Dad's natural superiority. With Mo, it was different. Sitting there, opposite Dad, in his baggy jeans and over-sized shirts, he thought nothing of speaking his mind and "telling it like it is". I liked him very much. Sometimes he spoke about his children, Taylor and Esme, but there was none of my father's super-charged positivity about them becoming well-rounded individuals. It was all, "Poor old Taylor, not a lot up top, but he's a charmer." And: "Esme thinks the world is made of unicorns and fairy dust – she's gonna come down to earth with a bump!"

My favourite times were when he talked about the block of flats in which he lived on the sixteenth floor. He made it sound as though Saxon House was dilapidated to the point of near collapse, but I could tell he was proud of it. I imagined something so tall, Mo could look at the whole of London from his balcony. He told me he could see the London Eye, and every New Year's Eve he had a free ticket to "the best firework party in the world".

He had always lived in those flats, he said, born in a stalled lift somewhere between floors eight and nine to a single mother with three older children. "Never even took me in to hospital to check me over," he'd said proudly, "just bundled me up and went back to the flat." A few weeks later, baby Mo and his family were "promoted" to a bigger flat because they needed more space. "Imagine that happening now!" he exclaimed to us one night, and then putting on a posh voice, "Oh, Ms Bailey, you had another baby? Please, let us rehouse you immediately!" And then Mo had laughed so hard he'd snorted and spilt some of his beer. Dad had laughed too. I knew that if Uncle Rob had made a comment like that, the talk would have turned to politics and the "diabolical state of the country" but with Mo, it was just funny. Everything was funny with him, even the serious stuff.

He told us about his neighbours and his block sounded to me like a wonderful rainbow of a place, full of eccentric characters and laughter. At first, Dad would try and change the subject but when Mo waved him away with:

"C'mon, man, you *know* they ain't all bad!" he would sigh and relent with a shrug. There was "Druggy Dan" next door who smoked a lot of anything he could lay his hands on and frequently knocked on Mo's door to ask if he could use the phone; the flat above with a cockroach problem which Mr Arnott proclaimed had absolutely nothing to do with his failure to empty the bin, or indeed to use the bin in the first place; Sammy Dwyer downstairs had what she termed "a genuine issue with authority", which apparently meant she was not able to hold down a job, or stay out of trouble with the police, or the council, through absolutely no fault of her own; Damian McNeal constantly had women of various ages, shapes and states of undress leaving from his flat across the hall; and Mo suspected the flat immediately next door was being used to house a bunch of refugees because so many people seemed to live there that he rarely saw the same face twice. Everybody in Mo's block had an issue; it was a different world from ours and I loved hearing about it, especially as Dad thought I was too young to understand.

"Have you got one of those tablet things then, Naomi?"

Mo had learned quickly that Dad preferred the use of my proper name and he was making a special effort to remember.

"No," I replied, and though I wanted one desperately I added, "I'm not that fussed though, I prefer to read." It was the right thing to say because Dad smiled across the table at me.

"Naomi is an avid reader. She is quite happy using her imagination for entertainment, aren't you, Naomi?"

Mo raised a quizzical eyebrow at me but lowered it quickly when he noticed Dad waiting for my answer.

"Yes. A few of my friends have them." I didn't say that *everybody* had one because that was the kind of comment to make Dad even more adamant to steer clear. "But I'm really not that bothered. My cousin Violet lets me use hers sometimes, but I can't really see the attraction."

Dad drew his shoulders back and rubbed a hand across his chin. "You see," he said, "the problem is that kids become addicted to these things to the detriment of everything else. Mo, you said yourself, kids should be looking around them, not staring robot-like at a screen."

"Damn straight," Mo said quickly. "Although I guess... well, there's a place for entertainment... just every now and then. I mean, I was thinking of getting Taylor and Esme one to share... sayin' that, it'd probably be more trouble than it's worth, the arguments it would cause! But no... anyway, they're too little. And I wouldn't want them on it all the time."

I loved Mo then, for I knew he was just appeasing Dad the same as I was.

"As for YouTube," Dad was saying, "I believe they can't have an account until the age of twelve."

"Yeah, but even if they ain't got no account, it don't stop them looking at the videos..." Mo was getting into his stride now, empowered by the positive reaction he was getting from Dad. "You don't even *know* what they seein'... Man, the other day, Esme come running down the stairs bawling her eyes out 'cos she gone and seen some Killer Clown sh... rubbish on her mum's computer and it's freaked her right out… now I gotta go and check under her bed like twenty times before she go to sleep…"

"Well, Naomi doesn't watch anything like that… for the very reason you just exemplified."

Mo had been chewing gum and suddenly he stopped, leaving his lips twisted to one side. Eventually the chewing recommenced with renewed vigour and he nodded thoughtfully. "Yeah, I make you right. The internet's got some scary stuff, innit?"

I don't believe he agreed at all, but Dad had this way of making people seek his approval, and Mo, for all his swagger and charm, was not exempt.

Sadly, my popularity at school waned much quicker than I had expected and the following Monday, Molly forgot to ask me to sit with them at lunch. Had I not enjoyed the sense of inclusion quite so much over the last few weeks, I would probably have accepted it, but I was not prepared to go back to being invisible just yet. With new-found bravery, I grabbed Imogen and frogmarched her over to where the girls sat huddled over ham sandwiches and crisps and announced that I had something to tell them all. There was a moment's hesitation, and then Molly nodded and gestured for the girls to create space at the table. Suzy edged across to the end of the bench and Nadia moved in the opposite direction so that Imogen could squeeze in between them. I took my place on the other side, next to Molly. The girls continued to eat and only stopped chewing when I leaned in so that I could keep my voice low.

"So, before Mum died, she gave me a box of stuff…"

I had no idea of the effect my words were going to have but I got braver as the girls widened their eyes when I described the tampons and what it meant biologically to get your period.

All except Molly who rolled her eyes. "Oh, my God! As if we don't know all this anyway."

I could tell that Nadia and Imogen didn't really know but it was Molly I was out to impress, so I went a little further.

"Urgh, gross, why would you let a boy do that to you?" asked Maia, the most timid of the group.

"You might not let him," I said knowingly, "you might get taken advantage of."

Now I had their attention. Mouths stopped moving and sandwiches went uneaten as I ushered them in close so that our heads were almost touching over the table. And then I slowed right down, making the most of my audience, the shock on their faces a drug which kept me talking, and I went into detail, far, far more detail than I had intended.

It was the first time that I'd been sent to Mr Jackson's office. I waited patiently by the door studying a noticeboard displaying details of upcoming events: a PTA meeting scheduled for Wednesday, a cake sale to raise money for a school in India, a school disco (which I would not be attending because Dad believed standing in a school hall listening to pop tunes for an hour and a half and paying for the privilege was ridiculous) and an advert for the local Brownies group. I wasn't nervous about seeing Mr Jackson for I had a full explanation of events mapped out in my mind (as far as I was concerned I had only stated facts and you couldn't argue with the truth), but I had a knot in my stomach caused by the blatant betrayal of my new friends. It had been my masterplan, a way to maintain their interest and friendship, and yet I had barely finished speaking when Molly threw her sandwich down and declared that I was gross, narrowing her eyes to venomous slits. Nadia and Suzy needed no further encouragement and they too packed their uneaten food away with a series of "urghs" and swept poor Maia away from the table in a whirl of disgust. Imogen and I were left alone and even she then said that I'd gone too far.

Mrs Palmer appeared with Dad who stood taller than ever as he followed my teacher down the carpeted corridor.

"Naomi, would you like to follow us through?" Mrs Palmer was holding the door of the headteacher's office open for Dad who had yet to look at me. I could hear a smattering of voices as a class moved from one part of the building to another and then an adult voice making that weird "*Errr*" noise that all the teachers did to get the attention of the children before telling them to be quiet. I followed Dad into the office and felt my defiance wane a little.

Mr Jackson had a large nose covered in red veins and a wiry white beard which covered the bottom of his face right up to his ears. With his round glasses and bald head, he reminded me of a baboon. He shook Dad's hand and indicated that we should sit on two chairs on the other side of his desk. Mrs Palmer took a seat next to the baboon and smiled at me sadly. I often caught her looking at me in class, but it was usually with a degree of puzzlement as though she couldn't really decide whether she liked me or not.

"Mr Rose, I do apologise that you have been called away from work at a time when you are no doubt incredibly busy." The baboon was referring to the *exam period*, a matter of weeks away at the university and the cause of much angst for all heads of department.

"Indeed," Dad said, "my students are really up against it, so if we could—"

"Quite so, quite so." Mr Jackson pushed his glasses up his nose and stroked his beard. "I don't wish to keep you long so I'll get to the point. At lunchtime today, our midday staff were approached by a small group of girls, rather upset I must add, claiming that Naomi had been talking about… well, something of a delicate nature and… I'm afraid, rather inappropriate considering the age of the children involved."

"I see." Dad turned to me at last. "Naomi, would you like to explain?"

But I no longer wished to explain. Faced with the disappointed expressions of three adults, all earlier bravado had dissolved and I wanted to disappear under Mr Jackson's messy desk and curl into a ball. "It was just," I began, my voice high and quiet, "it was just about something… that happens to girls. I thought they would already know anyway."

Mrs Palmer chose that moment to take pity and she leaned over to rest a hand on my shoulder. "I don't think we need to make Naomi go through the exact words, we can assume she was referring to the changes that girls go through during puberty. Periods in particular."

Mr Jackson pursed his lips and picked up a pen which he rolled between his fingers. My cheeks were burning; I lowered my head and stared at a yogurt stain on my skirt.

"And I suppose ten-year-old girls discussing bodily functions is so out of the ordinary that you felt it necessary to call me in?"

Dad's tone was curt and I looked at him in surprise.

"Forgive me, Mr…"

"Jackson."

"Forgive me, Mr Jackson, Mrs Palmer… but I assumed this was about something serious."

Mr Jackson dropped the pen and chased it as it rolled across the desk. Mrs Palmer caught it and placed it back in a wire pencil pot. "Mr Rose, the issue is not the nature of the topic in question but rather the… detail to which she felt it necessary to go into."

"What do you mean?"

"The menstrual cycle is not something that every girl is comfortable talking about but we understand it is only natural that some girls are at a stage where they feel the need to question and discuss the changes they may or may not be experiencing. But the point is, in this instance, Naomi felt it appropriate to go into more detail, to explain the purpose of the menstrual cycle and also, the reasons why a cycle may stop."

"You mean pregnancy?"

"Yes. Pregnancy and the means by which a girl may fall pregnant. Even…" a vein twitched on his right temple, "even broaching on non-consensual activity."

At this, Dad hesitated. I held my breath.

"I see. Naomi, is this correct?"

My breath escaped in a tumble of words. "Yes, but I read about it. I thought all the girls knew already."

"And I'm sure most of them did."

"Mr Rose, we have children of varying levels of maturity, and in this case there were two girls who were very upset. I wonder now whether Naomi would like to leave us to talk this through?"

"Hold on, you talk about pregnancy and periods in front of her and now you think she should leave the room? Naomi, do you want to leave?"

He was staring at me but though his brow was heavy, I was gripped for the first time by a sense that it was us against them, against the world, and I liked it. I shook my head. "No thank you, I'm fine."

"Okay, as you wish," said Mr Jackson, looking decidedly uncomfortable now.

In the six years I had been at the school I had never witnessed my headteacher being challenged. He was generally well respected; parents, pupils and staff alike were keen to please him and yet here was my dad calling his authority into question over something as trivial as a book.

"Mr Rose, do you monitor what Naomi reads?"

Dad bristled and folded his arms across his chest. "My daughter is a voracious reader, it would be impossible to check the content of every book she picks up."

"Indeed. However, it has been brought to my attention that Naomi may be reading material that is not suitable for her age."

"Brought to your attention? By whom? When?"

"By two members of staff on two separate occasions."

"Right. But it hasn't been of such concern that you needed to contact me earlier?"

"Well… no, an oversight perhaps."

"And what exactly are these materials that concern you so greatly?"

Mrs Palmer smiled encouragingly. "Naomi, where did you read about the things you talked to Molly and the other girls about?"

I shrugged.

"Naomi, earlier you told me the name of a book by… oh, who was it now?"

I shrugged again and felt sorry for Mrs Palmer who was trying to show she was on my side.

"Naomi, you are not in trouble, we just want to make sure that you are reading age appropriate books."

When I failed to respond she addressed Dad. "The conversation today apparently stemmed from a teenage book dealing with puberty and things of a… sexual nature. Personally, I was more concerned last week when Naomi mentioned she was reading *To Kill a Mockingbird*, the themes of which, I'm sure you're aware, are rather adult in nature."

"I see." Dad had his hands face down on his knees but his back remained poker straight. "It is a long time since I read it myself, but I know my wife, my *late* wife, thought very highly of it indeed. I'm not aware of the other book."

Mr Jackson took his glasses off, polished them briefly before placing them back on his nose and then placed his palms together, pressing them to his lips as though in prayer. "Mr Rose, the quality of the fiction is not in dispute but perhaps you would agree that Naomi is a little young to be reading books such as these. Of course, given your recent circumstances, it is entirely understandable that certain things may have been overlooked and I very much hope you will view this intervention as helpful—"

"Intervention? For Christ's sake, the child has been reading decent literature; you're acting as though she had been caught with a copy of *Mein Kampf* under her arm!"

"I can assure you, Mr Rose, it is not our intention to—"

"No," Dad was shaking his head from side to side and smiling dangerously, "no, let me tell you what your intention is… your intention is to produce a set of children who think the same, look the same and adhere to non-existent guidelines about when they are mature enough to cope with the details of life. Well, let me tell you something, my child has just lost her mother, and I'm pretty sure that reading a couple of stories which happen to mention the menstrual cycle and pregnancy are not going to do her much damage. If she has shared her knowledge in an inappropriate way then we can deal with that but I am not going to censor her choice of fiction. Just to be clear, you have a school which allows mobile phones to be brought in to class—"

Mr Jackson looked affronted. "For safety reasons, you understand?"

"Oh, yes! I've heard the spiel about children walking home from school needing to be contactable – utter nonsense! Mobile phones do not make children safe; they make the streets a mugger's paradise. You encourage mobile phones and the use of social media and, what was that new club I read about in the newsletter last week, *Film* Club? The online world is actively supported regardless of the consequences while the education authority is lamenting the fall in basic literacy standards and *yet*, when a child chooses to pick up a book, an *actual* book, she is reprimanded for reading at a level which might extend her capabilities!"

There was a silence, broken only by the rhythmic thud of Dad's heel against the floor.

"Mr Rose," the headteacher levelled his voice, "I can assure you that Naomi is not being reprimanded for reading, most certainly not. Naturally we encourage children to further their own progress but we must be seen to monitor the content of what is being read. I'm sure you appreciate that we take the well-being, both physical and mental, of our children very seriously. Now, I am more than happy to continue this conversation further but I strongly suggest we allow Naomi back to class as this situation must be extremely uncomfortable for her. Mrs Palmer, you are free to leave with Naomi and to relieve Mr Walker who I believe has been covering for you."

Mrs Palmer stood up. Her cheeks were flushed and she was fiddling with the thin silver pendant hanging around her neck. "Come on, Mimi, let's see what the other children are up to."

"It's Naomi, not Mimi," said Dad, rising to his feet, "and I believe the meeting is over. Perhaps in future, for matters as trivial as this, I could be contacted via email rather than being called away from work?"

chapter five

"NAOMI, WOULD YOU GET THAT? IT WILL BE Uncle Robert."

I sloped down the hall in my socks and opened the front door to find Uncle Rob shaking an umbrella and wiping his shoes on the mat. "Hi, Mimi, how's tricks?" he asked, dumping the umbrella and sweeping me into a bear hug.

"Urgh, you're all wet!" I exclaimed.

Dad appeared in the hall and I was released, my skirt left with a huge rain-soaked circle on one side. "Right, homework please, Naomi," he said, taking Rob's hand and giving it one firm shake.

"I don't have any."

He paused. "So... go and *read*."

I stared at my father, searching for a sign. He had not mentioned the earlier meeting with Mr Jackson, nor alluded to a time that he would. Dinner had been fish and chips in front of the news and our remarks limited to what we had seen on the screen. It wasn't right. I wanted to discuss it all; I wanted to recapture that feeling of solidarity that I had felt in the headteacher's office and now Uncle Robert was here there would be no further opportunity.

"You're just going to sit and drink whisky and *beer*?" I said sulkily.

Uncle Robert grinned and flicked my arm. "Of course we are," he said, "and we need to discuss very important things." He leaned down and whispered in my ear, "Although, to tell you the truth, your dad has a habit of waffling on…"

But I couldn't even be bothered to raise a smile.

Upstairs, I lay on the bed with Arthur kneading my back, pen poised to write about Mr Jackson's baboon face and poor Mrs Palmer. I really hadn't meant any harm; I had so wanted Molly and the others to be impressed and they *had* been. Trust Molly to make a big deal out of it and tell, she just didn't like it when the attention wasn't on *her*. When I reached the point where Dad had stormed out of Mr Jackson's office, I placed the diary back into the drawer of my bedside table and wandered back downstairs in search of a snack. The door to the living room was ajar, and I paused, curious by the silence.

A glass landed on a hard surface, then Dad's voice, low and determined. "It's just not something we've… I've considered, Rob. I mean… really? Counselling? What good would it do? She's better off getting on with things. Too much is made these days of *talking everything through* over and over again and *listening to feelings*… it's a waste of time, nothing but an invitation to dwell on the past."

"Hardly! Look, I don't want to speak out of turn but—"

"Then don't."

There was a pause. And then Uncle Rob changed his tone, making it a little softer. "All I'm saying is that it would be a shame to have anything hold her back. I know the waiting lists are huge but maybe, if we all pool together, we could get her seen privately."

"She doesn't need any extra help, mentally or academically… and certainly not privately! According to her teacher she is above… sorry… *exceeding*, the expected levels for her age already."

"Yes, but it's not enough to do well in class, she needs to be exceptional to pass the exam, and that means being in the right headspace too. There's so much competition now, not just within school but across the county. Many children will have been receiving extra tuition for the last two years in preparation, but it's not too late, not for a bright spark like Naomi."

"Listen, after what happened today, I don't need any more persuading that the education system is stifling our children. I was dithering a little before, but my mind has been well and truly made up now; she won't be sitting any sort of entrance exam. I want Naomi to attend a school that provides diverse opportunities, not a set of rigid targets."

"All schools have targets."

"I don't want her to feel she has to conform."

It was all so boring and as I'd heard most of it before, I headed off to the kitchen, leaving them to it.

My uncle was a maths teacher at the local grammar, and was proud of the excellent results his pupils received. But Dad was never impressed. He would laugh, "You may know how to teach to the test, Rob, but by the time they get to me a few years later my staff have to fill in all the gaps…"

They had first met when Dad had gone into my uncle's school to deliver a talk on the benefits of higher education. He said that loads of kids were deciding not to go on to university because of the government's decision to charge really high tuition fees, and it was his job to persuade them that studying was still a viable option. They had bonded over a pint after school and a few weeks later, Dad had introduced Rob to his sister. Their favourite topic had always been the grammar vs comprehensive debate and I could still hear them arguing as I rummaged around for a snack.

"Fine, I understand that but I'm still not keen. In many ways I agreed with Katherine. I want Naomi to make her own way, fighting against whatever the odds are. I don't want her to have special favours, or a leg up… no one is entitled to anything in this world, it all needs to be earned through hard work and discipline… plus I want her to experience the diversity that mainstream comprehensive education would provide… friends with different backgrounds, different social classes…"

"Oh, come on… social classes? Bit outdated, isn't it?"

"Call it what you like, it doesn't matter. What matters *to me* is that Naomi becomes a well-rounded individual who can cope in the world, not one who has been wrapped in a bubble of academia and protected from the harsh realities of life. School is what you make of it. She will have the same opportunities as the majority and then rise above the rest through sheer determination and stamina."

"Sheer determination and stamina!" Uncle Robert was laughing now, Dad wouldn't like that. "Look, I realise it's not fashionable to favour the grammar school system—"

"It has nothing to do with what's fashionable!"

"Then let her have a go at the exam, with my help we can—"

"She's my daughter, Rob. The answer is no."

As far as I was concerned, there was only ever one contender for my secondary education because Dad said the grammar school was for the kids who were "academically exceptional but unable or unwilling to integrate successfully into mainstream society". He said that these kids with their straight A*s or whatever would receive a mighty wake-up call when they eventually left education and realised that the workforce was not made up solely of "articulate, well-read people but by an eclectic mix of creative personalities with decent social skills". My last school report said I had an eclectic taste in fiction which apparently meant "wide-ranging", so I guessed I was halfway there.

I came across an unopened multipack of crisps and shuffled back down the hallway with the bag in my hands.

"Dad, can I have some of these?" I asked, sticking my head around the door.

"Naomi, come here a minute, will you?" Dad had both hands palm down on the table and I could tell he had started on the whisky because his cheeks were blotchy. "What do you think then, about school?"

"What do I think about school?"

"Yes, yes, school. *Secondary* school. On the one hand we have the grammar – promoting rules and rigidity and stifling personality – while on the other we have Harper Comprehensive... Naomi, school is what you make it. It is possible, and vital, that you reach your full potential alongside, and sometimes *despite*, outside influences. You're not there to follow the crowd and blend in, you are a bright girl who is capable of standing out and achieving excellence in adverse conditions—"

"The flower that blooms in adversity is the rarest and most beautiful of them all," I interrupted, holding out the crisps. "Can—"

"Absolutely! What a wonderful saying, where did you read that?"

"Nowhere. I got it from Mulan – the Disney film."

Uncle Robert erupted with laughter, but Dad looked incredibly disappointed. He waved his hand in front of him and continued, "The key to success is to mix with everyone, learn from everyone, be brave, listen and then make your own opinions heard."

"That's a lot to remember!" Uncle Robert said, recovering enough to roll his eyes at me and grin.

"Dad, can I eat these? I'm starving."

"You're not starving, Naomi, you're hungry. Children dying from hunger are starving. But yes, you can eat them."

I was mightily relieved not to be going to the grammar. My cousin Violet was having extra tuition to sit the entrance test Uncle Robert was talking about, as was Charlotte, a girl in my class whose pale eyes blinked rapidly whenever anyone ever spoke to her. No, my route was already set. Next year I would attend Harper Comp (a vast concrete and glass jungle which Dad described as architecturally pioneering and everyone else deemed a monstrosity) and develop a *well-rounded sense of self.*

Dad and I spent the following afternoon at the vast university campus library which housed books, journals and things called "periodicals" on every conceivable subject. I loved being inside that building and happily whiled away the time waiting for Dad as he burrowed amongst the imposing shelves in search of one elusive text or another. As a toddler, I had delighted in being able to run backwards and forwards down the aisles, letting my chubby fingers skim the tops of the books, though I was only permitted to do so in the breaks between semesters when most students were at home. Unlike the library in town which was now used, for the most part, as a training centre for adults learning ICT skills or retaking their Maths and English exams, the university library was as I felt it should be: dark, eerie and silent. I loved it.

We spent some time trawling the shelves for "an accessible classic". I realised that the outing to find suitable reading material was Dad's nod to what had happened at school, and I went along with it, resigned to the fact that it would never be discussed openly. When he selected *Oliver Twist*, I agreed, because even though I knew the story from the abridged school copy, Dad said there was no substitute for the real version. I was happy enough to read what he wanted and I still had *To Kill a Mockingbird* under my pillow as well as a whole series of books following the lives of teenage cheerleaders which I had found in the garage. Dad wouldn't have deemed them suitable because they were mostly about boys and parties and tiny skirts and, worse, they were *American*, so I kept them hidden behind shoeboxes under my bed.

Once we'd finished at the library we went for a walk around the university grounds. I clutched *Oliver* to my chest as we wandered away from the tower blocks which housed the students, along the mossy path towards the lake, home to mallards and coots as well as the occasional moorhen. As we manoeuvred our way past a pair of ducks who had taken a fancy to the path, their silky heads folded into their backs, Dad asked me how it was going with the girls at school.

"Fine," I lied, thinking how pretty the tabby mallard was. "Is that the girl duck or the boy?"

"That's the female. So... you're getting on alright then, with everyone?"

"Yes."

There was a pause while Dad considered his next question; to give him time I turned to look at the sun pushing through the leaves of nearby trees.

"Friendships are difficult sometimes," he began, "I remember finding that I had to try quite hard with people. Being sociable didn't... doesn't... come easily to me."

He often did this when trying to give me advice, refer to his own experiences rather than to mine.

"I'm alright. I have friends."

"Good. Good." He ran a hand over his hair and nodded several times in quick succession. "As long as you realise that you don't need to impress anyone, just be yourself. Okay?"

"I'm thirsty, can I have a drink?" And this is what *I* did when *I* felt uncomfortable; I changed the subject.

We had reached the other side of the lake by now and were winding our way back towards the campus. There was a café to the right of the library which served free refills of lemonade; occasionally Dad let me have two.

"Yes. Why not?"

And just as with the events in Mr Jackson's office, we dealt with the issue of problem friendships by not really discussing it at all.

*

"Naomi, sweetheart! I hope you don't mind me being here – Dad was in a bit of a fix..." I was pulled forward and crushed to my aunt's chest. Dad was always in a fix recently. "I thought we could bake some bread, and then I was going to concoct something yummy for tea."

Aunt Chrissy's cheeks were flushed from the heat of the kitchen, and her hair was in the process of escaping from the clip at the back of her head and forming damp wisps about her face. She had on her nervous *I want to make everything better for you* expression.

"Okay," I said slowly. Dad had once decided to bake bread every evening before realising by the second day that it was much cheaper to just buy it. "Where is he anyway?"

"He's gone to have a quick pint with Mo. I'm sure he won't be late. Now, why don't you go and get changed and I'll make you a snack to keep you going?"

"Get changed into what?"

"Oh." She looked suddenly perplexed, as though my indecision was a spanner in the works of her perfectly planned evening. "I don't know, do you not have comfy home clothes to get into rather than sitting in your uniform all evening?"

"Well, I do but… I normally don't bother."

Aunt Chrissy adjusted her expression and regained her sunny beam as she placed a floury hand on my left cheek.

"That's fine, you do whatever you normally do," she said, and I pulled a chair out from the kitchen table and sat down. "Now, can I make you a drink… maybe a chocolate biscuit too?"

We ate biscuits and baked bread and when she spilt flour down her dress, I laughed and she looked pleased. When it was time for dinner, I was given the choice of sitting at the table or having a "cheeky tray" in front of the telly and when I chose the latter, she hugged me and said, "Oh, good, I was hoping you'd say that."

At nine o'clock she tucked me into my own bed and kissed the top of my head. "Is there anything I've forgotten to do, sweetheart?"

"What time will Dad be home?"

"Ooh, soon I expect, but I'm going to stay over anyway. Now, uniform is ready, packed lunch is made…"

"That's everything," I replied, snuggling down under the duvet, "unless…"

"Yes?"

I paused, "Well, it's just that… no, it doesn't matter."

Aunt Chrissy leaned in and tickled my ribs. "It matters now that you've started… tell me."

I pretended to giggle even though I wasn't ticklish, and when she stopped I sat back up and shook my head. "It's just that I wanted to try and make my hair wavy… I was going to plait it before bed but I can't manage the back by myself."

Her sad eyes misted over in the dim light. "You want me to have a go? I can't promise to get it right but I'll try my best."

I pulled away and threw back the cover. Sliding off the bed in my knickers and vest and revealing my tardiness regarding pyjamas, I scampered about the room searching out hair bands and brushes. Aunt Chrissy laughed as I jumped back onto the bed, positioning myself with my back to her expectantly. "Okay, let's see what we can do."

The following day I got washed and dressed without any prompting, and Aunt Chrissy came up to my room to witness the unveiling of the wavy hair. Together, to the backdrop of heavy snoring from Dad's room across the hall, we gently removed the bands which secured ten neat plaits all over my head and then separated the hair out with our fingers. When I reached for a brush, my aunt stopped me.

"No, if it's one thing I know, it's that you don't brush styled hair without causing it to go frizzy. Just use your fingers, like this, see?"

I looked at my reflection in the mirror and couldn't help but smile at the way my silky hair zigzagged softly over my cardigan. Wearing it loose had the added bonus of covering my ears too; the girls would definitely be impressed.

"Is that what you wanted?" she asked, placing her hands on my shoulders and smiling at me in the mirror.

"Yes," I nodded, "it's perfect."

"You can't wear your hair down at school."

I had barely taken my seat at my desk when Molly appeared in front of me.

"What?"

"You can't wear your hair down, you might spread nits."

"I haven't got nits," I said, wondering when Molly would notice the beautiful waves and say how nice they looked. Molly's own hair was plaited today and pinned in a perfect circle around her head. She looked like Anne of Green Gables. Not the child Anne, the grown-up one; Anne of… Anne of *Avonlea*. I was about to mention it but Molly was already speaking again, doing that weird thing of looking around at other people even though it was me she was talking to.

"Might not be you that has them but you soon will if you wear your hair down," she said, smirking at Maia. "Then we'll all get them."

I looked at Imogen who had taken the seat next to me and was busy arranging a set of colouring pencils into the order of the rainbow on the desk. "It looks nice though," Imogen said to the pencils, "all wavy. Looks nice."

"I didn't say it didn't look nice," Molly countered, just to prove she was being thoughtful really, "just said you'd spread nits. I'm trying to be *helpful*."

Mrs Palmer entered the room and Molly wasted no time in going over to address her concerns about my hair. The teacher dropped a pile of worksheets onto her desk and looked wearily in my direction. She sighed and opened her desk drawer, rummaging around for a moment. Locating what she was looking for, she made her way over to our desk and handed me a blue hair band.

"I'm sorry, Naomi. It looks beautiful but I'm afraid Molly's right, long loose hair is a bit of a hazard. Let's scoop it up out of the way, shall we?"

She reached for my hair but I dodged sideways and glared at Molly. "I can do it," I said, pulling my hair as tightly as I could into a ponytail and securing it with the band. I didn't take my eyes off Molly and she seemed to grow uncomfortable under the weight of my stare, her mouth twitching into an awkward smile.

"Just trying to be helpful…" she said again, but her voice was quieter this time and she dropped her eyes. I took my seat as Mrs Palmer addressed the class but I didn't listen to a word. Instead, I picked up a pair of scissors and focused intently on scoring a thick groove into the edge of the table.

*

It didn't hurt as much as I thought it would. It hurt, definitely, but I hadn't cried, and I could still move the arm, just not all the way around. As the doctor tested me with a series of movements, I found I could almost pull the limb all the way to my chest before letting out an involuntary yelp.

"Dear, oh dear, how did you manage this then?"

Doctor Heller was a young blonde woman with an accent which made her sound fierce even when her words were sympathetic.

"I fell down the stairs."

The doctor glanced at Dad who was on the chair next to me, leaning forward onto his knees. I thought Dad smelt of whisky but he couldn't have, it was four-thirty in the afternoon and no one drank whisky in the afternoon.

"Well, accidents happen. I'm pretty sure it's fractured but I'm afraid an X-ray will be necessary and possibly a cast. You will need to take her to A&E and sit it out with the masses."

My heart soared at the thought of having my arm in a cast, but Dad looked stricken. "Really? But that could take hours."

Doctor Heller returned to her seat with a frown and began typing something onto the computer. "Indeed it might. Would you rather I prescribed painkillers and let nature take its course?" she asked, crossly.

Dad rose to his feet and ushered me to mine. "Absolutely not, Doctor. That's not what I meant at all. Naturally I'll take her along at once, thank you for your time."

A flicker of impatience crossed his face, but it was gone in a moment and we left the surgery and drove to the hospital in silence. It was standing room only in the waiting area and Dad sighed as he directed me to the children's section even though I was far too old to play with the coloured abacus or the wooden railway set. "I hope this is a lesson learned, Naomi. If you had just moved your shoes from the stairs like I asked you to…"

"I know, it's all my fault, I suppose I'm getting what I deserve." I let my shoulders droop and stared at the floor.

My words had the desired effect and Dad pulled me in close and kissed the top of my head. "No, that's not what I meant. Of course, you don't deserve a broken arm…"

I allowed myself to enjoy the brief show of affection before sliding down the wall and sitting on the floor. Tracing the pattern on the floor tiles with my good arm, I looked at the heavy creases on Dad's forehead and wished that I didn't make him so tired.

"Woah! What'd you do?"

There were a group of six or seven children following behind as I made my way over to the desk that I shared with Imogen, Suzy and Charlotte with the blinking eyes.

"Just fell. Didn't hurt much."

"Is it properly broken?" Suzy Longman asked, her teeth as prominent as ever within her open mouth. Today she had decided to scrape her curly hair back into a tight bun and I thought she looked very grown-up.

"Yep. Properly broken, although it's called a fracture rather than a break."

A boy called Manny who rarely spoke to any of the girls sauntered past and gave us a quick glance. "A fracture ain't the same as a break, it ain't as bad."

I glared at him, and Alfie, who was at the next table, grinned. "He's only sayin'."

"Well, he doesn't know what he's talking about, does he?" I said fiercely. "Probably never even broken a sweat let alone a bone."

Three other boys who had joined Alfie's table whooped and gave each other high-fives. "Never broken a sweat let alone a bone! That's *wicked*!"

I was pleased even though I hadn't thought up the saying myself – I'd heard Mo telling Dad about a work-shy chef claiming to have broken his wrist – but the others didn't need to know that.

Alfie swung back nonchalantly on his chair. "So what did you do then? Or did someone do it to you? Did ya get pushed down the stairs for not cleaning your bedroom… nah, for not doing your piano practice—"

"I don't play the—"

"Aw, is your dad missing your mum and taking it out on you?"

There was a sudden silence then a couple of low "Nah, that's out of order" and "Alfie, man, that's low…" and Alfie, to his credit, had the decency to look sheepish. I wasn't actually offended, nor particularly bothered. In fact, I was pleased that Alfie was showing an interest as he hadn't said much to me since the comment in the cloakroom. After a thoughtful pause, he added, "Nah, I reckon you didn't finish that new Charles Dickens novel or something…" and waited to see if he'd won back peer approval.

Manny reappeared on the periphery of the group and shoved Alfie's shoulder. "Charles Dickens is dead, you idiot. How's he gonna write a new book?"

Alfie flushed pink. "Duh, yeah, I *know*. Just meant like, a new book from the library, innit? Like I see her reading the other day." But it was too late to redeem himself, and the boys laughed again, pushing and jostling for space within their bubble of hilarity, all of them glad not to be Alfie.

Lowering my head ever so slightly, I squinted in concentration. The noise around me gradually subsided and I felt an arm on my shoulder.

"Nae? What is it? Is he right, was it some kind of punishment?" Molly's voice was filled with a dangerous concern. "Oh, my God, Nae, not your dad, surely?"

I waited for just the right level of quiet, timing was everything; and then, ever so slowly, I raised my head in time for my audience to notice a single tear escape my right eye.

"Naomi, I just want to know that you can tell me anything, anything at all. My job is to make sure you're okay. Do you understand?"

I stared at a tea stain on the desk and nodded. Mrs Palmer clasped her hands together and inclined her head, trying to catch my eye.

"I realise things must be very... difficult... at the moment. At home? And now with your arm... I mean; it must have been very painful. I'm sure you must have wanted your mum to be around?"

I nodded again, and Mrs Palmer stood up and came around to my side of the desk. She crouched by my chair and put a hand on my shoulder. "Would you like to tell me what happened?"

"I just fell."

"Are you sure? Some of the other children seem to think that there's more to it."

I sighed and kicked at one of the wooden desk legs. "I was supposed to move some shoes from the top of the stairs, and I forgot."

"I see." She fiddled with her little neck chain. "And I suppose Daddy was quite cross about that?"

I wasn't stupid, I knew what she was getting at. I had implied it, hadn't I? But now the reality of dealing with the consequences annoyed me. "Not really. He reminded me to move them, and I didn't. Then I tripped and fell down the stairs."

"What did Daddy do then?"

I looked up at Mrs Palmer and crinkled my nose. "He wasn't there."

"He wasn't there? But I thought—"

"Well, he was home but he was in the garden. He wasn't there on the stairs."

"I see." Mrs Palmer thought for a moment. "Naomi, did you tell the other children that Daddy pushed you?"

"Nope. Why would I say that?"

In bed that night, I recorded two new important facts in my diary.

Firstly, that I hated Molly Smith more than anyone in the world.

Secondly, that people would believe anything.

*

I guess that was the first time I'd felt something akin to power.

Power is perhaps the wrong word; control might be better. Yes, that was the first time that I felt something akin to control.

The roof of the clinic is now bathed in an orange glow and I can see people moving around in the upper rooms where the blinds have yet to be pulled. What's he doing now, I wonder? He might have gone for the day, I suppose, back to his little flat near the station, or he might be eating with the other staff like he sometimes does. He must know that I'm still here in Wellbridge – it's no secret and my name is on the intercom downstairs, plain to see. He probably thinks I'm no longer interested in him because people try to forget negativity from the past. Easier said than done though, isn't it? We remember pain more easily than we remember pleasure. Pleasure is there to be enjoyed for a fleeting moment before it flutters off to rest in the deep recess of our brain. But pain, pain is etched into the grooves of our consciousness, readily accessed so it may be relived during those quiet hours of the night when the rest of the world is asleep. But the cycle of reliving events has to be stopped before madness takes over, and so I've taught myself over the years to see nothing as negative. Everything, good, bad and in-between, is just part of a story and all stories can be revised and edited until the ending is perfect. Challenges, hurdles – I shape them all into the means to an end.

It was assumed that I would move away when the first book was published, at least to London, but people should learn not to assume. I felt no need to escape. A writer can write anywhere.

The interview Esme has set up for tomorrow morning is with the Wellbridge Gazette. It will be the fourth, maybe the fifth, time that the local paper has run an article and they're always so grateful when I spare the time. Not that I mind (publicity is publicity, and I have a book to promote), but I'm one of the few people left who physically buys the paper so I may as well be in it. Would I ever get used to reading the news online like the rest of the world? Probably not.

It's voyeuristically pleasing to keep abreast of local activity because you never know who might crop up. Usually it's a stranger holding a school fete, or winning an award for best regional hairdresser or, climbing Snowdon to raise money for their aunt's best friend's dog, but just occasionally, like the time Imogen was contracted to paint the subway under the railway, it's someone I know.

I lost contact with my former life for a while. I left to study in Glasgow and found distractions in editing the student paper and writing something long-winded and pretentious (which I refer to now as a "practice novel"); I discovered all-night raves where I hated the music but loved the euphoric antithesis to the endless hours spent in the library; I made hundreds of friends whom I never saw again, and survived mainly on a diet of noodles and cocaine. The city was swamped with student bars selling cheap shots and buckets of fluorescent cocktails but my taste for alcohol was always marred by thoughts of my father, so I stopped drinking for three years and survived the social scene by shoving vast quantities of white powder up my nose. When I eventually returned, hollow-eyed and skinny, I found Dad holed up in the kitchen, his skin an alarming shade of yellow (prompting the first of many appointments with a doctor, and further deterioration of our relationship), took a mind-numbingly dull job in the local library and wrote a second novel.

A light goes on in the main hall. Soon, the patients (or is it residents?) will begin taking their seats for the evening session. Lots of talking, lots of head-tilting and smiling... lots of "reconnecting with the past".

The Wellbridge Gazette played an unwittingly crucial role in helping me to reconnect to my own past. I'd been at home one afternoon, supposedly drafting a final chapter but in reality, just flicking through the local paper and being berated on the phone by Esme, again, for failing to update my Twitter feed.

"Thing is, I know you don't wanna hear it but it will take you, literally, five minutes... three even!"

I caught my breath and held it, one hand gripping the phone, the other smoothing the paper as best I could. It was just a grainy CCTV image captured from one of the numerous convenience stores that kept popping up on the high street, and the quality was terrible, but there was no mistaking it was him.

"*Maybe you don't think it's my place to be telling you what to do but actually, it is. It is my job to tell you that you need to keep up your activity on social media. Naomi?*"

I ran a finger over the image and sighed. Shoplifting. Of all the crimes. How desperately sad.

"*Naomi! Are you still there?*"

"*I'll call you back, Esme. Something's come up.*"

It was that moment when poor exasperated Esme had finally taken over my online persona. It made sense; the fact that she lived out her life on Instagram and Twitter compensated for my complete inability to do anything beyond clicking the occasional "share" when prompted to do so, and she loved to mutter "*… a novelist who can't come up with a bloody 280-character comment…*" frequently, which made me smile.

The image in the paper didn't shock me, but the nature of his crime did. It reeked of desperation and threatened to distort my memory, threatened to stir up mild feelings of something like guilt, not an emotion I have ever been familiar or comfortable with. Nevertheless, the issue was surprisingly easy to resolve – having a bit of money does that – and it meant I was able to regain control. Shape the challenge, mould it, make it fit my life.

I'd signed a lease for the office soon afterwards (despite Esme's protests that it was a waste of money – "*What do you need an office for? Surely you writers are supposed to be wandering around in fields or something?*") and combined writing with keeping an eye on the Wellbridge Substance Abuse Clinic's latest resident.

My phone beeps on the desk behind me. It's a text from Katerina, via her friend's mum's phone, asking whether she can stay later at Lottie's so they can practise running with bean bags on their heads in the back garden. I study the plethora of heart and prayer emojis which punctuate her mis-spelt sentences. How Mo would have laughed. I type back, "Not tonight, you need an early night before sports day," then pause, delete, replace the words with, "OK, one more hour," and press send.

Lottie is nice, and I'm glad she and Kat are friends (even if they spend an awful lot of time together taking selfies on their tablets and adding cat ears and butterflies and sending them to each other despite being in the same room) because it makes up for me not providing her with a sibling. I only wanted one child and so I only had one child – two would have impacted on my life far more than I would allow.

Do I worry about their access to technology? Probably not as much as I should. Last week, I caught the girls complimenting each other like teenagers – Kat telling Lottie how nice her eyebrows looked and Lottie reciprocating with a comment about Kat's French plaits (luckily for Kat, she inherited her father's neat ears and my healthy thick hair; she wouldn't have fared so well had it been the other way around) – and I admit to finding this focus on appearance odd, considering how young they are. Still, I do try to encourage them to play outside once in a while, offer to take them to the park, kick a ball, but they stare up from their huddle on the sofa as though I'm mad. Times change. Parks are out. Filters are in. According to Kat, denying her access to the internet (albeit to watch cartoons on catch-up) is to deny her access to the world, and therefore her human rights. Wow.

What had I wanted at Kat's age? I had struggled to find my place, and for a short time, perhaps I would have liked to blend in but it was never going to happen because I didn't have the skills; I didn't possess the patience or the tolerance required to just "be" like everyone else. I still don't. And Kat doesn't either but I'm not worried; Kat is already strong and intelligent and knows better than to pretend to be something she's not.

chapter six

I DECIDED MY TRANSITION TO SECONDARY
school would be marked by a period of reinvention. It was
as good a time as any and I was tired of being the awkward
girl who had lost her mother; I wanted to be known
for being bright (which everyone said I was), or funny
(though no one said I was), or pretty even, like Molly
Smith, because even though she wasn't nice, everyone
seemed to like her.

Imogen agreed. "There's no reason to tell anyone about
your mum," she said, experimenting with her hair which
had thickened up nicely, pulling it to one side and tucking
it behind her ears, "but they will find out eventually.
And once one person knows, it will spread like *crackling*

wildfire." Imogen was experimenting with being dramatic because she too wanted to change; she planned to discard her "timid caterpillar persona and become a butterfly".

It was the end of an unseasonably wet August and the holidays couldn't end quickly enough for me. Dad's students had dissertations due in a couple of weeks and he had spent most of the summer arranging last-minute tutoring sessions with twenty-year-olds who were all on the verge of mental breakdowns. I had spent most of the holidays alone in my room.

"The first thing I'm going to do at the start of term is join the art club," Imogen said, jumping onto my bed and striking an uncharacteristically vicious pose, "because art is a great way to express yourself. Plus, it's kinda cool."

We were in my bedroom, trying out different outfits but mostly prancing around in our underwear, proud that we both now had something to fill out our bras a little.

"Yeah, I know, you said. But about my mum, for now... just between us, yeah?"

She shrugged and pouted in the mirror, sticking out her chest.

"Don't do that, you look like Molly." And I ducked as she threw a hairbrush at me.

"Urgh, as if!"

We laughed, and then thoughts of my mother were buried beneath the more pressing matter of whether we could get away with shortening the length of our vile green school skirts.

We strode purposely towards our new school on the first day of term and the building rose up before us like a vast concrete submarine. I tried hard to see it as "architecturally pioneering" so that I could agree with Dad, but couldn't help thinking that it was, after all, a bit of a monstrosity. Not that it mattered, what mattered was my *fresh start* and taking my first steps towards developing a *well-rounded sense of self*; it was all incredibly exciting. I pictured who I would become. For so long, I had wanted to be Jem Finch's sister, Scout, but she had been replaced recently by Liesel Meminger from *The Book Thief,* because Liesel was much braver than Scout and I had been told a *million* times how brave *I* was, plus she had blonde hair and dark eyes so we had things in common. Unlike poor Liesel, however, who had to steal her books, I had access to any book I wanted, and just recently I'd been devouring them faster than ever. It wasn't to relieve boredom (though perhaps a factor), but an obsession to absorb as much information as I could, and I read and reread anything and everything: cereal boxes, newspapers (I liked the human interest articles – the little girl who went missing and the subsequent deluge of conspiracy theories, the canoeist who supposedly drowned five years ago and then turned up at a police station, the people who queued all night to be the first to own an iPhone), library books, Mum's old books... I'd even picked up some essays left behind on the kitchen table last week – something about Feminism and Realism and several other "isms" – but I didn't really understand them, and it was tedious trying to see past Dad's comments and arrows and numbers, so I put them back. Besides, it was fiction I really craved.

As it happened, the intention to keep my mother's death quiet didn't last long. After just a few weeks, Imogen let slip to a new friend over lunch that my stony expression was probably due to the fact that my mother was dead when, in reality, I had been put out that she was sharing chips with Skye who wore her fringe scraped back from her face and secured it with a childish plastic clip, but I played along and pretended to be sad. As expected, the news whipped around the entire school like "crackling wildfire". However, I was pleased to find that apart from a few gentle comments, there was no real level of interest as, having never met my mother, the vested interest of my busy, self-absorbed fellow students was pretty minimal.

The first couple of years at Harper Comprehensive passed in a blur of novelty. There were new timetables, new stationery, the freedom to leave the grounds at lunchtime and head off down the high street to the "chippy", and the first sneaky cigarette in the estate behind the school (Imogen choked dreadfully, I didn't). We got away with shortening our skirts, and, in an effort to fit in with her new arty friends, Imogen and I experimented with cheap hair dye from the local chemist. The school was as lax about the pink, uneven streaks as it had been about the length of our skirts, and it wasn't long before we changed to purple.

"I'm allowed to express myself, aren't I?" I said, to counter Dad's uneasy looks at me across the dinner table.

"Yes. Of course. I just find it odd that you would choose to do so by ruining your beautiful hair."

By the third year, Imogen was spending most of her lunchtimes in the art block. I floundered around on the periphery of different groups, never quite making the inner circle. There was Jayden Blackwater and his boisterous, baseball-hatted crew who dominated the corridors between lessons and the football pitches at break times, the art crowd (having adopted Immy) who mooched around the school with the same speed it took them to draw out their vowels – "That's just *amaaaazing*" and "How do you *doooo* that?" – and then the "Musos" who slunk around the school with guitars on their backs, earphones hanging out of pockets and the weight of the world on their shoulders. I liked this group best. They were a strange bunch, with their dark clothes and their heavy black eye make-up, always angst-ridden and "depressed" and drinking too much, or just pretending to drink too much. The girls scratched their arms with pencils and wore their thin, crusty scars proudly – sleeves rolled up, arms at prominent angles – and the boys wore their hair long and greasy. Everyone had "shit" going on at home that they "didn't want to talk about right now", and I watched wistfully from afar, knowing I could never be one of them because I really *did* have shit going on in the form of a dead mother, and to compete with that would have ruined their drama.

I wandered between them all. I watched Molly and the other girls making their way round the school picking up new friends as though they were choosing sweets in a shop. I had not forgotten how she had persuaded Mrs Palmer to make me put my hair up that time, or how she'd grassed me up to Mr Jackson for discussing pregnancy, but Molly had long since lost interest in me. I wondered which was worse, being disliked or finding yourself to be completely invisible.

Despite her lack of interest in me, I began to find Molly quite intriguing. She, and the girls in her group, had suddenly acquired the most immaculate eyebrows – stencilled thick, strong and dark – and they began wearing their hair loose (the irony) and rolling their waistbands over to make their skirts even shorter than mine. I watched them subtly from the benches on the concourse or from my seat in class and saw that the boys were beginning to watch them too.

On Aunt Chrissy's advice, I spoke to as many people as I could and played to my strengths, offering to lend stationery out or to help with homework. When the tall girl in my English class failed to think of a decent opening to her story, I offered a suggestion and she wrote it down word for word; when the loud boys on the table behind me in maths struggled to multiply three-digit numbers, I swivelled my chair round and scribbled an example in the back of my book when Mrs Blakely wasn't watching. The teachers found me to be intelligent and frequently called on me in class to offer my opinion or to read aloud from a text. They championed my suggestions and asked me to help other pupils when I finished work quickly, but I came to realise that my abilities were not going to make me popular. I heard kids whispering to each other. The term "teacher's pet" was bandied about and suddenly my offers of help began to be rebuffed. I'd turn and whisper the answer to a maths problem only for the recipient to look the other way or I'd offer my neighbour a spare ruler so that they might underline the correct quote only to be told they preferred to highlight freehand. Imogen explained gently that I could (just sometimes) come across as a tiny bit patronising, but when I mentioned what was happening to Dad, he disregarded Imogen's theory with a flick of his wrist.

"Not at all, Naomi. It's just that some of your classmates may be embarrassed that they need help, and the embarrassment comes across as hostility. You are a very able pupil and you should absolutely help in any way you can. Keep trying."

So, I did.

One lunchtime, as I wandered the school looking for Imogen, I caught Jayden Blackwater (who was usually to be found strutting about with a baseball hat pulled so low his eyes were barely visible *and* whom I had let copy my geography homework twice) standing outside of the headteacher's office. With Dad's advice in mind, I went over and asked what he was being kept in for.

"None of your business," he muttered, pulling his cap down lower still.

"Is it the maths project? I could help if you want." I knew he'd missed the deadline because the three pupils who had failed to hand it in on time had been named and shamed by Mrs Blakely at the end of the last lesson.

"Oh, fuck off, Naomi."

I blinked in surprise.

"You're so up your own fucking arse, go and help someone who actually gives a shit."

"I'm not up my own arse."

"Yeah. You are." He lifted his head a little and I saw his eyes properly for the first time, dark and menacing. "You think you're better than everyone else but you know what? No one gives a shit."

"I'm just trying to help…"

"Why? No one wants you to. You're just a fucking weirdo."

He pulled a phone out of his pocket and purposely ignored me, flicking through screen after screen of something or other. Jayden liked to take his phone out of his pocket at every opportunity just to demonstrate how incredibly important he was and that he didn't adhere to school rules. Ironic really, that he was accusing me of thinking I was better than I was. I clenched my teeth and scowled at his fingers busy typing something inane to one of his inane friends.

I could feel my cheeks growing hot in the face of his rudeness. "I'm not… weird," and my knuckles clenched ready for a fight that I believed I would not start, "I was offering to help," and still he stood there, one foot on the wall behind him, thinking he was better… why did they all think they were better…? "I'm not weird," I repeated, but I said it so quietly, I thought he hadn't heard.

What happened next was as much a surprise to me as it was to him. I gasped and let out a kind of nervous snort as the phone spiralled through the air, hit the wall behind him and split apart on the floor. Then only immense satisfaction when I saw the horror on his face.

Jayden stepped forwards and leant in so close to my ear I thought he might bite it. "You fucking mental little bitch! You better hope—" he spat.

"Jayden Blackwater? In you come, please." Ms Emery, the headteacher, was leaning halfway out of the door. She looked first at Jayden, then me, and then at the phone on the floor. "Everything alright here?"

Jayden narrowed his eyes and made a sound through his teeth. "Yeah, miss, everything's fine." He snatched the sad pieces of phone from the floor and skulked into Ms Emery's office.

I couldn't stop grinning, but my heart was pounding against my chest as I hurried off down the concourse. I stumbled through the double doors and, once outside, gasped for air. Collapsing down on a patch of grass, I leant back on my elbows and closed my eyes against the sun, waiting for my breathing to steady as the adrenaline rushed through my body.

"You alright?"

I opened my eyes and shielded them with one hand. A boy I vaguely recognised from another class was standing a few feet away. He had his hands in his pockets, his shoulders hunched forwards the way all the boys stood.

I nodded. "Yeah."

"Don't look it."

He was tall and skinny, with hair so dark I could see the beginning of a shadow across his chin. I exhaled deeply and shrugged.

"Well, if you're sure everything's cool…?"

Everything was *not* cool but instead of answering, I opened my school bag and rummaged around for nothing. When I glanced back up, the boy had sloped off; I just caught sight of his back as he disappeared into the building.

The run-in with Jayden Blackwater swiftly became public knowledge and by the end of the day, nobody was speaking to me at all. Even Imogen was impatient.

"Jesus, Nae. Why him?" she asked when I finally caught up with her after the bell.

"Who cares? He thinks he's something special, but he's just a twat." I tried linking an arm through Imogen's but she shifted the position of her bag to make it awkward.

"Yeah, but that's the problem, isn't it? He *is* something special. He's popular and—"

"He's special because he's popular?"

"I'm just *saying*… you didn't have to break his phone."

I stopped walking.

After a moment, she turned. "*Now what*?"

"Let me get this straight… I offer to help him and he tells me to fuck off… and *I'm* in the wrong?"

Imogen's shoulders sagged. "Yeah, okay. Alright, I suppose he was out of order."

"You suppose?"

"Fine," she relented and wandered back, pushing her arm through mine, "he's a twat. I just wish that sometimes you wouldn't make things so difficult. Like, just play the game, you know?"

"What game?" I asked, but Imogen just shook her head.

"She just talking about the Game of Life, you know?" Mo said, when I asked him his opinion later that evening. He and Dad had been for a "quick pint" and though Dad stank of beer when they returned and had taken himself off to bed, Mo was full of energy and rooting excitably through the kitchen cupboards, taking out various foodstuffs and lining them up on the worktop.

I stared at the odd assortment of dried pasta, lentils and baked beans. "What's the Game of Life?"

He ferreted around in the spice drawer for a minute before eventually holding up a jar of curry powder in triumph. "Ha!"

"And what the hell are you cooking?"

Mo spun around to face me and flashed his wide grin. "The Game of Life is the game we all play to one degree or another. It's how we learn to get along, it's about *social interaction*, about *conversing* and securing our place in the world. You understand?"

I leaned back on my chair and sighed. "Nope."

He filled a pan with water, placed it on the hob and then set about opening the bag of pasta with his teeth. "I think… if I can see the wood for the trees, I think what your insightful friend, Immy, is saying is you gotta let the others win sometimes."

"Why?" But my voice was sharper than I'd intended.

"Nah… calm down, listen. This Jayden sounds like he thinks he's a cut above, but… his time will come, you know? You gotta take care of yourself, don't be worrying so much about what others are doing and choose your battles, you know? Choose your battles."

"Oh… I see. I suppose I could try doing that."

"Good girl! It's all about the understanding and the seeing. You *gotta* be seeing. Now, as for your other question, just you wait. This concoction gonna blow your mind! Where's your veg at? This badboy of a dinner is needing some pure *goodness* in it."

On what would have been my mother's thirty-eighth birthday, we had a takeaway and Dad made a point of talking about Mum for a few minutes with a series of "Do you remember when…?" and "She always said that…", and when he ran out of anecdotes, he poured a large glass of wine, switched on the television and watched the news. I remained in the room until an appropriate length of time had passed and then slunk off silently to my bedroom.

Aunt Chrissy had been in, as was usual for a Friday, and everything was dust free and in its place. I reached around to the gap between my wardrobe and the wall and retrieved my current diary, brushing off a tiny piece of webby dust from the corner. From upstairs I could still hear the television and that newsreader who emphasised the wrong syllables in every sentence. I closed the door quietly and settled onto the bed, tucking my feet under my knees so that I was cross-legged.

I began several lines but crossed them all out. What usually came so easily was suddenly difficult; I knew I should write about the fact that it would have been Mum's birthday but I had little to say on the subject. Everything I wrote seemed false and awkward, as though I was writing for the benefit of someone who would judge my level of grief. I wondered what Dad would think if he ever read my diary and found that I barely mentioned Mum. He would probably think it best; grief was a tricky emotion and one best left alone – that's what he'd told Uncle Rob; "best not to stir things up". I sucked the end of my pen and all I could think about was the fact that Mum had found the act of living such a chore that perhaps dying had been a relief. But I didn't want to write that. I couldn't think of anything else yet still had the urge to write something so, leaving the diary to one side, I got up and went to my desk. Unearthing an old pad of lined paper, I bypassed several pages of doodles and drawings and found the next clean page. At the top of the page I wrote, "Amber and the Dark Heart – chapter one" and underlined it with a ruler. It was to become the first story that I would actually manage to complete, having previously only ever produced half-baked efforts, and as it turned out, Amber's heart proved to be so dark that she required two follow-ups and became something of a trilogy.

The teachers at Harper Comprehensive were a varied bunch. Some were as old as baboon-faced Mr Jackson and had apparently been at the school forever; others, like Mr Woods, the music teacher, looked like he was just out of school himself; then of course there was Ms Emery, the hugely fat headteacher and drama teacher and nicknamed Ms Emerald on account of her richly coloured skirts and tie-dye tops. Mr Adams, our new Year 10 English teacher, was somewhere in the middle. I noticed him straight away because he was always smiling and wore dark jeans instead of trousers and a shirt with no tie; Mr Adams noticed me straight away because I could write well and knew that George Eliot was a woman.

"And why do you think a female writer may have chosen to use a man's name?" he asked one morning, attempting, and failing, to seduce a bunch of fifteen-year-olds with *The Mill on the Floss*.

When no one raised a hand, Mr Adams turned to me for the third time in a row. "Naomi, any thoughts?"

"Because she thought she wouldn't have been taken seriously as a writer if people knew she was female," I said, doodling round the letter G on the handout in front of me.

"And do you think that would be the case nowadays?"

I continued onto the E before I realised he was still addressing me. "Oh, no. Nowadays women writers are just as respected as men."

"So, it's not about image then?" Alfie Richards called across the room.

"I'm sorry?"

"Just making a point, sir, that women shouldn't need to suddenly wear make-up and style their hair to get respect."

The class sniggered at Alfie's blatant reference to my newly sculpted hair and carefully drawn eyeliner, courtesy of an obliging Imogen.

"You're going to look hot!" she'd said earlier as she'd helped me apply a thin layer of foundation. She'd watched and nodded encouragingly as I'd drawn black lines around my eyelids and finished off with what I'd hoped were feline flicks in the corners. Then we'd pushed all my hair into a messy bun high on top of my head and secured it with a million wire pins.

"How's that?" she'd asked as we'd studied my reflection in the grubby mirror above the sinks in the girls' toilets.

"I look older. Maybe better…"

"Perk of having an *artiste* as a friend."

"I think an artiste is actually someone who—" but I'd caught Imogen's eye in the glass and stopped. "Thanks. I look pretty."

"Don't be silly, you were already pretty. But now you look *amaaaazing*."

I told myself she was right. I *was* pretty, in a kind of interesting way. I'd inherited Dad's cheekbones, which made me appear a little gaunt if I wasn't smiling, and my ears stuck out a little further than I would have liked, but otherwise there was nothing terrible about my face. I'd recently gone back to my natural blonde, cutting in a long fringe to conceal my forehead, and I'd finally learned to appreciate the contrast with my dark eyes. A bit more experimenting with make-up and I'd be set. I'd turned sideways and studied my profile with a smile; I was on my way to developing my *Self*.

Mr Adams was looking blank. He shook his head in confusion. "I'm not sure of the relevance of your comment, Alfie. I very much hope you are not being personal in any way?"

"Not at all, sir, just appreciating what I see."

Mr Adams waved the comment away and turned back to me. "And can you name another well-respected female author, Naomi?"

"Daphne du Maurier," I said, ignoring Alfie's suggestive smirk, although I couldn't help thinking how a few years ago, I'd have been only too pleased for him to speak to me.

Mr Adams' face brightened. "And… how about a more contemporary example?"

He had moved round to perch on the edge of his desk and was smiling encouragingly. His hair was short at the sides and slightly longer and wavier on top, and he had a habit of tapping the side of his head with a pencil when waiting for an answer. Like now. The class were silent but beginning to fidget furiously and I looked at Mr Adams clutching his copy of Eliot. I felt sorry for him and his insurmountable task.

"Lionel Shriver… Margaret Atwood… Tracy Chevalier?"

He nodded his delight. "Remarkable. And have you read anything by those authors?"

I picked up my pen and continued with my doodle. "Well, I read *The Handmaid's Tale* but it was pretty scary… I read *Double Fault* over the summer and I read *The Girl with the Pearl Earring*…" I paused and looked at the faces around the room. An acne-ridden boy sitting next to Jayden flicked a rubber across the room and it hit another boy in the foot. A couple of girls near the front of the class rolled their eyes and giggled. "Actually, I've only really just started *The Girl with the Pearl Earring*," I said and looked down at my handout. "I'm about quarter of the way through."

"Excellent." Mr Adams suddenly remembered the rest of the class and leapt to his feet. "Has anyone else read anything interesting lately? It would be useful to compare George Eliot's writing to the work of modern authors."

"I've been reading my gaming magazine, sir. It's full of useful stuff about—"

"Thank you, Jayden, but I'm looking for examples of fiction."

"That's discrimination, sir," Jayden said, his expression of mock horror causing the class to dissolve into jeers and laughter.

I kept my head lowered and avoided Jayden's eye. So far, I had managed to avoid retribution for the phone incident, but I certainly didn't want to antagonise him further.

Mr Adams rose to his feet and grinned. "Okay, settle down, settle down. It's absolutely not discrimination, Jayden. There's nothing wrong with reading a gaming mag, I'm merely suggesting the content will not be relevant as a comparison to *The Mill on the Floss*."

The class quietened and Mr Adams clutched the moment. "So..." he looked around the room, "let's see, Molly, what are you reading at the moment?"

Molly widened her eyes, pushed her delicate shoulders back and sucked her pen thoughtfully, allowing the tension to build around the room. We all knew what was coming, all except Mr Adams. Slowly removing the pen and crossing her legs beneath the desk, Molly smiled at her audience. "Facebook, Twitter and Instagram, sir."

That was it. The class erupted into giggles and whoops, and Mr Adams turned on his heels and threw his hands up in the air.

chapter seven

At the end of Year 10, I was given a lead part in the summer production. I was both amazed and impossibly pleased.

I liked drama lessons. I liked taking on a role and becoming somebody who could say something without being laughed at or having their words taken out of context; I found the whole experience incredibly freeing. I also liked Ms Emerald whose vast outfits draped over her body in a cacophony of colours. Her hair was huge and dyed bright red, and she wore it loosely knotted on top of her head where it seemed to want to escape and possibly would have done were it not for a sequined scarf looped over her forehead and pinned at the nape of her neck. She said, "Difference makes the world a better place" a lot, and I thought she was completely fabulous.

The class was spread out on the floor in the drama studio completing a breathing exercise. We were supposed to be in a space on our own but friends had drifted towards each other and there was a lot of sniggering between breaths. Molly and her doll-like friends were watching their rib cages rise and fall and competing to make their breasts look bigger against their skinny waists for the benefit of Jayden Blackwater and his ridiculous crew who were watching surreptitiously from across the room. Jayden had either forgiven me for the phone incident, or deemed me unworthy of the effort required to incite revenge. I suspected the latter. Ms Emerald might have said that difference makes the world a better place but mostly I encountered indifference – people were indifferent towards me, I was irrelevant to their lives.

"Right, for the purpose of the production, we will be linking up with the other Year 10 class who are currently lining up outside. I trust you can all sit quietly while I bring them in?"

It was a rhetorical question and Ms Emerald swept over to the door. We watched in suspense as the other form made their way to the back of the room and dumped bags and coats in a giant heap.

"Take a seat then, come on... find a space and sit. Mingle, mingle! You'll be best friends by the end of this."

Even though they were the same year as us, we had never shared a class and thus, barely knew each other.

True to form, both classes attempted to stick close to their allies despite Ms Emerald's insistence that we "mingle"; all except one who sat in a space next to me and stretched his legs out in front of him.

"Alright?"

I recognised him immediately as the boy who had spoken to me outside after the incident with Jayden. This time, though surprised to be acknowledged again, I managed a breezy "Yeah, you?"

"Oi, Ozzy, shift your moody arse over."

Alfie, who clearly knew the boy – from football, I surmised – shuffled across the floor and gave him a playful shove. I smiled and turned back to face Ms Emerald.

"Okay then, Year 10s; while you all lie back and relax, I'm going to announce the roles for the upcoming production. Remember, everyone will have a part of some description, and it's not a competition, but I've been very careful in my selection and chosen people who I think will really give it their all." Ms Emerald held a list in her hand as she floated between our bodies on the floor. She passed by my foot and the hem of her fuchsia-coloured skirt tickled my bare shins. The window box in the kitchen… hadn't that been filled with trailing fuchsia plants one year? Mum must have planted them. I tried to think of other things that my mother had done, but my mind went blank.

"There's a few girls in here I'd give my all to," said Jayden, causing me to snap back to the present, and the boys to disintegrate into jeers and whistles.

Ms Emerald, without looking up from her list, said, "Deeply offensive, Mr Blackwater. Be gone from my class."

She continued her walkabout as Jayden rose from the floor and swaggered out of the room to a series of catcalls and laughter. He made a face through the glass but quickly withdrew when he saw Ms Emerald lift her hand. Ms Emerald never lost her temper; she was capable of ridding the class of Jayden Blackwater with nothing other than a tone and a raised eyebrow. I caught Molly scrunching up her nose and narrowing her eyes in mock disgust. At the same time, she was rearranging her skirt so that it showed even more of her pale white thighs. Offended yet smug – the sum of Molly Smith's emotions.

"So, as you may know, the script has been kindly written for us by our very own Mr Adams." Ms Emerald paused by the window and swung around, her skirt fanning out dramatically. "Two protagonists – teenage sisters – both of whom wish to pursue a career in acting. Yet…" a raised finger at this point, "only one of them will succeed. It is a story to show the complexities of competitive sibling relationships."

My hand shot up without my meaning it to.

"Yes, Naomi?"

"I was just going to say that I wrote a story about something similar, a brother and a sister who both want a place at a top university, but the brother has social difficulties and in the end the sister feels—"

"And I'm sure it's wonderful." Ms Emerald was smiling but she didn't want interruptions. All eyes were on me and I put my hand down. Behind me, a whisper. "She's always got to make a point about *something*, don't you think?"

As the parts were read out, there were murmurs around the room as my classmates discovered their fates with a mixture of excitement and dismay. Molly, to the delight of her fans, got the part of Bryony, the older sister, and after a long pause, Ms Emerald stopped by my feet and said, "I believe the part of Alice, the other sister, belongs to Miss Rose."

"Me?" I sat bolt upright, my eyes wide.

"You." Ms Emerald was not exactly smiling but there was a definite crinkling around the mouth. "Mr Adams and I were in complete agreement; this part was made for you."

"Mr Adams said that?" I asked, trying to ignore the rather obvious signs of discontent around the room.

"*Ooh, Mr Adams said that?*" Molly mimicked behind me.

"Shut up, Moll," came another voice.

I knew it was Ozzy even before I swivelled round on the floor in time to catch him flick an elastic band at Molly's head.

"Ow… miss, Ozzy Mehmet just—"

"Enough!"

Ozzy Mehmet. … *Ozzy with the stubbly jawline and brooding eyes, Ozzy with his smooth, tanned skin and the already muscular shoulders…* I'd heard the girls talk about him but hadn't known exactly who he was. Ozzy Mehmet sticking up for me? Ha. Molly was going to hate me more than ever.

"Does that mean I have to spend a lot of time with *her*?" she piped up immediately.

"Not if you don't want to," said Ms Emerald, and then, without missing a beat, added, "you can give up your part to someone else if you'd rather."

Molly shot me a look of utter disgust but I held her gaze. The growing suspicion that Ms Emerald preferred *me* over *her* buoyed me up. I jutted my chin out defiantly; I was going to play this part to perfection and watching Molly crumble beneath me on-stage would be the sweetest victory.

chapter eight

THE FOLLOWING WEEK, MR ADAMS SET A PIECE of creative writing for homework. I was caught up in the buzz of learning lines, so rather than writing something new, I selected a story from the growing pile on my desk at home. It wasn't my best, but the three-page effort about a child befriending a ghost was all I could find to fit the "Supernatural" brief. It wasn't even particularly scary, more comical, yet something about it worked well enough to catch Mr Adams' eye.

"Naomi, have you got a minute?" he said, at the end of the lesson on Monday. Mr Adams was the only teacher who spoke casually like this, as though I had the right to turn around and say, "Actually, no, I haven't, sorry."

I nodded but laboured over the task of gathering my things together to allow the rest of the class to leave; I hated the idea of Molly or Jayden listening in. When everyone had gone, I perched on the edge of a nearby desk. "Sir?"

"Fantastic story, Naomi, really funny."

"Oh." *Really?* "Glad you liked it."

"I more than liked it," he said, coming around to lean against the front of his desk so that he was directly opposite me. Today he was wearing his usual jeans with a white shirt; he smelt clean and fresh and young. I wondered what my father smelt like to *his* students. "I thought it was extremely well-thought through, and you had me laughing out loud when your protagonist got his own back on the ghost!"

"Cool," I said, remembering how I had thrown the story together with no thought for a plot.

"So, I am putting you forward to represent the school at the awards ceremony at the end of the month along with Denise O'Brien who also submitted a good piece of work. How does that sound?" He tapped his ear with a pencil.

"Seriously?"

"Seriously."

I paused. "Will you be there?"

"Naturally! There's no way I would miss my star pupils getting the recognition they deserve."

"Star pupil?"

The tapping stopped and he leant forwards a little, his expression suddenly serious. He actually did smell lovely. "Naomi, you must realise you are in a different league from the rest of the class? You are incredibly well-

read for someone your age, and your writing skills...
Look," he placed a hand on my arm and I looked at it,
saw his long fingers resting on my green-jerseyed elbow,
"you have heaps of potential, heaps! It's my job to help
you unlock it." He removed his hand and laughed, a
loud and throaty sound. "Ooh, that sounds really corny,
doesn't it?"

I just studied his fingers, remembering what they had
felt like on my arm.

"Okay." He jumped up from the desk and began
collecting up textbooks from the tables. "So I'll give you
the details when I have them and we can organise travel
and so on. Oh, and be sure to let your dad know because
there will be extra tickets for relatives."

I stood slowly and pushed my bag strap up onto my
shoulder.

"How's the play going, by the way?"

"Yeah... good."

"Excellent. Well, I hope the script works?"

It took me a moment to remember that he'd written it.
"It's really good, sir."

Mr Adams grinned. "Go on then, or you'll be late for
your next lesson."

A different league from the rest of the class.

"What do you think of Mr Adams?" I asked Imogen
the next day. Her lunchtime art club had been cancelled,
and we were sitting on the low wall which divided the
football pitch and the netball court.

"What do you mean, what do I think of him?"

"Like, you know… compared with the other teachers… he's cool, right?"

"Duh, obviously, the rest of them are about ninety!" She looked at me and I turned away towards the footballers. "Don't tell me you fancy him?"

Jayden and Alfie were fighting for possession of the ball; Jayden gave a shove and ran off, leaving Alfie in a heap on the floor.

I whipped my head round. "Don't be stupid."

Something shifted in Imogen's face. "Nae, I don't want to burst your bubble but really? Mr Adams? He's a grown man… you're fifteen."

"Yeah, *obviously*."

Her eyes were hard as she added, "Anyway, he's got a gorgeous girlfriend. I've seen her pick him up after school."

"For God's sake, Immy," I picked at my thumbnail, "I didn't say I wanted him to be interested, I was just…" My hand was covered in biro doodles and I tried to rub them off. "I was just making a point."

"Yeah well, point made, he's better looking than the other teachers and better looking than all the gross boys… God, look at Jayden, he thinks he's something special, doesn't he?"

Jayden had scored a goal and was lapping the pitch with his shirt over his head, much to the delight of Molly and the other Year 10 girls who stood whooping on the edge of the pitch. I did not see the attraction. Jayden Blackwater was immature and arrogant; he had nothing to interest me. "You said he *was* special. Popular and special."

"And I was wrong. You were right, he's a prick."

"Mr Adams said I'm in a different league."

Imogen paused, considering her words. "Well, you are. Academically. You know that's what he meant, right?"

"Yeah."

"I think it's brilliant."

"What is?"

"That you're doing so well. I mean, other kids… they might have gone off the rails or whatever…"

"What?"

"Nothing. Forget it. But he's right, you have potential…"

"That's what *he* said."

"… and he's right. I wish I was half as clever as you." She laughed and rocked into me, making me smile.

I loved Imogen and her ability to be genuinely pleased for other people. There was not an ounce of jealousy in her entire body. We watched the football and kicked our legs against the wall.

"Okay, well, you know who else is nice?"

Imogen popped open a packet of crisps. "Who?"

I nodded towards the side-line to where Ozzy Mehmet crouched on his haunches, talking to a handful of boys.

"Oh, my God, not Alfie!"

"No, not Alfie… *him*."

Imogen followed my gaze once more and then shook her head, pursing her lips knowingly. "He's gay." She stuffed a handful of crisps into her mouth.

"He's not bloody well gay! But unfortunately he likes Molly Smith, I saw him talking to her in the canteen." This was true. Ever since he'd stuck up for me in the drama lesson, I'd been aware of Ozzy's presence around the school, and seeing him slouched against the wall at lunchtime while Molly giggled next to him had annoyed me.

Imogen screwed the crisp packet into a ball and stuffed it into her jacket pocket. "Everyone fancies Molly. Even the gay ones." She jumped off the wall. "Thing is," she said, her face deadpan, "she might have the looks, but she hasn't got the *longevity*... I'm gonna get a boyfriend who loves me for my creativity, and my art, and my sparkling wit... everything on my terms."

I laughed. "Cool. Do it."

Rehearsals for the play began in earnest but much as I relished having such a major part to play, some of my classmates did little to mask their annoyance.

"They think I got the part because the teachers feel sorry for me," I complained as Molly and her clique pushed through us one afternoon. Imogen and I were eating chips near the front steps of the school.

"No, they don't," Imogen replied, "they think you got the part because the teachers think you're amaaazing."

"So why are they so mean then? They barely speak to me."

"Obvious. It's jealousy, pure and simple."

I chewed a chip in silence.

"Do you think I'm weird?" I said, a moment later.

Imogen laughed. "Course you are! That's why I hang around, so we can be weird together." She pointed to her newly acquired nose ring.

When I didn't respond, she put her chips on the wall and an arm around my shoulder. "Forget the other kids, Nae. You don't usually let them get to you."

I shrugged her off. "They're not getting to me... couldn't care less to be honest."

She sniffed loudly. "Good. That's what I thought." She started eating again. "Anyway, it's going to be fun getting to work together on this," she said with a mouthful of vinegary chips.

Imogen was helping to create the set alongside other members of the art club. So far, they had painted a glorious backdrop which could be flipped halfway through the production; one side showing a girl's bedroom, the other the inside of a drama studio. At the end of the show, both would be removed to reveal a brightly lit stage adorned with spotlights and cushioned by heavy velvet curtains.

"Yeah, you're right," I grinned. "I've got to say, though, I'm not sure about the part where my character is heard singing by a talent scout walking past her open window... bit Billy Elliot, isn't it?"

"I don't remember Billy Elliot singing?"

"You know what I mean, it's all... a bit predictable, that's all."

"Come on, it's a school production; we all want a happy ending."

"If *I'd* written it, I would have had the other sister disappearing off into the sunset wringing her hands in despair, not sitting proudly in the audience like..."

Imogen laughed, tipping her head back, her curls losing their reddy tinge in the sun and becoming almost golden. "That's because you're such a doom-maker, Naomi Rose!"

At the end of June, a heatwave ensued which caused everyone, including the teachers, to become irritable and short-tempered. The only person who didn't seem affected by the heavy, thick air was Ozzy. Every time I saw him around the school, he was smiling and talking with the crowd who followed him as though he were some kind of Messiah. I understood the attraction. He had the confidence and mannerisms of someone much older and, despite his articulate speech and obvious intelligence, he'd found, and kept, his place as one of the cool kids, something I'd never achieve.

Because he was so popular, it took me by surprise when Ozzy sought me out one lunchtime to ask how I was.

"Perfectly fine," I said, automatically looking around for Jayden or Alfie, expecting them to jump out of a bush laughing. But no one was paying us any attention and Ozzy walked in step with me all the way round the perimeter of the school, making small talk about mock exams and homework until we reached the main entrance just as the bell went for afternoon lessons. He stopped walking and said I'd made him laugh the other day when I'd called Jayden an obnoxious little prick, then he patted my shoulder and jogged away down the corridor.

The next time I saw him was a couple of days later when we were both out late for break. Again, he walked alongside me, this time quizzing me on my interests and what I got up to at home. When I mentioned Mum, he didn't make a big deal of it but nodded thoughtfully and said, "You must miss her," to which I said nothing at all.

He told me the following day that he had moved from London a few years ago to live with his restaurateur uncle who would slip him a bit of cash for clearing tables or loading the dishwasher. "Jesus, it's twenty quid!" he laughed when I suggested he was legally too young to work. "Don't be so weird." But I didn't seem to mind Ozzy calling me weird. Ozzy, who managed to stay cool and confident without ever resorting to the belittling tactics of his peers, was, I believed, the only person in the school (aside from Imogen and Mr Adams) worth talking to. I was proud that we had developed a friendship of sorts.

The heatwave continued until all the green disappeared from the grass leaving the school playing fields yellow and patchy. Day after day, we trudged into the hot drama studio after lessons and flung ourselves down amidst remnants of stale sweat and the stench from the overflowing bin in the corner of the room.

"Miss, it stinks in here," Alfie complained pointlessly as we struggled into our roles amidst much lethargic flailing of arms and sighs of protestation. Ms Emerald did her best to rally us despite clearly suffering from the heat herself and got into the habit of supplying us with cold fizzy drinks from the staffroom fridge in order to appease us.

Molly and I were together a lot, and I noticed that her animosity towards me dissipated a little when we were alone. When one scene in particular was giving us trouble, we agreed to stay late one evening to work on it.

"I just don't think Bryony needs to stand there watching the whole time, it's weird." Molly was sucking on a lollypop and debating the same point for the umpteenth time.

"Well, it's in the script," I said, again.

"I don't think we have to do everything to the letter though, do you?"

She had never, ever asked my opinion and I blanked for a moment, reluctant to lose the moment. "I suppose not. Actually, I did make a couple of suggestions for changing the script... you know that bit where Alice comes home late and they end up arguing? I think it would be more exciting if Bryony falls, just by accident... like trips over something and then Alice could go and help... it would be more dramatic... and then more of a contrast when they make up."

Molly stared as she listened, then with a slow pop removed the sticky red lolly from her mouth and said, "That's actually not a bad idea. Although..."

"What?"

"Well, I don't reckon Ms Emerald or Mr Adams is going to let us make changes so close to the performance. What about if we practise it between ourselves and just surprise them with it on the night?"

"Are you *serious*?"

"Come on, it will be fun! It will show we've used our initiative and you could even rewrite the argument a little to give it more oomph. You're good at writing..." She was smiling shyly, her eyes wide under questioning eyebrows. "... I've listened to enough of it in English classes." And she stuck her tongue out, just a tiny bit, and winked.

"Right."

"Oh, come on! I'm only messing with you."

I lifted my chin a little and folded my arms. "Fine. I suppose we could give it a go."

By the time Ms Emerald arrived wearily to send us home, Molly and I had perfected the scene. Bryony and Alice would argue about the forthcoming audition and then, just as the shouting reached its peak, Alice would pretend to shove Bryony so that she fell backwards and, grasping the enormity of what might have happened, Alice would rush over to help and they would clutch each other, exhausted by the fighting and resolve to work things out. We practised the shove over and over so that my hand barely made contact before Molly stumbled back in precisely the right spot to land safely on a mottled sofa which formed part of the set. If I was worried over changing the scene without permission, having Molly onside made me brave.

Ozzy was outside as we left the building, leaning up against a wall and doing something on his phone.

"How'd it go?" he asked, pushing off from the wall and falling into step beside us.

I was surprised that he had been waiting all this time, but pleased. It would be nice to have someone to chat to on the way home, and he had promised to nick a portion of chips from his uncle's place next time we were passing. Perhaps when Molly left, I'd hint at how hungry I was.

"Yeah, it went okay," Molly was saying, swishing her hair over to one side and making a show of hitching up her socks. And then she righted herself, and I watched her snake an arm around Ozzy's thin waist and place her hand in the back pocket of his jeans. The breath caught in my throat, and I almost stopped walking. Had it not been for Ozzy's presence, I could have happily punched Molly in the mouth right there and then, especially after she cut me a sly, twisted smile. But Ozzy was beaming. I had to quickly pretend not to be bothered and look the other way.

"So, I'm guessing you know?" Ozzy drawled, giving my arm a light punch.

"Know what?" I really couldn't have been breezier.

"'Bout me and Molly."

Molly was still smirking, but I was damned if I would give her the satisfaction. We may have begun work on the foundations but there was a long way to go before that bridge was built. "Yeah, course. I'm glad. You make a great couple."

They absolutely did *not* make a great couple. Ozzy was worth ten of her.

It wasn't that I was jealous (Ozzy was attractive but he was no Mr Adams), it was that he deserved to be with someone as genuine as he was. He needed someone who stood up for what they believed in rather than hiding behind coquettish smiles like Molly did, pretending to be outraged whilst simultaneously encouraging Jayden Blackwater's misogyny. Ozzy would get bored, I was sure of it, and the sooner the better.

"And now that you're mates, we can all get along?" he asked hopefully, and Molly and I exchanged tentative nods and smiles.

"No reason why not," I said and Molly said something to the same effect. Then she pulled Ozzy's face round and kissed him firmly on the lips, just to make sure I understood exactly how things were going to be.

I arrived home to be met by voices coming from the living room: Dad, Aunt Chrissy. And then my heart sank as I recognised Violet's soft laughter fluttering across the hallway. Arthur appeared in the kitchen doorway and I crouched and held my hand out. Normally he sauntered straight over but he just stopped and lay down. Probably hot and bothered like the rest of us, I thought.

"Naomi, is that you?" Who else was it going to be?

My shirt was sticking to my back and I longed to go upstairs and strip off, but I discarded my school bag at the bottom of the stairs and obediently crossed the hall. Dad was standing with his arms folded and his back to the window. Aunt Chrissy was nestled into the sofa clutching a cup of tea while Violet perched on the edge with her hands primly in her lap.

I hadn't seen my cousin for some time. She looked different – taller, definitely, and slimmer. Her ginger hair was swept into a neat, low bun, not a strand out of place. She looked vaguely uncomfortable.

"Good, I'm glad you're home," Dad said, as though I might have gone somewhere else as I mightily wished I had. "Violet has popped over to share some exciting news."

I looked at my cousin and returned her sweet smile with my stale one. "Cool. Can I get a drink first?"

"No, I don't think we should make her wait a moment longer!"

"What's wrong with Arthur, by the way?"

"Nothing, he's fine. Now stop changing the subject." Dad was indicating that I should sit down so I collapsed dutifully into the armchair opposite and held my arms out, palms skywards, ready to receive the amazing announcement.

"Do you have to be so dramatic?" Dad asked with a frown.

"Oh, now come on, Oliver, the poor girl's been at school all day, leave her be." Aunt Chrissy beamed over at me but I kept my eyes on Violet's face, studying her perfect nose and pretty freckles and daring her to surprise me. Violet, to her credit, refused to rise to my pettiness and continued to smile shyly.

"I've been offered a work experience placement for next summer at the hospital."

I nodded, expecting more, but she stopped speaking then and I realised that that was it, that was the big news. Aunt Chrissy was quietly turning her teacup round in her hands and tilting her head to one side as though considering the quality of the design. When I looked over at Dad, his face was lit up like a beacon and he was grinning widely, showing all of his teeth.

"Isn't that just amazing?" he said earnestly, waiting for my awed reaction.

"Just admin stuff," Violet said into the void, "*obviously* I wouldn't be allowed to see actual patients."

"Yes, but what an opportunity!" Dad was still looking at me. "I mean it just goes to show, the sky's the limit, isn't it?"

"Oliver," Aunt Chrissy looked up from her teacup analysis, "it's just work experience."

"Rubbish!" Dad exclaimed. "It may be work experience for now but it's also the first step, isn't it? I wonder how many pupils at Harper Comp would actually consider medicine as a profession. What's so great about the grammar school is that it is so unashamedly ambitious... I mean, in a world that seems so intent on fairness and equal opportunities, the grammar stands out as one of the few institutions to still actively encourage bright kids into aiming high, to pushing the boundaries!"

What? Incredulity must have been scrawled across my face as I watched him pace the length of the room and loosen his tie. I searched desperately for signs of my liberal father. A few years ago, he had been anti-selective education to the point of mania. Had he not hated the principle behind grammar schools? And now he was showering praise upon his niece for securing a placement in a hospital, a placement no doubt offered *because* of the stuck-up school she attended.

"What do you think *you* might like to do for work experience, Naomi?" Aunt Chrissy asked, trying to refocus the attention.

I looked down at my hands and picked at a loose nail. "I dunno yet... I quite like writing... maybe something on a magazine?"

"Oh, that would be wonderful, wouldn't it, Oliver? Really exciting, you might get to work on one of the big glossies... meet all the celebs!"

Dad snorted. He had wandered over to the drinks cabinet and was pouring himself a large whisky. I watched the amber liquid settle over the ice and wished I could have a sip.

"Notoriously difficult industry to get into, publishing; only a few make it."

"Not as difficult as medicine," I countered, "and I'm not so keen on the publishing aspect anyway…"

Aunt Chrissy was leaning forwards, her round, soft face a vision of kindness. "So what is it you would like to do instead?"

"I just like writing. Stories mainly… but maybe I could write articles… and stuff."

Dad turned and held his drink aloft before tasting it, grimacing as the first sip went down. "The problem is just *that*," and he pointed a finger towards me, "articles and 'stuff', it's just all so vague, nothing concrete to focus on."

I winced. Even Violet was looking at me with something like pity now.

"Oliver, you're not being very encouraging." My aunt stood up and placed her teacup on the table and came and placed a hand on my shoulder. "Have you written much already, sweetheart?"

"Some. As I say, mostly stories," and then as an afterthought, I added, "although I am contributing to the script for the end of year production."

Dad looked at me sharply. "I thought you had a part in it?" he said, swilling the whisky around in the glass.

"Yeah, I do. But I'm also having a hand in the scriptwriting." I thought of the scene Molly and I had perfected that very afternoon.

"Well!" Aunt Chrissy got up and kissed the top of my head. "I couldn't be prouder! Both my favourite girls on their way to the top. Come on then, Vi, time to get home and put something in the oven for dinner."

And then, as my aunt passed my father I heard her whisper, "You're too hard on her, Oliver."

I scowled as the door closed on Violet's perfection and then I escaped upstairs to strip naked, leaving my crumpled, sweaty uniform in a heap on the floor.

After changing into a clean pair of shorts and a vest, I ventured back downstairs to find Dad scouring the kitchen cupboards in the hope of finding something edible for dinner. Our once highly structured evening routine had become somewhat lax over recent months. He looked up as I entered the room and offered a weak, unnatural smile. I could tell he was quite drunk.

"Sorry if I was a bit—"

"Doesn't matter," I interrupted, embarrassed to see him as anything other than his usual, together, self.

"It does matter. I just want you to realise your potential and I don't think… I think I may have… I worry that I haven't done enough to push you."

"I don't want to be pushed."

"You need pushing, everyone needs pushing."

"Just because I don't want to be a doctor, doesn't mean I won't have a career."

"As a writer?"

"Maybe."

I waited for the spiel about how writers rarely make a living from their work, about how they spend years honing their craft only for their work to be ripped apart by unscrupulous money-hungry agents, about how the life of a writer is romanticised far beyond anything reality has to offer. But Dad closed the fridge, took his glasses off and wiped them on his shirt sleeve. Once satisfied, he placed them back on his nose and looked straight at me, "Let's get a takeaway and then… maybe you'd let me read some of your work?"

I paused, waiting to see if he meant it, and then broke into a slow grin.

I was oddly nervous about showing him my writing and spent some time going through the piles on my desk before carefully selecting three of my best short stories. When I heard the doorbell, I swept down the stairs and smiled winningly at the delivery driver, telling him to keep the change from the money I'd taken from Dad's wallet.

"I'll sort it!" I called through to the living room.

In the kitchen, I dished up carefully, making sure that Dad had plenty of the Chow Mein and not too much of the bright red sauce which he said made him cough. I spooned out the chicken and added the lemon to Dad's plate because he liked to squeeze it over the plate. Then I placed everything on two trays and, with my stories wedged under one arm, I carried it all through with a flourish.

"Dinner is served!"

I stood staring at the sofa where Dad had passed out on his side, one arm draped on the floor and the other under his cheek. I set one tray on the table, crumpled the stories into a ball, turned and carried my dinner up to my room.

chapter nine

"I don't understand, Naomi. Help me to understand."

Ms Emerald's office was little more than a cupboard. It was dark and poky with barely enough space for a desk or the two chairs on which we now sat facing each other. Behind the desk, copies of *A Midsummer Night's Dream* towered precariously on a shelf, enough for the A-level class to have one each; next to them, a smaller pile of scripts, the title of which I failed to make out. The desk was surprisingly clear and held nothing but a single mug containing a stain of leftover coffee. I imagined Ms Emerald sitting in the claustrophobic silence after a long day and drinking from the mug. I had never seen her look anything other than vibrant and excited, even during those last hot weeks of rehearsals. Until now. Now she sat with her elbows on the desk and her bejewelled fingers splayed across either cheek. Her round face was flushed, and under the artificial light I could see shadows under her eyes.

"Well?"

"I'm sorry, Ms Emerald."

"I'm glad you're sorry but it doesn't help me to understand. I gave you that part because I had faith in you. I felt you deserved it."

"I know."

"I realise you had some misgivings about the script but, quite frankly, the honour of playing one of the lead parts should have been enough; I told you quite clearly that we would respect the original script and then you…"

"I'm sorry."

Now was my chance to tell Ms Emerald about Molly. It was just me and my teacher, no other pupils around to talk over me or make me out to be a liar, no one to dispute my version of events; I could say exactly what Molly had suggested and how she'd persuaded me to go along with it. I should have known. I bloody well should have known… I'd been naïve… how stupid… how unlike me… I'd make sure *that* didn't happen again.

The day of the performance had been hectic from the minute we arrived at school. Imogen and other members of the art department transported the final sections of scenery, sound checks were carried out and backing tracks tested, chairs were laid out for the audience and costumes hung on a metal rail in one of the nearby classrooms. There had been a buzz amongst the pupils that the fraught exasperation of the staff had failed to quell. By the time the audience arrived, the buzz had muted to a nervous shuffling behind the curtain.

The first half went without a hitch and we clattered backstage to await the set change. I dared to look out from behind the curtain, trying to spot where Dad was sitting but the audience were shuffling between seats, collecting drinks and queuing for the loo. Imogen skipped over with her friend Skye and they both said that I was "amaaazing". I smiled graciously and finished adjusting my hair. Over Imogen's shoulder I caught Molly's eye and grinned. Our big scene was coming up and I wanted to offer a little encouragement but Molly's glance was cool and distant; perhaps she hadn't really seen me. Of course, that's when I should have known, right then.

The lights went down and we took our places.

What I remember the most was the noise from the audience. It was sudden, collective – a wave of air as everyone gasped at the same time. I was centre stage. The sofa was where it should have been and everything else was in its place. Everything and everyone. Except Molly. She was lying on the floor in front of the stage, her newly curled hair splayed over her face, her hands clutching her ankle. She was whimpering. People were rushing forwards, Ms Emerald was sweeping in and floating to the floor and Mr Adams was telling people to stay where they were. Kids peeped out from behind the curtain to see what had happened but no one would say.

After a few moments, the noise quietened and I felt the eyes of a hundred people turn on me. But I was doing what I was told. I was staying where I was.

Now, facing my headteacher, I fought for the words to come out, words to redeem myself and make Ms Emerald's opinion of me revert to one that was positive. But the words wouldn't come. I hung my head. What was the point? When all was said and done, Molly had been the more accomplished actress.

Ms Emerald sighed. "I thought so much better of you, Naomi."

I knew how it looked. I could see now just how clever Molly had been in making the whole scenario look like an act of vengeance against her; everybody knew that we had history, and everybody now knew that she was going out with Ozzy, with *my* friend.

"I wouldn't have been surprised if Molly's family had wanted to take matters further... as it is, you've been incredibly lucky and they are putting it down to a trivial dispute between the two of you."

There flashed a mental image of Molly's parents sitting her down and asking for her version of events, of Molly shedding fake tears and telling them how I'd always had it in for her. I wondered whether they believed her or whether they knew the truth, that their daughter was a vicious cow who had set the whole thing up. Perhaps that was why they didn't want to take the matter further, in case it got their daughter into trouble. They were seeing through her lies but standing by her.

Ms Emerald massaged her temples and I watched the skin around her eyes grow taut and then relax in turn.

"But the saddest thing," she continued to massage, "by far the saddest thing, is your lack of respect for Mr Adams' work."

She had me there. Mr Adams and his kind words when I received the part, Mr Adams with his arm resting gently on my shoulder during rehearsals, Mr Adams, the only person in the whole school to actually give a shit. A lone tear slid down my cheek and rested on my chin.

"I can see you're upset, Naomi, and actually I'm glad because perhaps it means you do have the moral compass I thought you did. Is your father waiting for you outside?"

"Dad didn't come." I had stood under those stage lights and the scrutiny of the crowd and waited for my father to stand up and come to me. Several minutes had passed and Molly had been helped to a chair before I'd realised he wasn't there.

Ms Emerald was staring at me oddly. "I see. Well, I will obviously have to speak to him but perhaps that can be done over the phone. Go home. Think about how best to make amends. We'll talk again tomorrow when we've all had a chance to digest the evening."

Imogen was waiting for me by the front gate.

"Oh, Nae…"

I smeared the angry tears across my face with the back of my hand.

"What were you thinking?" she said, tucking a strand of hair behind my left ear.

"I didn't… it wasn't my idea…" but I couldn't finish my sentence because speaking created fresh tears and I wrung out my hands in frustration.

"You've got to admit it was a bit off?" she said, though not unkindly.

I stared at her, silently pleading with her to see the truth but the hopelessness of the situation was too much and I began to walk off down the road.

"Nae, I'm not trying to be…" she followed me and caught up. "I'm on your side, honestly, it's just, you know, with Molly and everything, you have to admit it looked like you pushed her on purpose."

"But I didn't! I barely touched her."

"But even so—"

"It was all planned, don't you understand?" Finally, my voice came through. "We were getting on… when she got with Ozzy I thought she was trying to be friends… like, for *his* sake. I wanted a bigger reaction for my character but it was Molly who suggested I push her… we practised and practised it so she wouldn't get hurt. There was no way she could have fallen from the stage without doing it herself, I didn't…"

"Nae, listen to me." Imogen's grip on my arm was firm and I stopped walking and stared at my feet. "If you say that's the truth, then that's the truth."

"It is."

"But even so, you took the piss by changing the scene and it fucked up in your face."

"Immy!" She might as well just have slapped me.

"I'm just trying to help. It's just… why do you have to be so…"

"What?"

"I don't know, like, so *awkward*?"

"Awkward?" I sniffed, genuinely baffled now. "Are you serious?"

"I don't want to hurt your feelings."

"You're not hurting my feelings, you're smashing them to pieces…"

"Nae… you're being dramatic."

"Hold on, you're basically saying that it's my fault that Molly is such a bitch."

"God, no. She is a bitch. I'm just saying that you make it easy for her sometimes."

"What does that mean?"

"Nothing. You know what? I'm sorry."

"I've only ever tried to help people, it's not my fault that it's always thrown back in my face."

Imogen blinked and fiddled with her nose ring. "Maybe the 'helping' comes over a bit like you're… I mean… you don't *always* have to know the answer to *everything*."

"So, everything's my fault."

"That's not what I'm saying. Sometimes it's just the way you say things."

"I can't believe this! I've gone from wrecking the school play to being… patronising. I thought you were my best friend."

Imogen snapped impatiently, "For God's sake, Nae, no one thinks in terms of best friends… we're not kids, no one has a best friend anymore, we're all just a group."

"Who?! Who is just a group? As far as I can see everyone is in a group except me."

"You have Ozzy."

I hesitated. Ozzy. How was he going to react to the news that I had supposedly pushed his girlfriend off the stage? "Yeah well, I doubt he'll stick around now."

"You're being ridiculous."

"Am I? Oh, I'm so sorry, I'll try and think about my behaviour in the future."

"There. That." She laughed, but her exasperation was obvious. "That's exactly the kind of patronising snotty language you use with everyone, can't you see how you come across?"

"Oh, fuck off."

And though I heard her calling me back, I kept walking and didn't turn. I didn't need her, or Ozzy, or anyone.

I stormed home, taking each step with such purpose and ready to kick anything that got in the way. Dad would surely have spoken to Ms Emerald by now. I wasn't going to take any of it though, not when he couldn't even be bothered to turn up; I would get in there first, pre-empt his shitty excuse about work.

He was at the door before I had fully turned my key. Aunt Chrissy was there too, standing in the hallway with Uncle Rob and Violet. Great, just what I needed.

"Good, you're home." But Dad's tone was urgent, not cross.

"What's going on? What are you all doing here?" I asked, shrugging out of my jacket and throwing it over the banisters.

"We just popped in to see you both but then we found—" Aunt Chrissy looked distraught.

"It's Arthur," piped up Violet, "he's not well."

I hadn't even noticed the cat basket by Dad's feet, nor that he had his coat on. "What?" I crouched and put my finger through the wire grill, but Arthur was curled into a sorrowful heap at the back of the basket. "I told you there was something wrong, didn't I?"

"Did you?" Dad's voice was vague.

"Are you taking him to the vets?"

"Your dad was just on his way," said Uncle Rob. "We were going to wait for you to come back, but now you're here…"

"I think you should come with me," Dad interrupted, "it's for the best."

I put my jacket back on without a word. Thoughts of Molly and Imogen evaporated as I took the basket from Dad's grasp and again, peered inside. Arthur's eyes were tiny crescents of yellow and I whispered through the grate, "Come on then, beautiful boy… come on."

It was acute kidney failure. It would be the kindest thing to do, considering Arthur's age; he would feel no more pain and the end would be quiet and dignified. That's what we were told, and I believed the gentle vet who smiled up at us as we stood hopelessly beside the examination table. I believed her because it was too painful not to but I was not prepared for the final glance from Arthur as he peered lovingly out at us. I reached into the basket and lifted him one last time, held him like a baby and kissed his tabby head.

I told him through my tears that he was going to a better, pain-free place and he purred trustingly in my arms. Dad patted me gently on the back and the vet looked at her feet.

Ozzy had sent me three messages by the time I arrived home with the empty cat basket. I called him back from the privacy of my bedroom and steeled myself for our first row.

"What the fuck, Nae? Molly reckons you shoved her off the stage."

Sinking down onto the bed with a sigh, I cradled the phone between cheek and shoulder whilst peeling off my tights. "She's lying."

"I thought you two were alright now."

"She was pretending to like me."

"Are you serious? Nae, if this is some kind of weird bullshit, I haven't got time."

There was traffic in the background and I pictured Ozzy strutting down the road looking furious. "It's not bullshit. She's lying." I rolled the tights into a ball and threw them across the room; they landed perfectly, right in the centre of the laundry bin. He was silent, and all I could hear were cars.

"Ozzy?"

"It's a tricky one, Nae. Molly saying one thing, you another."

"Believe what you want, Ozzy. I don't care."

"You what? So now you're too high and mighty to bother defending yourself?"

The crack in the ceiling became fuzzy. "I shouldn't have to… not to a friend."

"Nae…"

"And for your information, my cat just died."

I hung up.

If Ms Emerald had phoned as she had threatened to, Dad made no mention of it. He may have forgotten, or he may have decided that losing Arthur was enough of a punishment. Either way, I had a much worse fate to face.

I waited outside of Mr Adams' office at lunchtime and hung my head to an appropriate level when he called me in.

Perhaps I imagined it, but I thought there was just a hint of amusement across his face as he watched me sit down. He placed his elbows on the desk and leaned his face upon balled-up fists.

"Naomi. And to what do I owe this pleasure?"

I toyed with the idea of telling the truth, held a little fantasy in my head of Molly getting shot down in flames… but I soon deflated and made my apology instead. Brief, contrite, *sincere*.

He pulled open the plastic wrapping on his shop-bought sandwiches. "Don't be too hard on yourself, move on."

Ham and mustard. Good choice. "Um, okay?"

Mr Adams *was* finding this funny; I could see his face twitching with the effort not to smile and I sat up a little taller.

"Some people are not easy to like," he said, easing out the first sandwich and narrowly avoiding a white shirt and mustard disaster in the process. He wiped up the yellow splodge with a scrap of paper and placed it in the bin beside the desk.

"You mean Molly?" I asked.

He paused, chewing thoughtfully. "I will rephrase. Some people are not easy to get along with."

I nodded and watched his jaw working through the soggy bread.

"I'm not going to condone what happened but I have to say, I did like the way you altered that line."

"Which one?" I edged forwards, interested now.

"Just after Molly sniped at you, 'You'll never be good enough for the lead,' you shouted, 'and you'll never even be good enough for the chorus!' – Clever, I liked it. It added value to the scene."

Ha! Ms Emerald and Dad and all the kids who'd said I shouldn't tamper with the script… they'd been wrong. I hadn't shown disrespect… I'd *added value*.

"Which brings me nicely onto something much more important. The awards ceremony. You haven't forgotten it's next week?"

That was it, the big showdown?

Evidently it was and I floated out of the room a few minutes later, confident enough even to flash a smile at Ms Emerald as I passed her in the corridor.

"You've seen Mr Adams?" she asked, her expression a perfect depiction of stern.

"Yes, miss. And I'm really sorry for all the trouble I've caused."

Funny how easy it was to apologise profusely when the event no longer mattered. I didn't care enough about

Molly Smith to grass her up, not now I knew that Mr Adams didn't like her either.

"And *I'm* sorry to hear about your cat," said Ms Emerald, her face softening as she rested a hand on my shoulder.

Fate continued to be on my side as the scandal of the school production was obliterated by the news that Suzy Longman was pregnant.

"Who's the father?" I whispered to Imogen in Maths.

"Apparently, she doesn't know," Imogen whispered back, and we both took great pleasure in covering our mouths in mock horror. Suzy Longman, whose wayward teeth had long since been tethered back into their rightful position, had become a particular hit with the boys over recent months. Immy and I had watched, not a little wistfully, as she'd waltzed around the school with her army of admirers. Now, my jealousy had vanished and despite the relief that the focus had been taken from me, I felt a little sorry for the girl.

"So, you've heard then?" Ozzy appeared out of thin air as I was walking home. I tried not to show how immensely pleased I was.

"About Suzy? Yeah, poor girl."

"It's not mine."

I whipped round to face him. "Why would it be yours? You're with Molly."

He fell into step beside me and rubbed his chin. I could see he had been experimenting with his clippers because the facial hair of which he was very proud had been artfully cut into an impeccable goatee.

"Nah. We're taking a break."

I could have leapt high into the air and performed a series of cartwheels.

"Oh. Cool. Why?"

"Dunno."

My bag, overflowing with books, was slipping and I hitched it further up onto my shoulder. Ozzy, as usual, had no bag. He somehow managed to live an effortless existence in which he swung through school life borrowing the odd pen here, the odd book there, and achieving inexplicably decent marks along the way.

"You don't know?"

He stuck his hands deeper into his pockets and shrugged. "She's fit. But she can also be a bitch." And then he turned and winked, a look of playful amusement on his face.

"Huh. Is that your way of saying you believe me?"

He shrugged again. "I'm not committing to anything… but something tells me that you're alright."

"Alright?"

"Yeah. Maybe I was too quick to defend Molly."

That would have to do. "It's fine, she was your girlfriend."

"And you're my mate. If I got it wrong, I'm sorry. It won't happen again."

chapter ten

I CLAMBERED ONTO THE COACH BEHIND DENISE O'Brien. She reminded me a little of Charlotte with the blinky eye; not in appearance, (for Denise was short and robust with wide hips whereas Charlotte had been as spindly as a willow branch), but in her mannerisms – they were both like baby tortoises, just keeping their heads down until it was safe to emerge.

I nodded and sat next to her on the coach because to sit anywhere else would have seemed rude. As the coach moved off, heading for the town hall where we would get to read an extract from our stories and receive a prize fund for our school library, I began unravelling my earphones.

"Are your parents coming tonight?" Poor Denise's gentle smile melted away as soon as the words left her lips. She flushed scarlet and scratched her nose furiously. "Oh, oh my God, I'm so stupid…"

"It's fine, don't worry about it," I said.

"I… oh; I meant is your dad coming tonight?"

If Molly or Jayden or any of the others had made the mistake, I would have made some kind of sarcastic remark, but there was something so sweet about Denise, so genuine, I felt her mortification as though it were my own. "Honestly, please don't worry," I placed the earphones away in my jacket pocket again, "it's not like I expect everyone to remember anyway. Yes, Dad said he'd come tonight." (His exact words had been "I'll do my damnedest", so I was not going to get my hopes up.) "How about your parents?"

Denise relaxed her shoulders. "Mum is coming but Dad is working away at the moment." Then after a pause, she added, "They're divorced."

I looked at her innocent little face devoid of make-up and her uniform worn on the knee and buttoned up just as it should be; she looked very young, though there were only a couple of months between us.

"There you go," I said, patting her knee as though she were a small child, "perhaps I should have known that. See, no harm done."

"Yes, but I never even told—"

"Yeah, I know," I interrupted briskly, then softened my tone. "Let's forget it, okay?"

The journey was not a long one, and we managed to find enough to talk amiably about until the coach pulled up outside of the town hall. We alighted and made our way to the front entrance where Mr Adams stood waiting with hands in his pockets and a wide grin. Next to him stood a small, neat woman wearing a straight black dress which came to her knees. She was clutching a little sequined bag against her hip.

"Ladies, welcome! May I introduce you to Alice?"

Denise nodded dumbly and held out her hand.

"Alice, this is Denise and this is Naomi, the writers of the future!"

"Oh, it's such a pleasure to meet you both," Alice gushed in a silly, high-pitched voice. "Joe… *Mr Adams…*' she paused and giggled. I was embarrassed for her. "Mr Adams is always telling me about his students and I rarely get the chance to meet them."

I decided that Alice was like an older, darker version of Molly Smith – straightened hair and symmetrical eyebrows and no substance whatsoever. "Hi," I said, "it's really nice of you to come… though I would have thought you'd have had a million more interesting things to do."

Her smile faded a little but to her credit, Alice didn't miss a beat. "I like to show my support when I'm available," she said, pushing me back in line.

We had been told to wear our school uniforms, but Mr Adams had changed into a black suit and had restyled his hair so that it was slicked back away from his face. "Shall we?" he said, gesturing wide and inviting us to go ahead. Denise looked at her shoes but I pushed my shoulders back and smiled brightly at him. "Thank you," I said, and, pushing past Alice, I marched straight in.

The entrance to the hall was grand. A central staircase rose up from the marble floor and huge vases of flowers stood on either side. To the right of the stairs were doors leading off to unknown rooms which stood tall and forbidding. Our ceremony was to be held in the main hall. To get to it, we had to go up the stairs and down a long corridor adorned with paintings of old people I didn't recognise. As we made our way towards the hall, I kept a casual eye out for Dad, daring to hope he was somewhere amongst the hordes of parents, teachers and pupils milling about the building.

We took our seats in the middle section of the hall in the spaces reserved for the prize winners. The room was awash with chatter and then a young woman came onto the stage and hesitantly tapped on the spongy head of a microphone. I stared up into the gallery and then back down to the main floor; there must have been over 300 people in the room. Denise was waving timidly at a couple a few rows behind us.

"He's probably looking at you right now from wherever he's sitting and wondering why you haven't spotted him," Mr Adams said, leaning into my ear.

I spun back to face the front. "Who? My dad? It doesn't matter if he's not here, I'm pretty used to doing things on my own."

"I'm sure he'll be here if he can," he replied, patting me lightly on the knee.

"Seriously, I'm not fussed either way," I said, staring at Mr Adams' hand. I crossed my legs, angry that he felt sorry for me.

The ceremony was long and dull. Denise and I got to stand on the stage for approximately two minutes where we smiled and shook hands with the short, dumpy Mayor and received our cheque for £100. "It's not even like we can spend it on ourselves," I muttered behind my smile while we were being clapped.

"Well done, you two!" Alice was patting me on the shoulder like a dog as we stood together in an awkward huddle in the lobby afterwards. I moved away, out of reach.

"See, didn't I tell you they were talented?"

Mr Adams looked particularly puffed up as he placed an arm around Alice's tiny waist. Who was he showing off, us or her?

"It's a shame I didn't get to hear your stories, girls," Alice was saying. "I'd really like to though, if you thought that would be okay?" Her teeth were a dazzle of white neatness and I felt an urge to knock them all out of her mouth.

"Of course," Denise answered for both of us, "if you really want to?"

She was obviously of the same opinion as I was, that Alice must have better things to do with her time.

"Right," said Mr Adams, "let's see about getting you back on the coach, shall we?"

"It's fine, I'm going to walk home," I said, flicking my hair to one side.

He smiled kindly at me. "I'm afraid not, Naomi. More than my job's worth."

I felt my cheeks redden. "I'm allowed to, honestly."

"Not without written permission… come on, you know the rules."

I caught a glimpse of Alice as I sat down on the coach. She was laughing and nudging Mr Adams on the shoulder. Patronising cow. She must be thinking she was something special, coming along with her bright teeth and stupid giggle, pretending to be interested in us just to impress Mr Adams. But she didn't understand him, she couldn't possibly know his passion for writing like I did; she was just humouring him and he was too gullible to see. He deserved so much better. Just like Ozzy had. The coach moved off and I sank back into my seat, thoroughly miserable.

Aunt Chrissy was in the kitchen when I arrived home, decorating a slightly wonky sponge cake with chocolate icing.

"Dad called," she sang, "told me what a clever girl you were and I thought, well! What better way to celebrate than by having cake?"

I threw my bag down behind the kitchen door and dipped a finger into the bowl of icing. "Where is he then?"

"Held up, but he'll be here shortly."

"He was supposed to come and see me get the prize."

"Was he? He didn't say... oh, well, never mind, there'll be some sort of explanation."

"Yeah."

I took another dip and sucked my finger hard. Aunt Chrissy stopped layering on the icing and placed the knife down, wiping her hands on her apron.

"Come on, love, you know how busy he is."

"Yeah, I know. It's not a problem... I didn't want him there anyway. No other parents came... it would have been embarrassing."

She tilted her head to one side and drew her mouth into a soft smile. I turned away and reached into the fridge for a drink.

"I got you some cans of Coke, they're at the back."

I grabbed a can and released the ring-pull with my nail. My aunt returned to her icing and I sat down at the table, watching her.

"Why are you here, making a cake? Dad doesn't give a shit, why do you?"

"Naomi." Her tone didn't alter, so I knew she had already prepared her words carefully. "Your dad cares more about you than anything in the world."

"Uh."

"Try not to give him a hard time. I'm only here now and then to help out, it's not easy for him having to juggle work with being a parent." A splodge of brown icing escaped the knife and landed on the floor with a sad splat.

"Oopsie!" Aunt Chrissy tore a section of kitchen towel and swiped the mess away in one clean movement. I didn't offer to help.

"So, tell me all about it," she said, in a tone which suggested I was five.

"Nothing much to tell. We went into the hall; our names were called and we went up onto the stage and shook hands with some education bloke and the Mayor and then sat down again."

She turned to the sink and rinsed her hands. "I hear your story was quite outstanding."

I swigged from the can. "Not really. Nothing special."

Dad was profusely sorry. Of course he was. He had wanted so much to be there – "I was almost out the door!" But disaster had struck at the last minute and he'd had no choice but to stay behind. I understood, didn't I?

Had he not elaborated on the missing coursework (a study of female oppression within fairy tales) and the distraught student (a needy but brilliant girl by the name of Emily who, without her work would surely sink into deep depression), I may have forgiven him. But he was so intent on spinning out the excuse with intricate details of work-shy colleagues and outdated filing systems that he sucked the importance out of my night and blew it into his. I sat, pretending to listen, and thought about kind Mr Adams and how Alice didn't know just how lucky she was.

chapter eleven

I SAW HER AGAIN A COUPLE OF WEEKS LATER. SHE was in the school car park, leaning against her black mini and speaking animatedly on the phone. She hadn't seen me, and I stood watching as she laughed prettily and swung her car keys round on her index finger. What did she have that Mr Adams liked? I wasn't blind; I could see Alice was attractive, but being attractive wouldn't be enough for Mr Adams. There must be something else.

Mr Adams appeared at the school entrance and I took another step back. I saw Alice raise her free hand and give a little wave, then she opened the driver-side door and slid inside, knees together, no hint of thigh on show. Class; that's what she had. She was mature, and experienced; she knew how to make the art of being cool and confident and sophisticated seem as effortless as breathing, and she knew how to make a man like Mr Adams fall in love with her. One day, when I was mature and experienced, I would be like Alice. Only better.

For now, though, I was still me. It was Friday, and all day I'd listened to my classmates talking about what they were wearing or what they were bringing to Molly Smith's party later tonight. Imogen was going (probably with *Skye*), and needless to say, I was yet to receive my invitation, because despite getting away with blaming me for the school play fiasco, Molly still hated me. I had steadfastly refused to give her the satisfaction of calling her out on it, but both she and I knew that she had thrown herself off that stage. She had avoided me as much as possible since, barely speaking to me in class, but while the rest of the school thought it was because of the play, I knew that she blamed me for her split with Ozzy.

I very much doubted that Alice had ever been excluded from anything.

I turned away to avoid witnessing the inevitable greeting between Mr Adams and his perfect girlfriend, pulled my blazer tight across my chest and wandered off the school grounds. I didn't want to go home. Dad would still be at work or out with Mo, and even if he wasn't, it would be worse than returning to an empty house. He'd be waiting, preparing his conversation starters, preparing to pretend he was interested when we both knew he'd rather be drinking in peace.

I wandered circuitously through the warm streets, surrounded by people who were going home, or coming out to begin their weekends. At a zebra crossing, a trickle of sixth-formers slid past and I overheard Molly's name. Wow. She really had invited everyone. Even Suzy Longman and her unborn child would probably be there.

Restaurants and pubs propped open their doors; tables on the pavement littered with glasses and ashtrays and serviettes tucked under plates made it difficult to pass at times without stepping off the pavement and into the road. No one paid me any attention as I made my vague journey to nowhere, they just continued talking and laughing, eating, smoking, drinking; everywhere I looked people were happy and together. I stopped outside a charity shop and peered at the cluttered display of toys and books and all those records that were coming back into fashion now (Ozzy reckoned they were too cumbersome – "Why bother when you can just download everything?" – but Imogen and I liked the look of the grooved discs), and then I caught sight of my reflection and froze. My hair, sweaty and limp, was scraped back into a messy ponytail, my skirt had worked its way up further on one side than the other and, what I thought was the shadow of a bruise was actually a smudge of mascara on my right cheek. How *very* classy. The next pane of glass was patterned, and as I moved, my reflection distorted so that my face and body were misaligned. Another pane, this time opaque, making me vanish altogether. I moved from side to side – messy, disjointed, gone, messy disjointed... gone.

"Are you okay?"

A man had jostled past me and apologised, pushing small, round glasses back up his nose. I took in the concern on his face and opened my mouth to speak. I suddenly wanted to tell this complete stranger that my mother was dead, that my father found me... difficult, that Imogen was going to Molly's party with her other friend because I wasn't invited and that Alice was going home with Mr Adams. But I didn't. I didn't say any of those things because I wasn't *that* weird. Instead, I lifted my chin and pulled my shoulders back tall and proud.

"I'm fine, thank you," I said, and walked off stiffly.

"Oi!"

Ozzy was on the opposite side of the road, already changed out of his uniform and into the baggy jeans he favoured and a crisp white T-shirt. There was a break in the traffic, and he jogged across the road and stopped in front of me.

"Where you off to?"

I tilted my head a little and wished that I didn't look quite so horrendous. "*I*... am off to relax after the stress of batting away all of the invitations I've received for this weekend."

He grinned, and I noticed the dimple in his left cheek. Cute.

"Not going to Molly's then?"

It warranted a punch to his shoulder. "Very funny."

"You could always come as my plus one?"

Another punch. "Yeah, because that would go down *so* well." I began walking again and he kept in step.

"Not fussed about it myself, to be honest."

I smiled. "You don't have to say that. I'm fine, really."

"Nah, seriously, she'll be busy being popular. She won't notice if I'm there or not."

"Course she will. She still likes you," and then I couldn't help teasing, "all the girls like you."

"Yeah, well," Ozzy broke into an exaggerated swagger, "either got it or you ain't..." and then he turned back and put his arm around my shoulders. "C'mon, let's do something else."

"Seriously? I'm not even changed!"

"Look alright to me."

I followed Ozzy to Mehmet's Mezze Bar and waited outside while he swiped us a couple of cans of Coke.

"Got to be some perks to having my uncle run the gaff," he said, handing me a cold tin.

We wandered aimlessly but chatted easily. Ozzy told me some more about his family in London and I told him about Dad's friend Mo, even going so far as to do an impression – "that's the thing, man, that's what they don't understand... it's like, at the end of the day, it's night..." – and then I stopped because Ozzy wasn't laughing. "Sorry, probably not doing him justice... he's kind of someone you have to meet in the flesh to understand."

"I have."

"Huh?"

"Met him. Mo."

"Huh?" I said again, I was completely lost.

"He lives in the same block as my family. We know him really well."

"You know Mo? My dad's friend Mo?"

"Yeah, look… I wasn't going to say anything 'cos I thought you might take it the wrong way…"

"Take what the wrong way?" I had the can to my lips but I didn't drink. My eyes narrowed.

"Mo asked me."

"What?"

"Like he just wanted to know there was someone looking out for you at school."

"Oh, my *God*. He asked you… to be my *friend*, didn't he?"

"Not exactly…"

"Yes, he did, and that's why you came up to me after my row with Jayden, that's why you stuck up for me in drama class."

"No… well yeah, in the beginning but—"

"Oh, my God! Oh, my God… this is *so* embarrassing." I held my hands up to my head and marginally avoided tipping Coke over my hair.

"Yeah, but it was only in the beginning… I feel like we're proper mates now."

"You're actually hanging around because you *feel sorry* for me… Molly's party… wow, you must think I'm a complete loser…"

"Not… at… all," he said firmly, placing a hand on each of my shoulders. "Seriously, you gotta believe me. At first, I was happy to look out for you, happy to do Mo a favour, but now I don't think of it like that at all. You're not like the other girls, you got something about you… I would be hanging around even if Mo hadn't asked me to. I promise."

The sky was beginning to turn pink. I laughed thinly that we had pretty much walked the circumference of the town and were back to where we had started; the mezze bar was a few feet away.

"Don't change the subject. Are you okay? Do you believe me?"

I sighed. "I don't want you feeling sorry for me."

"As if. Smartest girl in school, what's to feel sorry for?"

"Okay. But you have to *promise*, don't just be nice to me for Mo. *Really* promise, you have to *really* mean it."

"I *promise*. Now… you hungry?"

I was, but I didn't want him to stay longer than he had to. "Shouldn't you be going? Molly will be wondering where you are."

"Let her wonder. Treat 'em mean…"

"You still like her then?"

Ozzy smirked. "She's not as bad as she makes out."

"I'll take that as a yes."

"She's misunderstood."

"You mean you still fancy her."

He laughed. "You saying I'm shallow?"

"Just saying it like it is." I looked at him standing in front of me, the epitome of cool with his trendy clothes and confident swagger, and tried to believe that he genuinely wanted to hang around.

"Wait here." Ozzy disappeared into Mehmet's bar and returned minutes later with two polystyrene cartons full of hot, crispy chips smothered in vinegar and ketchup. We sat on a nearby wall and ate.

"So, what's your type then?" he asked.

"My type?"

"Yeah. Big, small, fat, thin?" He jumped off the wall and posed, hand on his chin, legs wide. "Sexy and cool?"

I pictured Mr Adams and almost laughed at how far away he was from Ozzy's depiction of cool. His name was on my lips but I kept it there; Ozzy wouldn't understand.

"Is that the pose that did it for Molly?" I asked, throwing a chip at his head.

Ozzy rejoined me on the wall and mocked up a dramatic sigh. "Leave her alone, she's just insecure."

"Ah. Token excuse for a bully."

"Come on, she's hardly a bully."

"Whatever."

"You're probably the only girl in the school who doesn't try and fit in, plus you're really smart. She's jealous."

Chips done, I scrunched up the box and lobbed it into a nearby bin. "And why wouldn't she be?" I exclaimed. "You've either got it or you ain't." And we both grinned.

*

How did that story end, the one that earned me a place at the awards ceremony? For the life of me, I can't remember. I don't even think it was particularly good, but Mr Adams had put me forward because he'd wanted me to believe in myself, and look where I am now – I have a lot to thank him for really.

I leave the window and wander across the room to where I've had a makeshift kitchen area installed. I say kitchen; it's little more than a wide shelf holding a mini-fridge and a kettle. Down the hall, there is a communal kitchen area with all of the usual facilities which I never use because I'd rather stick pins in my eyes than make small talk with employees from the other firms on the floor. They all think I'm aloof and "up my own arse" (nothing changes) and Esme takes great pleasure in laughing about it, but it's fine; I have long gotten over caring what other people think.

I was a nightmare that night at the town hall, I remember with a smile. Mr Adams had been intent on impressing Alice with his well-mannered, intelligent pupils, and I'd been rude and obnoxious. Still, it hadn't put her off because she'd hung around for quite some time afterwards. Naturally, she'd let him down in the end like I'd always known she would. She can't have loved him. Not really. I did her a favour when you think about it.

Alice and Molly, peas in a pod, sauntering along and turning men's heads, drawing them in and leaving at the first sign of trouble. How many times had Ozzy been enticed back to Molly in the end? Three, four? His teenage hormones had not allowed for rationality; one sorrowful look in his direction and he'd skulked back. Not that I ever held it against him. Even back then, somewhere in my subconscious, I must have known that there would be a better way, that my time would come eventually.

Katerina catches my eye from the frame upon my desk; she is laughing, her hair wet from the sea, a smudge of damp sand on her cheek.

I was pleased when I discovered I was pregnant. Even though I had been young, there was none of the panicked drama that you see in films or soap operas, I didn't hang *my head or worry that I was on my own; I simply called the father and explained exactly how things would be. My intention to raise the child alone was (predictably) contested, but I was never fazed by the haranguing and pleading that followed. I had my child growing inside me and no one else mattered. The father accused me of being emotionally cold; those were his words, "emotionally cold and incapable of real feelings", but that was because I wouldn't give him what he wanted, I wouldn't toe the family line. Anyway, I proved him wrong, because when Katerina was born, no one could deny that I knew what love was. So, yes, I was pleased to be a mother, and pleased with my choice for the child's father.*

I have made a mug of coffee without realising; it's funny how second-nature things become. I'm back at the window in time to see the night staff arrive at the clinic. Give it half an hour for them to hand over and then there will be a trickle of people as the weary day team leave, only to do it all again tomorrow. They are saints, all of them. Alcoholism is a torturous disease for the individual, but it's also bloody hard on the people around them. No one thinks about that.

No. That's not true. Sometimes my anger gets the better of me. There is a lot of support out there for the families of alcoholics, a lot; it's just having the courage to take it. Sometimes you're made to feel like you're the one who is deluded.

Families are tricky at the best of times, aren't they? That's why I like to keep mine simple; just me and Kat. For now.

Dad tried his best but for all his wisdom, he had been narrow-minded and insular and thus failed to see what was right before his eyes. Now he is vulnerable and dependent on others. A sad state for a proud man.

Mo had been different, of course; you only have to look at Esme now to see what a good job he did as a father. And if I could, I would tell him what an amazing woman she has grown to be, and that if I could bottle and sell her confidence and self-assurance, I'd make a fortune. There are so many things I would like to tell Mo.

The staff have all gone now and I dismiss the stab of annoyance at not seeing him amongst them. I remind myself that I can't possibly know where he is all the time; the poor man needs a little privacy!

chapter twelve

I DECIDED TO GET SEX OUT OF THE WAY. NOT because I was particularly interested (there was no desperate curiosity), just a mild thought it might be best to get it over with, as though my innocence might be holding me back in some way. I knew that Molly and the other girls were doing it; perhaps it would help in my quest to feel a little more normal, or at least a little less "weird".

"I need you to help me with something," I said one afternoon.

Imogen and I were sitting on the floor of her bedroom picking through various photos with which she wanted to make a collage for her wall.

"What about this one?" she said, lifting a particularly

flattering one of her and Skye looking sultry, up to the light. Skye had blossomed from an awkward, hair-clip-wearing daisy into a tall, striking iris; she was all vivid colour and floaty hair – being arty suited her.

"Immy."

"Yeah, sorry. What?"

"I want to change my image."

"Again?" She tilted the photo to the right and placed another shot underneath so that it overlapped.

"Not my hair colour. I want to look... like the other girls."

I had her attention now.

"Ah." She dropped the photos back to the carpet and twisted her body round to face me properly. "You mean you want to look like Molly."

"No."

"Yes."

"Just help, okay?"

"Yeah, of course... I did before, didn't I?"

She had. But I hadn't been ready then, I hadn't been interested enough to maintain a new image and I'd washed the make-up from my face that evening and not bothered to reapply it since. I *was* ready now.

Imogen twisted her nose ring so that it turned a full loop; she did it so often I imagined the hole must be getting wider and wider, and that if she ever took the ring out, she'd be left with a gaping hole above the nostril. "But just as long as you know—"

"What?"

"Oh God, *you* know! You don't need to look like the other girls to get attention from the boys."

I frowned at her, furious to find I was so transparent. "It's *not* to get attention, I couldn't care less what the boys think of me."

"Good. Because you are clever, articulate... and funny... you can wow the boys with words—"

"Yeah, they're queuing up to hear me recite sonnets."

"So, it *is* for the boys then?" and then ignoring my protest, she went on, "Look, if you fancy a new image, then fine, why not? As long as it's for the right reasons."

"Yeah, of course." Whatever.

The first opportunity to try out my thick, dark eye-liner and contoured cheeks came the following weekend when Imogen sneaked me into the party of a friend of a friend of a friend of Skye's. We arrived late to a basement full of smoke and dark clothes and "alternative" music which was too loud but thankfully dulled my senses to the "amaaazing" and "sooo coool" phrases which hung in the air and made me feel like an extra in a seventies film. There were several people from Harper Comp and a whole heap of people I didn't recognise but I felt brave behind my new mask.

"Heeey, Imogen, who's your mate?"

Imogen had begun straightening her long auburn hair and she kept flicking it from one side to the other whilst addressing the boy stood before us. "This is—"

"I'm Naomi," I said for myself, "I go to Immy's school."

Admiring glances followed us as we navigated our way around the room. I was handed a drink and winced as the pink liquid burned my throat. "What's this?" I asked, leaning into Imogen's ear.

"God knows, some shit attempt at punch?"

We grinned, clinked glasses and downed the drinks in one.

In the corner of the room was a pile of furnishings: cushions, a throw, what looked like a sleeping bag. Two girls sat giggling amongst it all, surveying the scene until something, or someone, caught their eye, and they vacated their lumpy seats.

"Come and sit."

It was Alfie, holding my elbow and leading me over to the cushions. I blinked in surprise.

"I didn't expect to see you here."

He laughed.

It was odd seeing him out of school. His usual topknot was missing and his fair hair flopped to one side. He leaned with it as though it were heavy.

I followed and sat as he directed on an itchy, crumpled throw and we both leaned back and watched the party.

"You look good tonight," Alfie said. He said it as though it were a fact rather than an opinion. I simply nodded.

Imogen was dancing with Skye and some other girls in the centre of the room. They were singing loudly and looked as at ease as they would have been in their bedrooms – arms in the air, arms around each other, eyes shut, mouths open.

"So, what's this, the new you?" Alfie drew a circle in the air around my face and I shrugged.

"Maybe. What do you think?"

He just grinned.

Later, we stood in the kitchen in a loose circle, clutching bottles and glasses and cigarettes. There were a few girls, older, and cooler, but mostly boys. Imogen introduced me as her oldest friend. The boys studied me briefly and I knew I was a novelty. I talked fast. And loud. The vodka burned my throat and hit my chest, but it also travelled into my head and formulated clever, witty sentences, and I could see the boys were impressed. They thought I was *interesting*. But the conversation moved too quickly onto less familiar territory and I stumbled along, claiming to understand Grime and agreeing that the charts were monopolised by a handful of mainstream artists.

"I quite like them," admitted Imogen, "give me Jennifer Lopez over Skepta any day."

"Oh, my God, you are joking?" I exclaimed, knowing full well she wasn't because we had spent many a happy hour listening to Jennifer harp on about her ex, and neither of us had the faintest idea who Skepta was. Imogen slipped me a hurt look and I turned away to pour another drink. I was being mean, pulling her up on what I perceived to be her shortcomings in order to absolve myself of my own – like a fat child making fun of someone's weight.

When Ozzy appeared later, I was drunk. I could see him scanning the room for someone and, in my heightened state, I confidently decided that that person was me. I left the group in the kitchen, flicked my hair and wandered over to where he was shouting something into Alfie's ear.

"Hey," I said lazily, trying out the word for size.

Ozzy's hands were buried in the pockets of a dark green bomber jacket. His brow furrowed when he turned and saw me lolling my weight onto one foot.

"What *you* doing here?"

"Why? Am I not supposed to be?" I asked, purposely coquettish and barely refraining from twirling a strand of hair.

"You're drunk." His gaze lowered, and he seemed to take in the dress and the boots and the skin on show, but his expression did not alter as I'd hoped it would. "You're better than this."

"Seriously. Here I am… trying to be like *everyone* else…" I could feel myself swaying.

"Do what you want." And he wandered off without a backward glance.

I watched him make a circuit of the room, bend to chat to a mate crouched on the floor, high-five another. I watched him absentmindedly stroke the dark hair on the nape of his neck and square his shoulders before going in for a brief hug with the tall guy in the corner. And then, as abruptly as he had arrived, he left. My bravado evaporated and I felt a little ridiculous.

"And that's your lot for today." Alfie had reappeared at my shoulder and was watching me watch Ozzy. "Come on, time to refill your glass."

I staggered back to the kitchen to find Imogen and Skye giggling in the corner and sinking shots of clear liquid.

"Want one?" Skye asked.

I shook my head and followed Alfie who was busily opening a wine box with his teeth, his blond hair hanging greasily in front of his face. There was a thump and a ripping sound and suddenly he was shouting for me to grab a glass.

"Here! Put it here!" he laughed as wine trickled from the corner of the damaged box. I managed to laugh too and replaced the full glass with another until Alfie righted the box and stopped the flow. We performed a celebratory toast and leant back against the sideboard to drink. Very soon, the circle in the kitchen reformed to include the two of us and we joined in with what had become little more than pointless drunken whoops and inane laughter. I could feel Alfie's hand against my back and, ignoring the instinct to flinch away out of reach, I allowed it to remain. His thumb began stroking my lower back, tracing my spine up, down, up. No one else had noticed; they wouldn't have been able to see his hands and what did it matter anyway? Just a boy, touching me… get it over with… completely in control… my decisions, my choices… I thought of Ozzy and wondered what his thumb would feel like on my back… not that he ever would put his hands on me… he didn't want me… just as Mr Adams didn't want me… perhaps he didn't even like me anymore… no matter… I didn't like him either… I didn't need either of them… I had vodka… plenty of other boys around. I didn't fancy Alfie in the slightest but continued to let him touch my back because it was easier than making a fuss and really, who cared? What did any of it matter? And later, I would let him kiss me because some attention was better than none.

As a result of the basement party, Imogen and I secured an invitation to the next event which turned out to be a gathering of mostly the same people, this time in a field. Alfie was ignoring me because after saying I didn't need him to walk me home from the party, he'd caught me kissing Josh in the street. According to Imogen, he'd said that he wouldn't blank me forever, just until he'd mended his wounded pride.

"Quite mature of him, don't you think?" Imogen had asked on the way to the field. "He obviously likes you."

"Yeah," I said. But I wasn't thinking about Alfie. Or Josh.

Everyone was drinking, and someone handed us a bottle of vodka. "I'm not drinking it neat!" Imogen scoffed, but I took the bottle and swung it up to my lips, much to the delight of the chubby boy who'd given it to me.

"Go on!" he encouraged, so I took another swig.

"Nae..."

I ignored Imogen and wiped my mouth with the back of my hand. Handing the bottle back to the delighted boy, I marched off towards the throng of kids shouting and laughing under the trees. I was on a mission. A girl I remembered meeting briefly at the party last week launched herself at me as though we were long-lost friends and took me by the hand. I couldn't remember her name but I remembered her smell – a mix of cheap body spray and incense – and her bizarre choice of hairstyle, two long plaits which hung over her shoulders like Mildred Hubble. She introduced me to lots of people, most of whom nodded or waved but otherwise paid little attention, too busy drinking or kissing or lolling across the grass in spaced-out heaps.

"This is Iffy," the Mildred girl said, resting a hand on the shoulder of an older boy. He was dark-skinned, with closely cropped black hair and a wide grin.

"And who's this then?" the boy asked, reaching for my hand and lifting it gently to his lips.

"Oh, man, shut up!" a voice said behind me before breaking into boyish laughter.

"This is… what was your name again?" Mildred girl asked.

Taking control, I spoke directly to Iffy. "I'm Naomi," I said, "friends call me Nae."

"Well, friends can call you what they want. I'm gonna stick with Naomi. Posh. I like posh."

A group of us settled on the ground between a cluster of trees. Imogen found my side again. Alfie, Josh and a few more from school – including, to my dismay, Molly and Ozzy together – joined the circle, and soon everyone was passing bottles and spliffs and cigarettes in a bubble of shared spit and germs.

I tried to keep up my new, sociable persona. I remembered to laugh and to chat and not to say anything that might be construed as condescending but all of the time, I was minutely aware of Ozzy, and my laughter faltered every time I noticed Molly take his arm or touch his hand. He had barely spoken to me all evening and although I vaguely remembered him being annoyed at my drunkenness last week, there was no way I was giving him the satisfaction of calling him out on it. The one time he acknowledged me by handing me a drink, Molly threw me a death stare.

"He doesn't fancy you, you know," she hissed when Ozzy disappeared off to piss behind some trees.

"I know that," I replied steadily. "We're mates, that's all."

"Mates! If you say so."

But we *were* mates, even if it didn't feel like it right now. I hadn't imagined all those conversations or the shared chips on the wall; Ozzy was being off because she was there, that was all. I drank some more and smoked and laughed loudly with Mildred Hubble and Imogen and the other boys in the circle at all of the jokes that were not particularly funny and purposely looked away whenever Ozzy caught my eye. Molly continued to drape herself over him and he let her.

I stared at the open car door, hesitating a fraction too long.

"You're chicken."

He raised an eyebrow and a smile danced playfully on his lips. I stepped forward and got into the front passenger seat. "Scared? As *if.*"

"Nae, don't be stupid; come out of there and let's go," Imogen pleaded, her eyes wide as she watched me close the car door.

Iffy was gesturing at the back seat. "Plenty of room for another one, or would that take you out of your comfort zone, Ginger?"

Even in the dusk, I could see Imogen's cheeks flare red as she crossed her arms over her chest. "I wouldn't be stupid enough to get into a car with a dumb-arse like you," she spat. Iffy winked at me and nodded towards Imogen. "She's a fiery one."

"Yeah, fiery and bloody boring. Let's go," I said, looking straight ahead as Iffy got into the driver's seat. He slammed the door shut and accelerated away but I couldn't help glancing in the rear-view mirror at Imogen stood where we'd left her with a face full of hurt. There was another figure running towards her and gesturing at the car. Ozzy. He looked furious and was shouting something at Immy but I told myself not to care and they grew smaller and smaller until we turned a bend and then they disappeared from view altogether. Good. This would teach him.

At first, the road was dotted with teenagers making their way to or back from the field, but then the streets were suddenly quiet and empty. The car engine was noisy and when we paused at a set of lights, the whole vehicle vibrated excessively.

"Your name can't really be Iffy," I said over the noise.

"Why?"

"Because it's not a name."

The lights switched to green and we thundered off again, screeching at every turn. I held onto the handle above my seat as though it could possibly save my life in the event of a crash.

"Nervous?"

"Should I be?"

He glanced round and grinned. Then, with one hand on the wheel, he reached across to open the glove compartment to reveal a bottle.

"It's my name; use it or use something else, whatever."

"How about Cocky Little Shit?"

He laughed. "Sounds about right. Drink up."

I reached for the bottle, unscrewed the metal cap and took a swig. More vodka. The car lurched over a speed bump and liquid spilled from both the bottle and my mouth onto my dress. I wiped my chin with the back of my hand and this time I enjoyed the burn in my chest. "So where are we going?"

"Need to pick up a mate… do a quick favour… then I'm all yours."

"What makes you think I want you to be mine?"

He reached for his phone on the dashboard, swiped at something and threw it back where it slid immediately to one side.

"You got in the car," he said with a grin.

I stared out of the window and watched square terraced houses flash by in one long blur, then a break of blackened trees and the school and the hospital and yet more trees. I thought about Mr Adams tucked up in bed with Alice, and Dad asleep with his book across his chest. I thought about Imogen standing in the field looking disappointed and Ozzy stomping about furiously. I took another swig from the bottle and hated them all for making me feel bad. I drank to erase Imogen and Ozzy and Dad and Mr Adams, and then I drank some more to erase all my fucking potential, and then I drank again…

"Woah, leave some for me!"

"You can't drink, you're driving." My voice was beginning to slur.

"Is that right?" Iffy took the bottle with his left hand, eyeing me as he took a huge gulp and daring me to stop him.

He turned away from me and indicated right, slowing the car down and pulling into a darkened street. We followed the road to the end and then through a maze of intricate side roads until finally coming to a stop under a yellow streetlamp.

"This where your friend lives?"

But he ignored me and checked his wing mirror, leaving the motor running. The vibration of the car made me feel a bit sick and I tried to think of something other than the bitter taste of vodka in my throat.

"Wait here," Iffy said, suddenly opening his door, levering himself out and wandering off up the road.

I adjusted the rear-view mirror so that I could watch him – shoulders hunched, hands in the pockets of his jeans. After a moment he stopped, and a small figure, much shorter than Iffy but wearing a similar outfit, appeared from a shadowy hedge. They shook hands, and both said something that I was too far away to hear, and then the short man vanished back into the hedge and Iffy jogged back to the car. He said nothing and slammed the door. I expected him to hit the accelerator and screech off down the road, but it was as though the exchange had morphed Iffy into the model driver and he checked his mirrors carefully before signalling left and moving off gently from the kerb.

"Back to mine then?"

I chewed briefly on my bottom lip. "Sure, why not?"

Iffy lived in some kind of house share. We entered through a basement door where he turned and put his fingers to his lips before leading down a short corridor and into a small room. There was a bed and a television, a clothes rail and a chest of drawers but no evidence of a bathroom or kitchen.

"Who do you live with?" I asked, stepping over a pile of neatly folded clothes on the floor.

"People."

I removed my jacket and nonchalantly, so I hoped, threw it over the clothes rail. Then I kicked off my shoes while Iffy poured the remaining vodka into two glasses, lay down on the bed and positioned myself so that I was leaning on one elbow with my skirt hitched up to mid-thigh.

"Make yourself comfortable, why don't you?" he said, handing me a drink.

I wasn't nervous or excited. I was intrigued to see what all the fuss was about, to see what it was like in an adult world where men like Iffy picked up random girls and took them back to their grown-up flats just because they could. Alfie and Josh and the rest of them were a million miles away, probably still trying to get a girl to snog them behind a bush or allow them to touch a breast. And Ozzy... well, Ozzy was probably shagging Molly Smith under a tree. But I was going to do it here, in a bed, with someone who knew what they were doing.

Iffy joined me on the bed and we clinked glasses. I missed my mouth when I went to drink and laughed, throwing my head back and causing more to spill over the duvet cover. I could hear how loud my voice was and I consciously quietened it; for some reason it mattered that Iffy didn't think I was drunk. Reaching over, I placed my glass on the floor beside the bed. I turned back and ran a finger over Iffy's stubbly chin, letting my hand slide to the back of his neck so I could pull his face to mine. He leaned in and kissed me, slowly at first and with barely any pressure, and so I pressed my chest against his to make him know how much I wanted him.

"Hold on," he laughed, pulling away, "there's no rush is there?"

I narrowed my eyes and shrugged. He was amused and it annoyed me. "Yeah, cool. Whatever."

"Oh, come on…" He threw a pillow at me when I got up from the bed, "don't be like that!"

But I had my back to him, to turn at his request would show immaturity. So, what now?

Keeping my back to him, I focused on appearing sober as I unfastened the buttons on my top and gently edged it off my shoulders so that it fell to the floor by my feet. He was quiet now, and I knew he was watching so I loosened my skirt and took that off too. I had no qualms about letting Iffy see my body because I had already decided that I would never see him again. Plus, I had read a million sex scenes, and I was yet to read anywhere of a man being put off by a woman removing her clothes – from what I'd learned they were usually pathetically grateful.

I turned and faced him at last. He was sitting upright now, and I followed his eyes as they travelled down my body, sensing his growing excitement as I unclipped my bra.

"Come here," he said.

He had moved to the edge of the bed and pulled me forwards so that I was standing in front of him. I wished for a moment that I was wearing better knickers, something sexier than the childish white pants that I had thrown on this morning, but he didn't seem bothered. He leaned in and kissed my tummy button, looked up with a kind of smirk and then kissed it again. I concentrated on standing still as his hands inched over my hips, down onto my thighs, wondering all the time whether I should be doing something else. I didn't care that he was looking at my body, but I wished that he wouldn't keep looking up at my face; like he was waiting for some kind of reaction; it made me feel awkward. His eyes started to glaze over, possibly from smoking weed, but I told myself it was desire, and when he pulled me closer so that I felt his erection pushing stubbornly at his jeans, I knew I was right. I felt suddenly powerful, like I could get him to do anything. I pushed him back onto the bed and straddled him, looking straight into his eyes as I teased his belt undone and pulled at his zip. He was watching me, fascinated, and then he closed his eyes and his hands moved to my shoulders and then to the top of my head and then he was pushing my head firmly so that I had to shimmy my way down the bed. I knew what he wanted.

I must have hesitated a moment too long and felt his growing impatience in the force of his hands. But I needn't have worried for he chose to mistake my curiosity for lust, lifted my chin with his finger and said, "You want it, don't you?"

I very much hoped I looked seductive biting my bottom lip because it was the only way to stop the sudden urge I had to laugh. It felt as though we were in a film, playing out roles that we'd seen a million times before; I didn't "want it" at all, but I heard myself saying, "Yeah, I really do," and it wasn't even my own voice but something low and husky.

How easy this all was.

He didn't try to force my head down again as I'd been expecting. Instead, he drew me back up and whispered, "Well, then, because you want it, I won't make you wait…"

And then I worried that I had somehow failed because I had never heard of a boy turning down a free blowjob. He placed his thumbs over my nipples and roughly massaged my breasts and thought perhaps I should make some kind of noise to convince him I was enjoying it. But before I could, he whipped me over onto my back and suddenly he was on top of me.

And that was the only moment I felt slightly apprehensive. I wasn't sentimental about it being my first time, I wasn't worried about attaching anything meaningful – it was just sex and I wanted to get it over with – but I *was* concerned it was going to hurt.

With his face close to mine, he pushed the stray strands of hair from my face and kissed me, forcefully this time. I tasted cigarettes. My eyes closed and I tried hard to relax. The heady mix of vodka and aftershavey tobacco scent and lack of air made my head spin but I went with it, telling myself it would be over soon, and then the next time would be better and the time after that. I felt his fingers brush between my thighs and forced myself not to clench them together. I was no longer the weird girl; I was desirable – an independent woman who had a beautiful, older man completely under her spell. Iffy could do what he liked, and I was going to let him. I was in control and he was going to turn me into a sophisticated, beautiful, *better* version of myself. He was kissing me hard and pulling at my knickers. I could feel him hard against my bare skin and I told myself to enjoy it, though I wasn't yet sure which part was supposed to be enjoyable.

Suddenly he stopped moving and groaned. "Shit, I've got to stop… wait."

I snapped my eyes open and saw that he was damp with sweat already. "What's wrong?"

"Nothing's wrong, I just need a condom. You're so hot, it's not going to take long."

"For Christ's sake," I muttered. But Iffy was oblivious and shifted across the bed to rummage in a drawer. "What the fuck?"

His weight lifted from me completely and I snapped my eyes open. He was leaning on his elbows, no longer looking at me but at something in his hand.

"What?"

"Are you actually taking the piss?"

"*What*? What's wrong?"

"*This* is what's wrong!" He jumped up from the bed and threw something small and rectangular at me. It was my school ID card, which must have fallen out of my jacket pocket and landed by the bed.

His nakedness was vulnerable and suddenly incredibly unattractive. I tried to sound patient. "So?"

"What do you mean, *so*?" he was shouting now. "It says you're *fifteen*!"

I smiled sweetly, sat up and tucked my hair behind my ear. "Nearly sixteen."

"It makes no fucking difference. Why would you tell me you were seventeen if you're still a kid?"

His tone shocked me, and I reached for the bedcover. "I'm not a kid… it doesn't even matter, it's just a number, I can still—"

"It doesn't matter? It bloody *does* matter! It's the difference between being with a fucking kid and being with an adult."

"I'm still the same—"

"It's not about *you*, you stupid cow, it's about the law. Fuck!" He began pacing the floor, picking up various items of clothing and throwing them at the bed. "For fuck's sake, get off my bed and out of my room."

"What?"

I thought he was going to sling me out there and then onto the dark street and I shrank back against the headboard, lifting my knees up to my chin.

"But how will I get back?"

"For fuck's sake," he muttered again, running his hands over his head and reaching for his own discarded shirt. "Get up and I'll run you home but—"

"What?"

He stopped still and his eyes narrowed as he leaned over the bed so that his face was inches from mine, "I swear to God… if you've got any sense of decency, you'll put this right."

"How?"

"You tell no one, you understand?"

"But people saw me leave with you."

"You tell them I drove you straight home, right?"

"But what if they don't believe me?"

"Then you make them believe you. Shouldn't be hard, you're good at lying."

"Why are you being so mean to me?" I said, searching for my knickers which I found twisted up in a little ball on the floor.

"*Why are you being so mean to me?*" he mimicked coldly. "I'm being mean because it's girls like you who get boys into trouble, stupid little girls playing at being grown up, you haven't got a fucking clue about how the world actually works. Where do your parents think you are?"

"My mum's dead."

"For fuck's sake," he said without pausing.

He drove me home in silence and left me at the end of the road. I climbed out of the car, horribly, horribly sober now, and leaned down to thank him for the lift.

"And not a word to anyone, right?" he replied before hitting the accelerator and screeching off into the dark.

I was left shivering in the cool air.

*

She'd ignored my messages all weekend so I waited for Imogen at the school gate on Monday morning. After ten minutes, I was about to give up when she finally appeared at my side. She had straightened her hair again so that it hung in bright curtains over her shoulders. I could see she was sulking furiously.

"Hair looks nice," I said, taking a strand between my fingers and running it through my hand.

She pulled away.

"I'm sorry, Immy. I was a cow."

"Yep."

"I don't know what I was thinking, I just wanted to have a good time."

"You need to be careful."

"Of?"

"Looking like a slapper." Her tone was clipped and cold.

"Imogen!"

"Well, I'm just looking out for you."

"Did someone say something?"

"*Everyone* was talking about it."

I tutted, immediately defensive. "Who I decide to have sex with is none of anyone's business."

She stared me straight in the eye. "So, you did have sex then?"

"No."

She studied my face, looking for signs that I was lying.

"I swear."

"What happened then?"

"Nothing at all."

"Are you *sure* you didn't sleep with him?"

"Of course I'm sure, it's not something I'd forget!"

"I just don't want you doing stuff just to be like—"

"Like who?"

She began walking and I grabbed her arm.

"The other girls. 'Cos even though they say they've done stuff, I don't reckon they have and anyway, what's the rush?"

"I'm not trying to be like them."

"Good, because you don't need to act like—"

"Yeah, I remember. Wow them with my fascinating vocabulary instead," I snorted but Imogen wasn't going to let me off lightly.

"You shouldn't have gone off and left me."

"Yeah, I know. I'm sorry. And I'm sorry for what I said."

We wandered towards the school together and I tentatively put my arm through hers. "How did you get home?" I said, edging my chin against her shoulder.

"So, you do care then?"

"Of course I care."

"Alfie and Josh walked me home."

"Did they? Cool."

"Oh, just to warn you though…"

"Yeah?"

"Ozzy came over and asked where you were going. He was proper stroppy."

"Yeah, I saw him in the mirror as we left. What did you say?"

"Well, I was angry so I told him the truth – that I didn't have a bloody clue!"

I had to put things right. I cared what Ozzy thought, but more importantly, if I was going to be judged for something, I wanted it to be something that had actually happened. Anyway, I had promised Iffy that I would set the record straight.

Ozzy was sitting on one of the benches near the football pitch watching a match between a group of sixth-formers. His eyes locked with mine as I approached but he offered such a minuscule nod of acknowledgement, I almost missed it.

"Hey," I said breezily, "enjoy the party the other night?"

"It was alright. Glad to see you're still alive."

"Of course! He literally gave me a lift home, that's all."

Ozzy's head snapped round. "You don't even *know* him."

"Course I do, I'd spoken to him earlier."

Ozzy was right. I'd known Iffy for approximately two hours before getting into a car with him. But so what? I was showing I could loosen up a little, be spontaneous... exciting.

"Oh, here she is, we were wondering if we'd ever see you again..." Molly had appeared from behind me and begun the process of draping herself over Ozzy, "what with you going off with strange men and everything."

I gritted my teeth and smiled. "So, are you two definitely—"

"Back together? Yep." Molly pulled Ozzy's head round and kissed him hard on the mouth. "Can't keep away," she added, but I didn't know whether she meant the pair of them, or me.

"Cool. I'm happy for you both," I said, standing to leave. "For the record, Molly, I didn't have sex with Iffy."

Molly barely bothered to conceal a smirk. "Okay."

"She didn't," said Ozzy, "he gave her a lift home."

Molly's finger paused on Ozzy's jaw. "I said… *Okay*."

In the end, it did prove simplest just to have sex with Alfie.

It wasn't difficult to manipulate a situation where we were alone, and it was almost worth it to see poor Alfie's expression change from one of amazement, to lust, and finally to immense gratitude. When he eventually rolled his sweaty, skinny body off me, I pulled his grubby bedsheet over my naked body and waited. He scrunched his hair back into a topknot and still I waited. He pulled his jeans on and kissed my forehead and still I waited.

Nothing.

Since the very moment Alfie Richards had pushed up my skirt and tugged roughly at my knickers, I had waited for everything to make sense, to feel that connection to another human being that I had read about time and time again, but there was nothing but a brief physical pain. Afterwards, Alfie made a show of being sickeningly affectionate. He got back on the bed and tried to snuggle up, but I kept the cover tight against my body, moving only to avoid having my cheek stroked lovingly.

"That was amazing," he whimpered next to my ear.

I felt nothing so said nothing.

He reached for my hand and tried to thread his fingers through mine. "I'm so glad this happened… I think it means more, you know?"

"What?"

"Like… the first time should be with someone you like and respect. I like and respect you… so I'm glad, you know?"

"Okay."

He lay his head on my chest so that my right breast was squashed uncomfortably beneath his ear. I tutted and pushed him away.

"What? What's wrong?"

"Nothing. You're hurting me, that's all."

"Sorry."

For a moment I felt bad. "It's alright, just, you know…"

"Yeah, yeah… course. We're both new to all this." And then he laughed, and it was such a sorrowfully needy sound that I cringed and suddenly I couldn't wait to get away from him. "Hey, you know what? I have to go."

"Are you serious?"

"Yep. Dad's expecting me home."

"Okay… maybe we can…"

"No, we can't. I'm sorry."

"Did I do something wrong? You know, the first time is never that great… next time will be better…"

"It wasn't my first time, okay?"

"Oh." He rubbed the palm of his hand over his cheek and looked absolutely crushed.

"But you didn't do anything wrong."

"Oh."

I left. And felt utterly unchanged.

I hadn't intended to lie but I also hadn't expected Alfie to think having sex with him meant any more than what it was. It was just sex. I'd had to stop him creating a great romantic scenario because that was never the plan. He was a cog in the wheel. Collateral damage. He'd get over it.

chapter thirteen

THAT SUMMER, THE SCHOOL HOLIDAYS STRETCHED on forever. Ozzy was either with Molly or helping his uncle in the restaurant, and Imogen was away with her parents, and so I whiled away the endless hours reading under a tree in the garden, or on my bed, or if Dad was out, I sprawled along the sofa holding the book above my head until my arms ached, forcing me to change position.

Dad had taken on yet more exam marking and spent the little time he had at home sitting at the dining room table with papers spread out before him. On these occasions, I tended to go out. I would either go for long walks with my headphones on or, if Ozzy wasn't busy, I would hang about while he pilfered supplies and then we would sit on a wall and smoke or drink cheap vodka and talk about nothing in particular. I was always careful not to say anything bad about Molly and he was careful not to mention Alfie even though I knew perfectly well that Alfie had told him we'd had sex.

"Everything alright at home?" he'd ask now and again.

"Yeah. All good," I'd reply before rapidly changing the subject.

Sometimes I longed to tell Ozzy about how empty the house felt, how Dad was either at work or working from home. I wanted to confide that sometimes I dreamt about running away and going to live with Mo in a bright, tall tower block where daily life was colourful and happy and everybody talked and laughed and really *lived*. I wanted to ask whether he thought my mother had found parenthood too demanding and whether, perhaps, had I been a different kind of child, Mum might have fought on for a bit longer. But I didn't say any of those things, and it seemed, that summer, as though ours was a friendship built around things we didn't say.

Time eventually passed. Imogen came back, Dad and I prepared for our prospective new terms and I had sex twice more with Alfie Richards. I didn't particularly want to but I felt it was the polite thing to do; I didn't want him feeling used.

It was the last night of the holidays and the taxi ride was taking forever. Alfie, who had claimed the front passenger seat, was chatting away to the monosyllabic driver. "Mate, did you know that if you pour vodka into your eye you get drunk almost immediately? Of course the problem is how to get the vodka in there in the first place 'cos you *know* what would happen, *right*?"

"Nope."

"Yeah you do, the eye would close of its own accord, wouldn't it? The eye would be like, *fuck me, man, why you pouring fucking alcohol straight at me*? Am I right?"

"I 'spose."

"No supposing about it, your eye would be—"

"Yeah, yeah right, I get it."

On the back seat, I was wedged between a singing Josh to my left and a subdued Ozzy to my right.

I could tell he hadn't wanted me to come.

Imogen and I had been leaving the cinema together when Alfie had appeared out of nowhere and swung us both round in a circle.

"Fuck's sake, you've caught my tights," I shouted, looking down as a hole widened over my right knee.

"Soz… Come and have a few drinks and I'll make it up to you?"

"Nah, not tonight," Imogen replied, pulling away and looking at her watch.

"Nae?"

Ozzy appeared a few feet away, in deep conversation with Josh.

"Maybe just a couple then," I conceded.

"Nae! I thought we were going back to mine?" Imogen was already furious, knowing full well that her pleading would be futile.

"Immy, Immy, Immy," Alfie wrapped his arms around her waist, "come and have some fun! Oi, Ozzy, you don't mind if the girls come too, do you?"

Imogen shoved him off and muttered moodily that she'd see me tomorrow.

Ozzy looked over and shrugged. "Whatever."

Now, in the taxi, he was silent.

"What's wrong now?" I leaned forward a little to try and get Ozzy to look at me; I was beginning to grow bored of trying to second guess his moods. "You don't mind me coming back with you guys, do you?"

Ozzy continued to stare out of the window. All along the high street, people were spilling out of the brightly lit bars and making their way towards clubs, fast food joints and the taxi rank. He shrugged. "Don't really see why you want to, that's all."

I was stumped. "Well, I— I don't want the night to end, you know… I'm just getting started, a few more drinks and then…"

"Why do you do that? What's happened to you?" He turned sharply to face me and frowned.

"What?"

"Why are you pretending to be something?"

"I… sorry, I really don't understand what your problem is."

"You're covered in make-up again, massive hole in your tights… you should be going home, getting an early night."

"And you shouldn't? Jesus, I just meant we could hang out and have a laugh, nothing else!"

He was silent for a moment. "Sorry." His tone had softened. "Just forget it, yeah? Course it's alright for you to come back with us."

I wilted back into the seat. As the taxi pulled up outside Mehmet's Mezze Bar, I stared out at the darkened restaurant where the last of the diners had long since gone and tried not to take Ozzy's mood to heart. He got out first and I waited for him to hold the door, but he left it and wandered off. Alfie paid the taxi driver as I got out and smoothed my dress.

"Cheer up, Nae, it's time to play," sang Josh, coming up behind me and snaking his arms around my waist. "Let's have some fun."

"Leave her alone, you idiot." Ozzy had reappeared to lead us round the back of the restaurant to a side door. I followed, realising too late that I *did* look out of place in my short dress and ripped tights.

"So, you want to be part of it, you wanna hang around with the boys, see what we get up to?" he muttered in my ear.

I stared at him quizzically, trying to work out if he was joking or not. "Couldn't really care less what you do." I sounded much more confident than I now felt.

"And yet…" his smile was cryptic now "… you're here."

I had a sudden recollection of being in the car with Iffy and shuddered. As I followed Ozzy through the door and along a narrow corridor full of cardboard boxes and vending machines, I had to be cautious to avoid dislodging the precariously stacked clutter and step sideways along the cheap lino floor.

A dim light escaped from underneath another door and I could hear male voices from within. If I hadn't been uneasy before, I was now, but with Alfie and Josh hushing and shoving behind me, it was too late to turn back without causing a fuss. We entered a large room with no windows; it certainly wasn't part of the restaurant and at first I thought it must be some kind of storeroom, but in the absence of food or drink or even boxes, I gauged it to be something else entirely. Around the perimeter of the room, perched on rickety wooden stools, were three young men – were these *Ozzy's cousins?* – and then an older one whom I guessed, by the mutual nod of acknowledgement, to be his Uncle Mehmet. There was a strong smell of weed.

In the centre of the room, suspended from the ceiling, was a large blue and white punch bag. Ozzy pushed it to one side to allow me to walk past and indicated that I should sit down on one of the stools. Josh and Alfie tumbled through the door with a series of whoops and exclamations as I took my seat.

The men in the room fell silent and once the high-fiving had quietened, I felt the eyes in the room turn on me.

"Ozzy?"

But he was busy whispering something to his uncle. I turned back and smiled, even gave a little wave to a man next to me. Josh and Alfie seemed completely at ease; they scavenged a joint from somewhere and proceeded to share it between them in the corner of the room. The man next to me, I realised, was no older than Ozzy. He was squidgy and pale and his round face grew wider still when he returned my smile, his mouth opening out to display a set of discoloured, chipped teeth. I nodded, and tried not to look terrified.

"Drink," Ozzy said, but it wasn't a question and he disappeared from the room. I turned back to the round-faced boy.

"Hi, I'm Naomi… a friend of Ozzy's." My words were met with silence but a tentative hand reached over and passed me a hand-rolled joint, the end glowing a blackened red. I shook my head and raised my hands in refusal, just to be really clear. Round-Face retracted the joint and proffered a regular packet of cigarettes instead. I took one because it seemed rude to refuse twice.

I was about to light up by leaning into the flame that Round-Face was holding out when Ozzy reappeared at the door clutching two bottles of beer. "What the fuck you doing?" He marched over and snatched the cigarette from my mouth.

"I was only joining in," I said, hating how pathetic I sounded.

"Joining in with what? Smoking with a group of men you don't even know?"

The uncle stood up and said something in Turkish. Ozzy turned, and his shoulders drooped. Sucking the air between his teeth, he handed me a beer and waved a hand dismissively towards the man. "This is Ahmet, my mother's brother. He wants to teach you something. Best go along with it."

Ahmet stood in the middle of the room with black hair slicked backwards like a shiny helmet and a cigarette dangling between his lips. His skin was deeply pock-marked under the yellow lighting but I was more interested in his eyes; he had the same elegant sloping lashes and dark thickened brows as Ozzy – the family resemblance was strong.

Without warning, Ahmet raised his right arm and gave the punch bag an almighty whack, sending it high into the air. He turned and winked, gesturing for me to come over. I shook my head vigorously but he reached over and pulled me to my feet.

"Go on," Ozzy sneered, "go and *join in*."

As it was, I had little choice, for no sooner had I looked away than Ahmet was behind me, gripping my shoulders and lifting up my right arm.

"Hit," he instructed.

"What? I can't."

Ahmet moved so that he was behind the punch bag and steadied it with both hands. "Now, hit."

I giggled nervously and shook my head.

"No, not laugh. HIT."

"I can't, I don't know how."

"What there is to know? HIT!"

I glanced desperately at Ozzy but he was ignoring me now and chatting with his cousins. Alfie and Josh had located a kind of African-looking drum from somewhere and were simultaneously beating random rhythms and laughing hysterically.

"What you wait for? It is so simple, no?"

Ahmet had released the bag and was back behind me, one arm on my shoulder, the other gripping my right arm.

I could feel the cool leather of his jacket on my bare skin. Taking something from the floor, Ahmet reached round and forced my hand into a bright red boxing glove.

"So, you are nervous, yes? See, this…" He beat his own closed first on top of my gloved one. "This will protect your hand. You don't worry now, you just hit, yes?"

If I hadn't felt so utterly ridiculous, I would have tried a little harder. And if Imogen were here, we would have both laughed – the sheer absurdity of standing in the back room of a Turkish restaurant in the middle of the night wearing a tiny dress and a boxing glove. But I couldn't laugh because Ahmet was now pushing at my arm, one hand under my elbow so that my gloved hand jabbed repeatedly at the punch bag with quick, even movements. After a moment he stopped and reached for another glove and held it while I forced my other hand inside.

"Now you, alone, go. Hit."

I did as I was told now and gave the bag my full attention, striking it repeatedly with alternating arms. I was aware of being watched and aware that I was a source of amusement, but having placed myself in this situation willingly, I felt compelled – out of pride, out of politeness – to ride out the ridiculous charade.

"No! This is not good. You will not hurt a flea with this punches." Ahmet mimicked my feeble taps and Round-Face sniggered in the corner. I caught sight of Ozzy who was back watching me now, leaning forwards onto his knees, his face unreadable.

"I'm no boxer, I'm sorry." Urgh, the squeak of my own voice – silly, high and apologetic. I'd wanted to impress

Ozzy with my confident independence – "I can stay out until whenever I want, I can fit in, I can handle myself" – and now I felt stupid.

Ahmet stubbed his cigarette out in an ashtray by his foot and began to remove the gloves from my tired wrists. "No, you are not good boxer but I did not ask you to be. I ask you to learn. You don' want to learn though. You don' want to protect yourself."

"Protect myself?"

"Yes! From anyone!" Ahmet gestured around the room at the rabble of young men. "You know these people?"

"I know Ozzy. I know Alfie and Josh."

"You know them well? You put yourself in dark room with strange men and you feel safe?"

"Of course."

"No! You say this because you feel like you should say this… like you will offend… but I am not offend. You do not know these people. I know them, and I know these are good men who will not hurt you but not everys man is like this. Why you not want to protect yourself?"

"I…"

"What if I attack you, like this?" And he grabbed my hands and pulled them behind my back with lightning speed, pulled me down so that the curve of my spine was against his stomach. I gasped as he put one hand on my throat. "No, don' worry, I not hurt you, I just *show* you. So I got you like this, what you do now? Hold up your hands and say: *Please don' hurt me*? What this do? This do nothing, *nothing*. You have to fight back. I teach my daughters this and I know they feel safe." He let me go and turned to his young audience. "Though my daughters not go back to strangers' houses with strange men."

How do you know? I wanted to say, crossing my arms and kicking at the floor.

"No, I don' understand this country, you all dressed up and ready for good time, and I say 'Yes! Good for you...' but learn to protect... not everyone nice like these boys here."

I surveyed the room with all the "nice" boys and saw that Ozzy could not look at me. "I want to go home now, I'm going to get a taxi."

Ahmet ignored me. "See now, my restaurant is best there is but why you come when it closed? You pretty girl, you should be out on nice date with nice boy eating nice food in my restaurant, but instead you turn up after hour in dress and stocking with hole and think it okay to come in back room with strange men and drink and smoke when you don' even like the smoke. What does your mother thin' you are doing now? She thin' you are tuck up in warm bed?"

"I'm going home."

"Ah, so, you all defensive now because I tell truth? Where your mother thin' you are?"

I pushed my shoulders back. "My mother is dead, actually."

There was a pause while Ahmet shook his head sadly.

"Oh, this get even worse now. Your poor mother lying dead in the ground and you not think this behaviour would break her heart? You think your poor dead mother would be proud of you?"

I narrowed my eyes. "You have no right to ask me that." I threw Ozzy a look. "And *you*... thanks for nothing, I'm getting a taxi."

"Get a taxi, *get a taxi*?" Ahmet was gesturing wildly with both arms. "From where is this taxi? What you do, walk the street alone and stick out your arm and hope? Pray to some god you don' even speak to until you need something? No. I will call taxi, you will wait." He searched his pockets and located a mobile. As he keyed in a number, Ahmet stormed across the room and slapped first Ozzy, then Josh and Alfie across the top of their heads with his free hand. "You boys, it is you who should be calling the damn taxi for your friend, what you think she okay out there on her own? Selfish! Why you not being gentlemen? Why you bring girl back and then... hello? Hi, hi, yes I need taxi soon... Mehmet's Mezze Bar. Yes. Come now."

I peered at my skin in the bathroom mirror and picked at a scab which had begun its life as a spot. I searched out some cleanser and a tub of foundation and a dark eye-shadow and fished around for an eye-liner, growling when I discovered it was blunt. It bored me, this careful construction of my face every morning with lotions and potions and make-up, and with a sudden flash of delinquency, I swiped the contents of the bathroom shelf into my make-up bag and settled for a tiny smear of lip gloss.

"Better," said Ozzy, when I met him outside the library.

"What's it to you?"

187

He ignored the remark. "So you got back alright then?"

"Naturally." I knew I sounded sulky, but the night in the restaurant had left its mark and I wasn't going to let him get away unscathed.

"Dad give you grief?"

"Nope." Dad had been sound asleep when I'd returned and we'd barely had time to say "good morning" when our paths crossed on the landing.

We moved into the library and took adjacent seats. As sixth-formers, we were expected to organise our time and use free periods for study, yet I counted only five other people in the room with us. Everyone else was outside, hanging around the football pitches or grabbing breakfast in the local McDonald's. Ozzy took out his phone from his jeans and began playing a game. The last time I'd seen him playing it, Molly had been next to him, her glossy head nestling against his shoulder, his face sullen, hers, pouty and smug.

"*She* wears a lot of make-up," I couldn't help commenting as I pulled out a token textbook and placed it on the table.

"Who?"

"The Moll Doll."

"She always has. It's who she is."

"Right."

"It suits her."

"Uh-huh."

"Look, it's up to you what you do to your face. I just personally think you look better without so much make-up. You're naturally pretty... don't try so hard."

I sighed. This wasn't about bloody make-up.

Usually, I liked Ozzy's quietness and his considered use of words and his indifference to what people thought of him, but today I needed something more.

"Aren't you going to say anything?"

"Sorry."

"What for?" I asked. He was going to acknowledge his behaviour if it killed me to get it out of him.

"I was out of order last night."

"*Thank you.* And, yes, you were."

Now it was his turn to sigh. "It's just… I don't know… I just knew what it would be like, that's why I didn't want you to come."

"What do you mean?"

"My uncle – he can be a bit full-on."

"Nah, he's alright… well, yeah, he was a bit."

Ozzy was still clicking buttons, sending the snake left, left, right, up a bit and down. "Thing is, he thinks everyone secretly wants to be Turkish."

"Really, why?"

He looked up with a smirk. "Because it's the best country in the world?"

I grinned. "Obviously."

At last, the phone was finally laid to rest on the table and Ozzy leaned back in his chair. "He hasn't really grasped that things are different here. Like, he's from a big city and everything, not a tiny village, but he still thinks families should live together and look out for each other more. He doesn't get it that kids can do what they like without their parents worrying themselves stupid. He finds it hard here."

I stared at this nugget of insight into Ozzy's family life as though it were a tangible object. I pictured Ahmet arriving in England, expecting cobbled Victorian streets full of extended families only to be confronted by drunk, barely-dressed teenagers descending on his business and his home with no thought for anything other than where the next vodka was coming from. I felt bad, like I was solely responsible for his disappointment.

"No, it's me who should be sorry. I should have been more respectful… considerate."

"It's weird 'cos I'm younger and everything, but… I still agree with a lot of what he thinks."

"Yeah, of course."

"Like, there's a right way and a wrong way to treat people… and I see a lot of disrespect, not just for girls but the other way too."

I thought about all the times when Ozzy had played peacemaker at school. Never one to be guided by friendly loyalties, he would always stand by the person in the right.

"Do you remember when Molly put chewing gum in my hair?"

"Yep."

"You told her she was out of order."

"Because she was."

"Even though you fancied her?"

He looked quizzical. "She's a pretty girl… doesn't mean she can treat people badly."

Of course it didn't. But I wondered if Ozzy's influence would ever have a lasting effect on Molly.

"You're good for her."

Ozzy smiled. "Maybe."

I folded my arms and pouted. "She still hates me though, even though she pretends to make an effort."

"She doesn't hate you, I told you... she's envious. She knows how to get attention but it's short-lived... she'd love to get your grades in English, love to be bright."

"So why doesn't she work harder then?"

Ozzy tilted his head to the side and smiled through a sigh. "Because she doesn't have the confidence to fail."

"What do you mean?"

"Like, to Molly... everything is about appearance..."

"Clearly."

"... no, not just her physical appearance, how she comes across to other people. She cares what they think... and it's easier to play the popular, sassy girl rather than to actually try because to try might be to prove that she can't do it."

I sat and pondered this for a moment. Really? Was he that insightful? All the time I had spent disliking Molly made it hard to view her with sympathy and I was reluctant to let Ozzy have his point so easily. "It must be so comforting for her to feel that her academic inadequacy warrants having the personality of a bitch."

I picked at a nail and waited for him to pull me up on my snobbishness. He didn't disappoint. "There is nothing comfortable about feeling inadequate," he said, and I knew he was right. He was somehow able to make a point without actually minding if you agreed or not and it was this indifference that gave him power. Bloody perfect Ozzy, forever standing in someone else's shoes before passing judgement.

"You're so irritating," I said.

And he grinned and flicked a pencil at me. "I know."

chapter fourteen

"Naomi, a word, please."

Dad was standing on the threshold of my bedroom with one hand on the doorknob, the other outstretched in the direction of the hallway, an indicator that I was to come downstairs to hear this "word".

"Now, please, I don't have a lot of time."

His mouth was twitching; a sign it was not a time to argue. I slid off the bed and skulked past him with a sigh. A waft of whisky. He followed me down the stairs, his light steps contrasting to my heavy stomps and then, into the kitchen where I launched into a chair, placed my elbows on the table and proceeded to chew my nails. A habit he hated.

"What?"

He didn't sit but leaned back against the sink and rested his hands on the counter top either side. His hair, usually styled so neatly, was sticking up on one side and he moved his hand repeatedly over the stray tuft in an effort to tame it.

"I don't want you going to that shop again."

I stopped biting and looked at him with genuine surprise. "Which shop?"

"The kebab place, the restaurant… whatever it is."

"How do you—"

"It doesn't matter how I know, I don't want you going there and I don't want you associating with those people, do you understand me?" There was a dangerous edge to his voice.

"Why? What do you mean, *those* people?"

And then I jumped as Dad's fist made contact with the table.

"Just do as you're told, damn it!"

There was silence as we both reeled from the moment. This was new. A fist on the table. *Damn it.* This was not my father. I stared at him, his complexion mottled and sweaty, a vein throbbing on his temple. He removed his hand from the table and swept it across his forehead.

"Please, Naomi, if you could just do this one thing…"

"But… I only want to know why, what's so bad about the place?"

"It's not the place, although I cannot imagine why you would want to visit a closed restaurant, it's the people. You don't know them."

I laughed nervously. "Of course I know them, Dad, I go to school with most of them!"

"But they're all boys, you said you were going out with Imogen."

"I know… change of plan. So what if they're all boys though, can't I have friends who are boys?"

"Not Ozzy."

"*What*?"

"Not Ozzy, I've—"

"How do you know Ozzy?"

"I… don't, I've just heard things…"

"Like?" Genuine puzzlement made me brave.

Dad sighed and turned away to look out of the kitchen window. The late afternoon sun was low and showed just how much the glass was in need of a clean. A fat tabby spider made its way precariously from one corner of a lopsided web in need of repair. "I know his uncle… or rather, Mo knows his uncle."

"I know. Ozzy told me. So?"

"They were neighbours in London before Ahmet moved out this way with his sister and nephew."

"Right?"

"I just don't think they're the kind of people you should be associating with… I don't want you getting side-tracked from your studies…"

"No, that's not what this is about."

"It is, I want you to concentrate now… you've wasted so much time—"

"Study, study, study… that's all that matters."

"Not at all. I want you to have a well—"

"A well-rounded education, yes, you've said. A million times."

"Don't be facetious."

I sighed. "I just don't see what Ozzy has to do with my studies, it was one night, we had a few drinks… it's normal teenage behaviour, you know?"

"You should invest more time in your friendship with Imogen… and the other girls."

I laughed again. "The other girls! Like… let's see now… Molly? The one who's hated me since primary school… or how about Suzy Longman? The one who's just had a baby."

He spun around from the window and cut me off. "Naomi, this is important. I need you to trust me on this. You're not to mix with those people."

It wasn't that I had any particular desire to visit Mehmet's Mezze Bar again, but this lack of reasoning, this lack of explanation… I shook my head in frustration and then paused dramatically. "Oh… my… God."

"What?"

"Oh, my God," I repeated, still shaking my head, "I can't believe it, I never thought I'd see the day."

"What are you talking about?"

"Bloody hell, you're…" I paused for maximum effect. "You're a RACIST!"

It was not true. We both knew it wasn't true. But I hoped that the sheer shock value of my liberal, intelligent father being accused of racism would be harder for him to stomach than whatever the truth actually was. Dad's eyes were wide pools. His mouth opened and then shut twice and he lifted his hands, clasping them together on top of his head as though he were waiting to be shot. He was breathing heavily and took a moment to speak. I watched him consider his words. My father – reasonable and rational at all times.

"Naomi," his voice was level now, "I think we both know that racism has no place in this house. I can also see that you are trying to provoke me, and I refuse to be provoked. I am your father and, though you are growing up, I still happen to know best at times. This is one of those times. What I need is for you to trust me and do as I've asked."

"But you're not giving me a decent reason!"

"DRUGS! There's a reason for you… Bloody drugs, Naomi!"

I almost laughed. "Huh?"

"You heard. Mo said Ahmet's flat was full of drugs. All the time."

"*Mo* said that."

"Yes."

"Those actual words."

"Well, something about popping in for a cup of tea and floating out on a cloud, actually."

Now I did laugh. "Dad, he just means that they have the odd spliff or something, nothing dre—"

"And *there* you have it, right there." He was pointing a finger towards me now, towards my mouth as though he could see the words. "It's a slippery slope. 'The odd spliff' as you so eloquently put it leads to other things, much more serious things and I won't have it, I will not have my daughter mixed up in all that crap."

"Dad, seriously. Loads of people do it, it's no big deal."

"No big deal?"

"But for the record, I don't. And neither does Ozzy."

"That you know of."

"That I know of."

"Anyway, it's done. I've passed on a message to Ahmet via Mo that you are not to mix with Ozzy or that family in the future."

"You've what?" I jumped up with such force that my chair tipped backwards behind me and thudded to the floor. "You had no right, I decide who I'm friends with, you are so bloody embarrassing."

"Don't use that language, Naomi."

"YOU use it! You said 'bloody' literally thirty seconds ago, you're nothing but a fucking hypocrite!"

"NAOMI!"

But I was not waiting around to hear anymore. I kicked the chair leg out of the way and stormed out of the kitchen and back up to my room where I slammed the door with such force, the ballerina nameplate fell off and landed by my feet.

*

Mr Adams was no longer my teacher. He taught the other A-level English class and since the beginning of term I had had to content myself with glimpses of him from afar – through the little square windows of classrooms or hurrying down corridors, arms filled with copies of *Romeo and Juliet*. He was even more desirable at a distance and I missed the attention he gave me in class but I had never forgotten his declaration that I should seek him out for help whenever I needed it. After all, I was a star pupil.

I could hear him talking inside the office and kicked my heels impatiently against the corridor wall. Eventually, Ms Emerald laughed her way out of the room. She was always laughing. She was always in his room.

"Naomi, are you okay?" she asked, finding me lurking.

"Fine, miss. I need to check something with Mr Adams about… some homework."

She put her head to one side and stared at me. "Really? That's unlike you to need help."

I wished she would go away. "Oh, I don't need help," I said innocently, "just want to check the hand-in date."

She frowned, made some sort of non-committal noise and walked away, her skirt swishing around her pudgy ankles as she made her way down the corridor. I waited for her to disappear around the corner and then slunk through the open doorway.

Mr Adams was standing behind his desk and sweeping a pile of orange peel into his left hand. He deposited the peel into the wire bin behind him and looked up.

"Miss Rose, something I can help you with?"

Without waiting for an invitation, I collapsed into the chair facing his desk and let out a dramatic sigh – I was getting good at those.

"What's wrong, has something happened?"

"Sir... I just... I don't know who else to talk to..." I looked down at my hands. The tissue which I had been absentmindedly pulling at had begun to shred white fluff onto the floor.

His chair made a scraping sound as he stood up and rushed round to my side of the desk. He placed a hand on my shoulder. I sighed again and Mr Adams' fingers flattened as he began rubbing the area between my shoulder blades, his skin separated from mine by a mere millimetre of white cotton.

"Come on, now, why the long face?"

"It's everything."

"Everything." He drummed his fingers on my right shoulder now. "So... the fact that it's sunny is making you sad? That it's nearly the weekend? That you will probably get the highest mark for your English coursework in the whole of the county?"

I smiled weakly. "Dad."

"Ah. Dad."

"I just thought he might have made more of an effort to understand me."

"The curse of the generation gap. He won't be the first father to fail in the understanding stakes, I'm afraid."

"Yeah, but, you know, what with losing my mum and everything..." *Had he forgotten?*

He moved away and placed his chair gently in front of mine, so close that when he sat, ours knees almost touched. "You think he should make double the effort?"

I shrugged.

"Come on, what's he done... or not done?"

What could I tell him? That Dad had overreacted about the possibility of Ozzy's uncle smoking the odd bit of weed? It wasn't that important and I wasn't really bothered anyway. "I just thought... I hoped my dad would have been at the ceremony, that's all."

It was lame, and I felt Mr Adams' confusion even though he masked it in his face. "The awards ceremony? But that was... a while back..." he cleared his throat, "but yes, of course... I think we'd all expected him to attend. I'm sure he must have had a good reason, perhaps something came up unexpectedly. Did he explain?"

I pictured frail little Arthur in his carrier and Dad's worry over my reaction.

"Just work. The same excuse as always but I think he actually just forgot." I forced a tear and Mr Adams leaned forwards, his face inches from mine.

"Naomi, I honestly don't think he would ever set out to hurt you. I'm sure he would be absolutely devastated to know how awful you were feeling, do you think... would it help if I spoke to him perhaps?"

I shook my head forcibly. "No, he doesn't listen to anybody."

"I see."

I waited for a few seconds to pass. "Mr Adams?"

"Yes?"

"Did you mean it when you said I was in a different league?"

"Absolutely, one hundred percent," he replied with a laugh. But his face altered suddenly and he became serious. He stood up and took his hand away from where it had moved to my arm. "What I mean is, that you... *along with Denise O'Brien*... are most definitely on target for some fantastic grades."

I ignored the mention of Denise and concentrated on keeping my eyes level with his. Mine, watery; his, puzzled... or nervy – no, why would he be nervy? "You're sure? A different league?"

Mr Adams stood up and took a step back. "Come on, love, let's have no more of the tears now. Maybe you would be more comfortable talking to another teacher, a female one perhaps?"

"Why?" There was an unintended sharpness to my voice. "This is not a female-related problem."

"No, no it's not but... look, I'm more than happy to help where I can but... actually, how about this? I think it might be a good idea to write some of your thoughts down on paper, it's a process I use myself to... well, it can help to order things."

I pictured my stack of diaries behind the wardrobe at home. "If I write my thoughts down, will you read them?" I asked.

He shuffled some papers on his desk – an unnecessary action. "Thoughts are private things, I'm sure you wouldn't want me to know everything. It's more of a therapeutic process."

But I left his office with what I needed to hear taped firmly inside my head and disregarded everything else. Love. "Come on, *love*."

Imogen and Ozzy were laughing at something on Immy's phone. "What took you so long? I'm soaked through," she complained, glancing up. "Look at my hair, it's huge!"

It was only a light mist of rain but Imogen's hair had a life of its own when there was moisture in the air and I laughed an apology.

"What were you doing?" asked Ozzy.

"Talking to Mr Adams."

"Again?"

"About the homework."

"Jesus, anyone would think you had a thing for him. Right, I'm off to see Molls." Ozzy turned to walk in the opposite direction. "Only so much time I can spend with the teacher's pet."

"Yeah, go on," I laughed, "go and see your pretty little doll."

He turned and stuck his middle finger in the air but he was grinning.

Imogen and I mirrored each other as we walked down the busy road, tattered navy-blue bags covered in doodles hanging off our shoulders, arms folded across our chests, heads lowered against the damp air.

"So, what's your excuse this time?" she asked coldly.

"I told you, homework."

"Yeah right."

chapter fifteen

"How come your aunt didn't move out this way with your Uncle Ahmet?"

We both had our feet up on the seat in front and were actively ignoring the disapproving looks from the other passengers. I had paid no heed to Dad's demand that I stay away from Ozzy and today we were heading into London so he could visit his family. While he was doing that, I planned to surprise Mo. The last few times he'd been over to see Dad, I'd been out and I missed him.

"You're kidding, right? She was glad to see the back of him."

"But they're still a couple?"

"Yeah, course. At weekends. Auntie says she's never been happier."

I picture Ahmet with his punch bag and dingy room and his forceful nature. I thought about his lovely traditional family values and how convenient it was that he only chose to live by some of them himself.

"But what about—"

"Don't." Ozzy held his hand up. "I know what you're going to say, but I don't have the answers. All I know is that when they lived together, you were lucky if you managed to avoid being hit by a book or a cup – one time, Auntie threw a frying pan across the kitchen… with the omelette still in it." He grinned at my raised eyebrows. "But now, they get together at weekends and it's like they're teenagers again."

"Really?"

"Yeah. It's gross actually… think I preferred the omelette."

The train slowed for a signal and I looked out over row upon row of neat terraced houses. "But how do they afford to keep up with two lots of rent?"

"Don't know and I don't ask," said Ozzy. "It's better not to."

Dad and his misgivings about Ahmet and the use of drugs in the restaurant sprang to mind. Maybe the business was a smokescreen for a more lucrative enterprise… clever, really, to move away from the family home so there was no link… or perhaps Ahmet's wife was in on the whole thing, she might be the brains behind it all… and *maybe* Ozzy was the *mule*! I studied him subtly, trying to figure out where he might be hiding tiny cellophane packages or wads of bank notes…

Saxon House was minutes from the station and I trotted alongside Ozzy as he led the way towards the imposing grey structure. Balconies were strewn with washing and bicycles and discarded furniture; on the third floor, a couple of kids were leaning over and watching us with interest. Heavy bass music blared from an open door on the fifth and every balcony that could be reached from the ground was littered with graffiti. I stood at the bottom and looked straight up – level upon level filled with families and lives, just like Mo's.

I had imagined knocking on his door and waiting to surprise him but we'd barely stepped into the front lobby when I heard his unmistakable voice coming from a nearby stairwell.

"Mate! It's like I said, you know? At the end of the day… you just gotta go with it."

And then the door to the stairs swung fully open and a beautiful girl with a halo of caramel curls rushed past us, dragging a wide-eyed boy behind her.

"Esme! Get back here! Mate, I gotta go but take my – ESME… I *swear* to God!"

But I had already seen the open lobby door and had hold of the girl's arm before she'd had a chance to pull her brother through it.

"Ge'off, ge'off, ge'off!"

She looked about twelve but she was remarkably strong and when I wouldn't let her go, I felt a sharp kick to my shin.

"Ow!"

"Mimi?"

Esme stopped kicking and stared at her father. Mo looked from me to Ozzy in confusion, "What are you two doing here?" And then to me, "Does your dad know?"

"I thought I'd keep Ozzy company… and maybe pop in for a chat," I said, but my voice fell flat when Mo's reaction wasn't quite as rapturous as I'd expected.

"And your dad?"

"Dad doesn't need to know."

"Did you *run away* from your daddy?" Little Taylor's eyes were wide.

I crouched down to his level and laughed. "No, of course I didn't, just like you weren't about to run away from your daddy." I glanced at Mo before adding, "You see, I'm a big girl now. I can do what I like."

"Well, I'm eight."

"Eight? So, you're getting pretty big too then. Where were you off to?"

"Esme wanted to go to the park, but Daddy said—"

"As if!" Esme spat. "I'm blatantly too old for the park."

"You *did* want to."

"Shut up, you idiot!"

I stared at Esme and marvelled at how a face could be so beautiful yet so venomous at the same time. "Well anyway," I intervened, "I'm Naomi, how's about you show me your flat instead? I've heard so much about you both."

The five of us crammed ourselves into a lift which smelt of urine and stood awkwardly in silence. Ozzy got out on the tenth floor after agreeing to meet me in an hour and the rest of us continued up to the sixteenth and then a few moments later, we were sitting in a strange line along one sofa, Mo and I at opposite ends, the kids sandwiched between us.

"So how do you know my dad?" Taylor asked, swivelling a finger gently around the inside of his nostril.

Esme kicked her brother on the ankle. "You're so gross, stop picking your nose."

Mo levered himself up and pulled the children to their feet. "Right you two, enough. I'm going to make a drink for our guest and you can play on the laptop in my room. Go."

"Yay!" Taylor jumped and ran out of the room, no longer interested in the stranger on the sofa. Esme followed more slowly. "Whatever… but we're not playing any of those stupid games."

I smiled at their retreating backs. "They're really cute."

"They're being little shits 'cos their mum's gone away for a few days."

"Oh?"

"Her dad's ill."

"Oh."

There was an awkward silence. Where was the easy, brash Mo who never ran out of things to say? The man in front of me now was nervous and shy, as though I were the adult and he the child. I saw that I'd wrong-footed him by turning up unannounced.

"Nice place," I said. And it *was* nice. Small and compact. Everything in its place; no clutter or mess, just two sofas, a TV, a small coffee table with an ashtray and a remote control. I thought of our living room at home full of books and piles of essays, the ironing pile which sat in the corner and never seemed to decrease in size and the heap of shoes by the window and the glasses and cups which littered the side tables until one of us realised that there were none left in the kitchen.

"Coffee? Tea?" Mo was pointing at the kitchen as though demonstrating where the kettle was.

"Yeah, tea, please."

We made small talk while the kettle boiled but once we held our cups in our hands the air changed between us.

"Why are you here, Mimi? I mean, without telling your dad?" It was funny how he reverted back to using my childish nickname in Dad's absence. I liked it. "You know he doesn't want you hanging around with Ozzy – I gotta say, I disagree with him 'cos Ozzy's a good kid – but you should show a bit of respect."

"Respect?"

"Yeah, like you should at least tell him where you are. The man'll be going outta his mind."

I laughed at this and Mo shifted uncomfortably. He leaned forwards and rested his forearms on his knees. I had never seen him so serious; where was the loud laughter, the gold shiny teeth?

"Dad doesn't listen to me. Ever," I said. "I've tried explaining stuff… he's only interested in my education."

"There's plenty of kids who'd be grateful for that."

"I should be grateful?"

"Not grateful, no… just… make a few allowances."

He must have seen the confusion written on my face because Mo placed his cup on the immaculate table and turned to face me entirely, his expression earnest.

"Mimi, your dad finds it hard to show emotion but that's not a crime. Plenty of people are like that…"

I shrugged.

"… look, you know I tell it like it is, right?"

"Always."

"I don't beat around bushes or use unnecessary, fancy words to say what I wanna say."

I smiled but held back the laughter in my throat.

"Your dad is a proper decent bloke. Out and out, through and through… one of the best. There's things he's done that most men would run a mile from."

I was interested now. "Like what?"

But Mo shook his head. "Not important right this minute. What's important is that you know he's doing his best. He's always done his best."

"But—"

"Wait, listen. I know what he's like but he found himself in a situation that maybe he wasn't prepared for and it's like he's acting out a role, putting his foot down about stuff because he thinks that's what parents do."

I considered this for a moment. It made sense but still… "It doesn't explain why he doesn't like Ozzy."

"You got to see the bigger picture, see the wood from the trees." Mo waved his arms in the air, I guessed to demonstrate the woods and the trees. "Ozzy is a good kid, I've told him that, but there's a difference in values, in *interests*."

"You mean that Dad thinks Ozzy and his family are all off their heads on drugs?"

"No, no, no." The arms were waving again. "Well, yes, he has his suspicions."

"It's ridiculous," I said, getting to my feet and pacing the wooden flooring. "So they have the odd spliff—"

"It's ridiculous to you but... look, everyone does it around here so it's no big deal, but your dad thinks it's a slippery slope, the calm before the storm, the road to ruin..."

"*Okay*, I get it."

"Just telling it like it is."

I sat back down and Mo patted my knee.

"The thing is," I said pointedly, "Dad drinks, like *all* the time, and surely that's worse?"

Mo looked at me like I'd just made a joke. "Not in the eyes of the law."

I lowered my eyes, not because I felt silly but because I felt a twinge of guilt. It felt disloyal, discussing Dad's failings with his oldest friend.

"And certainly not in the eyes of other people. Drinking is socially acceptable and your dad is all about doing the right thing socially, morally..."

"Why do you keep doing that?"

"What?"

"Talking about him as though he's some kind of saint."

But we were disturbed by the manic rattle of Mo's letterbox, swiftly followed by a kerfuffle in the bedroom and then the hallway as Taylor and Esme fought to get to the door first.

"Oh, it's just Dan," Esme called through, her voice calmed by disappointment. "Can he use your phone?"

Druggie Dan! I almost followed Mo down the hallway so as to catch a glimpse of the man I'd always pictured to be a skinny, sallow-skinned wretch in a raincoat, but I was distracted by Taylor slithering into the room on his tummy.

"Pretend you can't see me," he instructed, making his way around the sofa and towards the kitchen.

"Who said that?" I played along, glancing around the room and searching under cushions.

"Pretend you can't hear anything." The snake had managed to right itself against the kitchen counter and grow hands and fingers. I heard the crumple of plastic.

"Taylor, put those biscuits back *right now*." The front door was slammed shut and Mo suddenly appeared in the room.

"Pretend you—"

"I'm not pretending anything. Taylor, get your hands out of the packet."

I couldn't help laughing as the snake vanished and Taylor emerged on the threshold of the lounge, floppy arms by his sides, curly head so low we couldn't see his face.

"Did Dan use the phone?" he asked petulantly.

"Yes, he did," replied Mo.

"But you *said*…"

"I know what I said but sometimes people change their minds, don't they? Like snakes deciding to help themselves to biscuits after saying they wouldn't do that anymore."

The head fell even lower.

"Go on, back to your room. Esme's had the laptop for ages, it must be your turn now."

Taylor scuttled off, and Mo leaned back with a furtive grin. "Little shit," he muttered, but I could still hear the pride in his voice.

"You knew my mum, didn't you?"

Mo rubbed the back of his bald head. "I did. She was something special, proper natural pretty... didn't cement herself in make-up like the other girls. Hair like yours before you started messing around with dye."

Instinctively, I pulled a section of hair forwards and inspected it. I'd begun dying it again, but the last shade hadn't taken properly and it was now a mishmash of blonde and brown.

"What was she like?"

"You don't remember?"

I paused. "Sometimes I think I remember wrong."

Mo nodded as though this made perfect sense. He stretched his arms up and rested his hands behind his head. "Like I said, she was different to the other girls round here. Soft. Yeah, she was soft and there was, like, I dunno, like a vulnerability about her. Everybody saw it. Some people used to take advantage—"

"Advantage? How?"

Mo hesitated and scratched his chin. He shifted position. "Yeah, well... but for your dad, it was what made him fall in love with her. It can be rough round here, worse then than now, and your dad wanted to pick Kathy up and carry her off like a frail character in one of them poncey Victorian novels."

I tried to imagine my dad doing this, but it was such a romantic image, I failed.

"Why did she even need rescuing though?" I gave the rescuing physical inverted commas.

"Like I said, she was soft. Sometimes easily led. Your mum got caught up in things that were second nature to us, but to her... well..."

"Are you talking about drugs again?" Surely not. My mother had barely had the energy to make dinner, I couldn't envisage her ever bouncing off the walls in some nightclub.

"There are different sorts of drugs, Mimi," Mo said, reading my mind, "and some, though harmless to most people, can have a lasting effect on others."

"You're saying my mum was a druggie?"

"Absolutely not. Not in a million years. A dabbler, maybe... a couple of times... but sometimes one bad episode is all it takes."

"A bad trip?" I said, remembering the term from somewhere. No one used it now.

"If you like. Made her proper down, like, she couldn't lift her mood for *weeks*... then they found out she was pregnant."

"Me," I said softly.

"Yes. Her parents didn't want to know after that. Kicked her out. Bad times they were, bad times."

I couldn't get my head around any of this. I knew there had been some kind of family rift as I'd never met any of my grandparents but...

"Your dad proper stepped up. Took control. Moved you both out of London, saying he wanted you to have a better life. We all laughed, said he thought he was better than us but I can see now he was just scared."

I imagined Dad swinging in, Robin Hood style, and scooping my pregnant mother up and away from the heroin-needle-wielding addict.

"Your dad wasn't local, not really. But that's army families for you, can't never become a local, not really, never in one place long enough. He did his best to fit in, but…"

"He didn't," I concluded.

Mo shook his head with a smile. "He was like a fish out of water. All that money he reckons his dad spent on private tuition so he didn't fall behind, when what he proper needed was a lesson in social skills!" Mo laughed. "He used to say he wanted to teach in a London school, for the challenge of making a difference to all the disadvantaged kids. Said it was his 'moral duty'… he even moved into the tower for a bit, you know, to live amongst us poor disadvantaged… you know, be the rich, white saviour…"

I cringed, and Mo smiled.

"… but you know, even when he came across as patronising, it was unintentional. I could always see the good under the bluster and so could your mum."

"And so that's why he's so scared of Ozzy… he's scared of the connection to this place?"

"I guess. At first, he wanted to 'connect' and 'integrate', but reality isn't as sugary sweet when it negatively affects the people you love."

I pondered this, trying to see Dad's side, but all I saw was a man taking the easy way out and leaving his friends behind. It wasn't such a bad area surely? "But you're still here. I mean, you didn't feel the need to run away?"

"This is my home and I have a perfectly happy life. Your mum was unlucky and your dad can't see past that."

"And you're alright... and Taylor and Esme..."

"Yes, and I'm lucky. I never had someone I love get caught up in a bad way. Taylor and Esme, they're smart kids, like Ozzy. They know better than to get involved in anything dodgy."

"But you let Druggie Dan into your home!"

"They laugh at him, Mimi, they feel *sorry* for him."

"But still..."

"Dan is still a *person*, Mimi. He's part of my life... my neighbour for fifteen years. Just because I didn't up sticks and move, doesn't mean I don't have the same values as your dad, I just choose to handle situations differently."

Mo was being more honest with me than Dad ever was; he was making me understand. I had come here for sympathy, to offload about my indifferent, insensitive father, and yet I was suddenly clear-headed; it all made sense now – Dad had flipped out because he was scared, he couldn't separate what had happened to my mother with what might, or might not, happen to me.

"Mo, you said that Dad wanted to take care of Mum and protect me."

"That's right."

"But if he wants me to have the perfect childhood, why does he treat me like... like some sort of... acquaintance? Why doesn't he ever sit me down and talk to me like you're doing now?"

"Now who's the romantic one?" Mo laughed but his eyes were gentle. "Parenting isn't a one-size-fits-all procedure. Some people find the emotional stuff hard and focus on the practical... money, education... you know? You just gotta look harder, it's like that saying, 'if you're not looking, you're not finding.'"

"I've never heard that saying before."

"Because I just made it up! But at the end of the day, it's night. What will be, will be."

I must have looked puzzled then because Mo punched my arm and laughed, loudly this time. "Stop trying to figure everything out. Sometimes I'm so wise *I* don't even know what I mean!"

When I peeked into the bedroom and said goodbye to Esme and Taylor, they barely looked up from the laptop. At the front door, Mo placed a hand on my shoulder and pulled me into a tight hug.

"He's a good man, Mimi, a good man."

For the first time in months, Dad and I sat down to eat together. I'd prepared spaghetti bolognaise and a fresh salad so that it was ready and waiting for when he arrived home. I wanted to be honest with him from the outset and had practised what I was going to say but when he asked where I'd been that day, I found myself dodging the question.

"Around. How was your day?"

He was still wearing his reading glasses and he reached for them and took them off with a look of surprise.

"Don't know why I've still got these on." And he folded

the slim frames carefully and put them to one side. "It was fine. Thank you. Busy time of year."

When wasn't it a busy time of year? If it wasn't exam season, it was coursework preparation or training sessions or start of year inductions. Even the holidays were spent planning or marking or just planning to plan. It was endless. Dad looked tired and hollow-eyed as he lifted his wine to his lips. When he caught me staring he offered a subtle, self-reproachful smile. "Would you like a glass?"

"Of wine?"

"Yes, why not? It's civilised with dinner."

I wavered, unsure of the right answer. No, I didn't want a drink, but would it soften him to have me join in? Of course, there was nothing wrong with having wine with dinner, but I knew it wouldn't stop there. He was set now for the evening; he'd probably already stopped for a drink on the way home and when this bottle was finished the whisky decanter would beckon – *not against the law... socially acceptable* – but how was this any different, really, to Ozzy's uncle smoking the odd bit of weed? One drug leads to another... one drink leads to another, no differentiation other than Ahmet looked to be fit and healthy whereas Dad was looking crumpled and weak. Did Ahmet pass out on the sofa?

"No, I'm fine with water. Thanks, though."

He twisted spaghetti around his fork and placed it carefully in his mouth. Dad never slurped his pasta through his teeth, never spilt sauce down his shirt. Careful and considered movements at all times.

"Dad?"

"Mm, this really is delicious. What a treat to be cooked for."

"I went to see Mo today. With Ozzy."

He carried on eating and I waited, anxiously pushing the remains of my food around on my plate. It would be easier for me if he flared up and shouted, and surely more normal? But no – careful, considered, measured... even in anger.

"I know."

My hand froze on the fork. "You know?"

"Yes. Mo called me, as I would expect any responsible adult – and friend – to do, to let me know you were safe."

I felt betrayed after what had been such an intimate and open conversation. Mo must have phoned the minute I'd left the flat... how *could* he?

No. I was wrong to think badly of Mo. His loyalty was first and foremost to his friendship with Dad, he had just been trying to ensure there was no unnecessary worry. My anger was no longer directed at Mo but at Dad for saying nothing, for allowing me to sit eating my dinner with the knowledge of what was to come hanging over my head like a big raincloud. But I had to play Dad's game, I had to be calm, intelligent, measured. My fingers tightened around my fork. I closed my eyes and took a deep breath.

"I'm sorry for lying to you, Dad." This was good. Open with an apology, demonstrate that I am mature enough to make my own decisions.

"But..." No. Don't use "but". "I feel that I am in a better position now to understand your concerns. Mo explained why you were worried and I really do get it, you're scared that I'll get caught up in…" What should I say? It wasn't as though Dad and I had conversations about drugs, the word "weed" sounded ridiculous in my head. "… Caught up in stuff, but you have to understand, Ozzy is not interested in any of that… stuff, he's a good friend, and I haven't always found it easy to make friends." The sad reality of this struck me with surprise, as though I'd only just realised it myself. I looked down at my plate forlornly and waited for Dad to say something. Would he contradict me, tell me I was being silly, that I had lots of friends?

"Naomi."

"Yes?" There was ill-disguised hope in my voice.

"You may be right about Ozzy. Perhaps I haven't been altogether fair on the boy."

He had finished eating now and placed his cutlery neatly in the centre of the plate. I watched as he gently clasped his hands together and rested his chin on the tips of his fingers. But he still wasn't looking at me; his eyes were on the table, the salt pot, the wine glass, anywhere else but on me.

"I have no issue with you spending time with him in the future. I trust Mo's judgement."

What about mine? I was tempted to ask. *What about my judgement?*

"And I appreciate his attempts at explaining my motives…"

The impending "but" loomed large and every muscle in my body tensed.

"... but you cannot and will not ever 'understand'. Whatever you feel to the contrary, you are a child and you cannot possibly understand what it is to have a child of your own and feel so ludicrously inadequate against the evils of the world that your only option is to uproot and start again."

The "evils of the world"? What on earth was he talking about?

"Dad—"

"Enough now."

"But I think you're over—"

"You're going to say, of course, that I'm overreacting."

I swallowed the rest of my sentence in silent fury; the taste of blood when I bit the inside of my cheek giving me minor satisfaction.

"See, I already know how you're going to react before it happens." He took a long sip of wine and sighed. "Your mother was the love of my life and you were the love of hers, even before you were born. But it had a hold of her, even after I took her away... I worked and worked to give her a better life, not just an existence but a life – a career, a house, a clean slate – and still... *still*, it took her from me."

"She was still... was she like, a proper—"

"No!" His eyes twitched and he rubbed at them furiously, pulling the skin taut around his temples and releasing. "No." He lowered his voice. "She literally dabbled once, maybe twice – against her better judgement and most definitely under coercion. No, your mother had a terrible reaction from a limited exposure... but it was to have a lasting effect on her. The drugs may have been out of her system but they had taken a part of her… I couldn't lift her out, she was sinking into a black hole and I couldn't… by the time she became physically ill, I could see… I could feel that it was almost a relief to her." He choked on the shock of saying it out loud and I held my breath. "It was as if she had an excuse to give up."

"Dad…"

I sat completely still. The half revelations spun through the air and I tried to make sense of them. So Mum had mixed with a dodgy crowd… drug-use… depression… I hadn't been enough to get her out of that. *Why* hadn't I been enough to get her out of that? I needed to know more, I needed details and further explanations.

"Please, Dad, I need to understand."

But he was crying now. Free-flowing tears onto his fingers, into his wine glass. "I can't…"

"Please!" I was suddenly desperate and forced my hand to touch his across the table.

"Enough! I don't want to talk about this… there was a world before you, you know?" And he pulled his hand away and bashed his tightened fist upon the table, sending my knife to the floor and causing the wine bottle to rock precariously.

He stopped to collect himself. He sniffed and rubbed at his eyes again, breaking into a watery smile. "I'm behaving unforgivably, Naomi. Don't listen to me, it's the wine talking. Of *course* you understand, you are a clever, clever girl. Please, you don't need to let events before your time affect your life now. We cannot control the past but we can have a say in the future. I know you understand."

My expression remained blank because I didn't know what to do with my face. I could feel my legs trembling under the table because he was so wrong. I didn't understand any of it. But, disastrously, I had finally run out of words at a time when they would have been most use to me.

chapter sixteen

THE SKY HAD DARKENED CONSIDERABLY BUT SO
far proffered nothing more offensive than a fine mist
which dampened my blazer but didn't even soak through.
I'd hoped for real rain.

At last, the double door at the end of the English
block opened out and he appeared and looked up at the
sky. Hugging a pile of books to his chest, he adjusted
his jacket to protect them and broke into a jog towards
his car. He grimaced as he dropped his car key and bent
down awkwardly to retrieve it from the ground. From my
position at the gate, I watched him raise his knee against
the driver's door and balance his books to unlock the car
manually. The books were thrown onto the back seat and

he was in, facing away from me as he started the engine. Timing was everything now.

I left my post and, keeping an eye on the car, hurried out of the gate and across the road. The driver of a blue van leant heavily on his horn as I dashed in front of him, scarcely clearing his path in time, my bag inches from clipping his wing mirror. On the opposite side of the road was a bus stop and I hovered, pretending to check the timetable.

"I don't think they've updated that one, love… where is it you want to go? The twenty-seven will be along in a minute."

A small lady in a sandy-coloured raincoat was seated on the bench under the bus shelter, her bright, round face beaming out from under the plastic rainhat knotted under her chin.

"Is it the twenty-seven you're after, love?" she said when I didn't answer.

I clocked the car edging out of the school gate and pausing at the junction to allow for a gap in traffic.

"Um, no, I think I'll walk," I muttered and when the car moved off I skipped swiftly along the kerb in the direction that I knew he would take. It began to rain more heavily but I made no attempt to keep dry and left my blazer open and my collar down. Then, when I judged he must be moments behind me I allowed my ankle to buckle to the right and I lurched forwards, throwing my bag to the side and, though I couldn't stop my arms from pushing out in front of me, I managed to land awkwardly with my knee hitting the edge of the pavement with a painful thud.

"Oh dear, are you alright, my love?"

For God's sake. The old lady was scuttling towards me as I picked myself up and hobbled back onto the pavement.

"I'm fine."

"Naomi?"

His car had stopped as I'd hoped. With his left indicator flashing, he was leaning across the front passenger seat and calling through the open window. I looked up and smiled my feigned surprise.

"What are you doing, are you alright?"

"Yeah, just tripped, sir… I think I've jarred my knee."

The old lady had a hand on my elbow now and was fussing around me. "Oh dear, you need to be careful, love, you could have fallen right into the path of a car… always rushing, you young people!"

"Sir, can I get a lift home?"

But before Mr Adams could answer, the interfering old bat was exclaiming, "I don't think so!" And to my dismay, she strengthened her grip on my elbow and began steering me away from what she clearly perceived to be imminent danger.

"It's okay," I reassured her, "I know him, he's my teacher."

"I don't care if he's a professor at Oxford, you read all sorts about teachers and their pupils these days; youngster like you gets into a car with him and I'll be reading about your abduction in tomorrow's paper! No, you come with me and I'll get you cleaned up, I've got a packet of wet wipes in my handbag for emergencies."

Cars were having to pull wide to avoid Mr Adams' awkward position on the road and a horn beeped from somewhere. The rain was heavy now. If this was going to happen, I had no choice but to make it. Pulling my arm away from her clutches, I muttered a thank you to my wannabe saviour and limped over to Mr Adams' car where I opened the passenger door and got in.

"What are you doing?"

"I need a lift. Please, sir?"

But the lady from the bus stop was not going to give up easily. She was giving short, hard taps to the window with her umbrella and shouting something that I couldn't make out.

I giggled, but Mr Adams looked horrified. "Open the bloody window," he hissed, "for God's sake, you're going to get me shot."

"Woah," I said, holding my hands up, but I did as he'd asked.

The old lady shoved her umbrella through the open window and almost poked Mr Adams in the eye. Before she could shout again, I pushed the umbrella away from my nose and smiled sweetly. "It's fine, he really is my teacher. Look." And I pointed out the identity card hanging around Mr Adams' neck.

The lady paused and closed her quivering mouth but I could tell she was only temporarily placated.

"Honestly, thank you for your concern, but I'm fine."

Mr Adams leaned towards the open window from the driver's seat and held his ID card out so it could be inspected more thoroughly. "I work just over there, at Harper Comprehensive. I can assure you that I will get Naomi home safely, Mrs…"

"Lee. Mrs Lee."

"Thank you for your help, Mrs Lee," I said, tapping her

gently on the hand. "I don't know what I would have done without you."

"Well, only if you're sure." Mrs Lee still looked doubtful. "You can't be too careful nowadays." She adjusted the knot under her rainhat and peered at us with narrowed eyes. "You read all sorts in the papers, don't you? Old men preying on young girls... I wouldn't be able to forgive myself..."

"Please," I interrupted, "you'll miss your bus. Thank you for your help but everything is fine here."

Mr Adams was rubbing his temples. The number twenty-seven arrived behind us and pulled in awkwardly to avoid hitting Mr Adams' car.

"Will you at least take my number and give me a quick call to let me know you got back safely?"

I realised that she wasn't going to go anywhere until I agreed so I nodded and waited while she rummaged around in her handbag for an ancient-looking mobile. "Now hold on a minute, I'll have to look the number up, my daughter keyed it in somewhere... oh." There was more waiting while she located a scrap of paper which immediately got damp and a pen. Finally, she leaned into the car again, scribbled the number down and forced it into my hand. "There. Now don't forget to ring me. I won't sleep tonight unless you do!" And when at last she turned to get the attention of the bus driver who kindly reopened the doors to allow her to clamber on board, I breathed a sigh of relief and scrunched the scrap of paper into a tiny ball, stuffing it into my pocket along with everything else I'd discarded throughout the day.

But Mr Adams didn't sound relieved, he sounded angry. "Right," he said as he indicated to pull out into the traffic. "Right. Fine. I will drop you home, but I want you to call your dad and tell him. Do it now, please."

"And say what?"

He flapped his hands against the steering wheel. "Say that I'm giving you a lift because you hurt your knee. Which is the *absolute truth*."

"Calm down, he won't mind."

"Just do it. Please." He sounded almost desperate.

I huffed and made a show of searching through every possible pocket and section of my bag before locating my phone in the pocket of my blazer where I'd known it was all along.

"No answer," I said triumphantly.

He glanced across at the phone. "Leave a message."

I sighed and called again, discreetly ending the call before I spoke.

"There. All done."

He nodded and we drove off, merging with the traffic and following the road for a while before I directed him to turn left.

"Sorry," Mr Adams began to say, "but can you see how easily things can be misconstrued?"

I shrugged and looked out of the window. What did it matter what other people thought? I turned the handle and the glass edged downwards – "workout windows". *Wow, how old was this car?* It felt right sitting in the passenger seat next to him, as though we were equals. I wished I wasn't wearing my school uniform. "How's Alice?" I asked without looking at him.

"Alice?"

"Yes. Your girlfriend. Alice."

His eyes flicked from the road to me and back again. "Alice is good. *Alice and I are both good.*" I could hear the unease creeping back into his voice. "So, how's everything going? Coursework? Home life? Hobbies?"

Hobbies. Now he was trying too hard to sound breezy and it annoyed me. "It's impossible to get anything done at home. Dad needs me to do everything. He's always working."

We were silent and Dad's distraught face swam before me. I had pushed too hard. I knew he had behaved out of character but there had been something so utterly terrifying about seeing such an outpouring of emotion, however short-lived. He couldn't see that I was growing up, that I could share some of the burden, take away some of the fear; in fact, he barely saw me at all. I understood, I really did; he felt he had failed her, and for a man who prided himself on doing the right thing at all times, that must be a mammoth cross to bear but... I wanted to reassure him somehow and he wouldn't let me. Why? Everybody said I looked like her but I don't believe Dad ever made a connection. And if he did, it wasn't positive... perhaps I had been part of it all, just another problem for my poor weak mother to deal with.

I gestured for Mr Adams to turn left. Then we were there, far too soon, pulling up outside my house.

"I hope you're still writing stories?" he said, pulling up the handbrake.

"Now and then." This wasn't a lie. I wrote a lot; not just stories or in my diary, but long, nonsensical prose where words flooded the paper like blood on a tissue.

"Good. That's good." And then when I didn't move, he added, "Well, I'd be interested in reading anything that you'd like a second opinion on… that's what *us teachers* are there for."

"Right." What on earth had I imagined would happen? I felt ridiculous suddenly and my knee was beginning to throb.

"Try writing something that really shows who you are."

I nodded sullenly and manoeuvred myself out of the car.

"Oh, and don't forget to tell your dad what happened, I wouldn't want him to worry," he called just before I slammed the door.

God forbid Dad might worry.

I didn't see Mr Adams the following week. Twice, I waited outside of his empty office, and both times I was intercepted by a (I felt) slightly cool Ms Emerald, who told me that he was busy with his other pupils and I shouldn't bother him. And was there something she could help with? She annoyed me; always there, trying to come between us even though Mr Adams had *specifically* told me I could come to him whenever I wanted. Even when I explained this to her, *again*, Ms Emerald made a ridiculous comment about some people being too accommodating for their own good and how I hadn't any call to speak to him because he was no longer my teacher. She thought she could just pass me over to someone else and clearly had no understanding of the connection I had with Mr Adams. She was probably jealous. It was a shame really, I used to like her.

chapter seventeen

Ms Emerald stood and proffered her bejewelled hand to Dad and then sat back down immediately after a brief handshake. We were in a different office to the one I knew, and everything was wrong with the scene: the formality of the desk, the bland décor of the office, the polite handshake and Ms Emerald's wide frame forcing itself into a black swivel chair. Dad adjusted the knot in his tie and crossed his legs. I crossed my arms. We both waited.

"Mr Rose, thank you for coming in."

I stared at the strange woman in front of me. Gone were the wide smiles and the gregarious banter from the classroom and in their place, a stony expression and unfriendly tone. I studied her face, searching for the lost kindness from her eyes, even a hint of an upturned mouth, but she would not look at me. Her attention was fixed on Dad as though I wasn't even in the room.

"Mr Rose, I have asked you to come in today to discuss a matter which is causing a member of staff here to feel incredibly uncomfortable."

"Please, elaborate."

"One of our male members of staff believes that Naomi may have formed some kind of attachment."

"Attachment?"

"Naomi, are you aware of whom I am talking?"

"Nope," I replied, looking her straight in the eye.

"And neither am I," said Dad. "What exactly are you talking about, Ms Emery?"

"Mr Adams, Naomi's English teacher, has commented on a couple of occasions that he has been a little *uncomfortable*— "

The word stung. Why would Mr Adams feel uncomfortable? I was his star pupil…

"Can you please be a little more specific, Ms Emery? When has he felt uncomfortable? I sincerely hope this is not to do with what she chooses to read, Naomi is surely old enough now to cope with any material."

Ms Emerald looked blank at the past reference. "Not at all, in fact Mr Adams is impressed with Naomi's academic performance in English, *as we all are*… it has more to do with times when it is just the two of them."

"The two of them? I'm sorry, I don't understand, why would a situation arise when it would be just the two of them?"

"Well," Ms Emerald seemed to be considering her words carefully, "sometimes Naomi chooses to speak to Mr Adams after class when the other children have gone…"

"Right?"

"… and she often comes to his office to ask for help… I've seen you myself, haven't I, Naomi?"

I shrugged.

"I don't see how any of that is unusual, other than it perhaps being a little odd that Naomi needs help with English."

"Precisely."

"Precisely?"

"Naomi *doesn't* need help." She turned to me at last. "Do you, Naomi?"

"Sometimes I just need to check dates and stuff…"

"But that's not all," Ms Emerald interrupted me. "Last week we had a phone call from a member of the public voicing concern that she had seen a pupil from our school getting into a teacher's car."

Shit. The old lady from the bus stop. Stupid, bloody, interfering old cow! I was never going to bother calling her but I hadn't counted on her chasing me up. For God's sake.

"I beg your pardon?" Dad uncrossed his legs and leaned forward. I could see the muscle on the side of his head twitching rapidly.

"Apparently, Naomi had a fall on her way home as Mr Adams was driving home and he kindly gave her a lift."

"A male teacher *kindly* gave a female pupil a lift?"

"Mr Rose, I can assure you it was a genuine act of kindness on the part of the teacher in question."

Dad and Ms Emerald were both tense and a couple of moments passed in which neither of them said a word. I looked between them, wondering whether I even needed to be in the room; I was a key player in the unfolding drama yet I was also seemingly invisible.

"I want to speak to Mr Adams," Dad said at last.

"That really won't be necessary—"

"I think I'll decide whether speaking to a male teacher who thinks it's appropriate to drive my daughter around is necessary."

"Mr Rose—"

"He wasn't driving me around, Dad."

They both looked at me with a start, reminded of my presence.

"I fell over, he was driving past, he stopped and helped me and drove me home so I didn't have to walk. A lady was at the nearby bus stop, she came to see if I was alright. It was probably her who phoned the school. She gave me her number. I was supposed to ring her to say I was okay."

But Dad ignored my explanation and turned back to Ms Emerald. "Is it usual practice for teachers to give lifts to pupils at this school?"

"Absolutely not, Mr Rose. I can assure you that Mr Adams has been spoken to at length and is fully aware that his behaviour was inappropriate, but I can also assure you that his intentions were honourable."

"Ms Emery," Dad smiled his fake smile, "as you are probably aware, I am a professor at the university."

"I am aware of that, yes."

"The students are at least two years older than Naomi, sometimes they are much older. I have never offered a lift to any student, male or female. It is not professional, it is not appropriate, and it would potentially put my career at risk. In this current climate, any person in a position of trust towards young people would be a fool to take such a risk."

"Mr Adams, on his own admission, has perhaps been a little naïve."

"That would be putting it mildly!"

"But would you rather he had left your daughter nursing her grazed knee on the pavement?"

"It wasn't really grazed, I just jarred it a bit…"

"I would rather he had had the common sense to give me a call so that I could pick her up myself."

"He said that Naomi phoned and left a message." Ms Emerald raised an eyebrow at me.

"Um, yeah, I did but I must have got cut off." I didn't sound convincing.

"Right, because I don't recall a voicemail." Dad looked slightly smug. "But anyway, that's not the point. He could easily have walked Naomi back into school where she could have waited in safety for me to answer."

"I don't think we need believe that Naomi was in any danger."

"We would be having a very different conversation now if she had been whisked off to a love nest in Scotland!"

I wished very much that I had been. Dad was back in role and delivering an Oscar-worthy performance, not of an outraged parent, but of an incredulous peer – *why would a man in this profession place himself in such a dangerous position?* People do all manner of things on the spur of the moment, plus I hadn't really given Mr Adams much choice… but I knew for a fact that this situation would never happen to Dad. He wouldn't have let it.

"Mr Rose, with all due respect, I think we mustn't let scare stories from the media influence our reactions here. There is nothing going on romantically between teacher and pupil in this instance, just a member of staff looking out for the well-being of…"

"Of course there's nothing going on, Naomi is far too sensible for that. My point, however, is that…"

I zoned out.

Sensible girl. Full of potential. A* pupil. I'd won an award, for God's sake!

Those were the things that mattered.

I could whip up an outstanding essay on Keats or Dickens, I could write stories standing on my head, I knew how to play the star pupil game. So why did I feel like I was losing?

I studied Dad's face. His mouth was moving but his eyes were expressionless. He was excellent with words. Whatever he was saying would leave Ms Emerald questioning everything, including her own reaction, and she would have no choice but to give Mr Adams a really hard time. But why couldn't he look at me? I was a pawn in his self-righteous game, I was serving a purpose, giving him something to be outraged about.

What had my mother had that was so special she deserved to be rescued from the life she had made of her *own* choosing? What could *I* do? What would Dad need to see in order to rescue *me*?

*

The interview doesn't last long. They only want the chance to snap a couple of recent photos and ask, like they usually do "Are you influenced by the local area?", which really means "Do Wellbridge and/or its inhabitants ever feature in your novels?" The Gazette seeks to make a connection because I am the closest thing they have to a local celebrity. I always reply in the affirmative to make them happy but, truth be told, the latest novel to be published is the first I've written with a local connection.

The protagonist, tall, dark and kind, is a successful man whose life spirals out of control. The reader will feel sorry for him but eventually they will come to understand where he went wrong; they will see that he is not entirely blameless.

"This one seems darker than your previous work, would you agree?" the young interviewer asks at one point, tucking her hair behind her ears and sitting forward eagerly.

"Yes," I reply steadily, "life does not happen to us. We are not passive bystanders in our own destinies. We choose how to behave, we make decisions, but everything has consequences. That is what I would like the readers to take from this book."

"Uh huh, uh huh, and…" her head is nodding and I can feel the next question before it comes "… is this character inspired by someone in particular?"

I smile sweetly. "Of course."

"Your father called," Esme says as she follows me out of the office. "Wants to know if you can make his counselling session."

"Today?"

"Yes."

"Then no, obviously. I have Kat's sports day. He'll have to cope."

chapter eighteen

Ms Emerald was silent, her eyes boring a hole into my head. I studied the mayhem of her desk and counted five unfinished cups of blackcurrant tea. It must have been a stressful day.

"Well, what are you going to do about it?" Dad had his arms crossed; his confrontation mode. His right leg jigged up and down as he rearranged his face into various patterns of outrage.

Ms Emerald was wearing the same floaty smock dress as yesterday when we had been sitting in the exact same seats discussing my lift in Mr Adams' car. Funny the things you notice: same top, same office, same seats, different topic. I had done this, though, hadn't I? I was the source of this new upset. I was the cause, the reason, the person to blame. No point attributing blame to anyone. I knew that. Didn't I? But. I *had* pushed and prodded and poked until, finally, (finally!), I had got my reaction. Wow. I was quite the storyteller! In another scenario, I might even have been proud. Not my fault though, no one's fault.

What a shame that everything must have a consequence. I would have quite liked to stop the clock last night, right there when the little hand was on the eight. I would have liked to freeze-frame the shattered whisky glass and Dad's look of horror (from expressionless to monstrous in the blink of an eye – quite remarkable) and allowed myself time to enjoy the moment. But time has that annoying urgency, it must press on, always things to do.

"He did *what* to you?" Dad had never studied my face as intently as he had last night. He was searching for the truth, but I was already too good at masking it. And then, as I began recounting events, I really got into my stride, adding details and embellishments just to witness the changing expressions on Dad's face, his total absorption in me and the words which were tumbling out of my mouth. Reality was already merging with fiction as I began inwardly assessing my own fantastical story. Maybe it really did happen like that. It certainly sounded convincing.

"Sit down," my father had said, "sit down and start from the beginning."

So I did. And as I said the words, they became the truth.

Ms Emerald rose slowly and straightened her top. "Wait here, please," she said in a tone I didn't recognise.

She was gone for an eternity. By the time she returned, Dad was pacing the floor and I had reduced my thumbnail to a painful stub.

"Mr Rose, Naomi, if you'd like to follow me?"

We abandoned our positions and filed to the door obediently. Dad fiddled with his tie and cleared his throat, ready for a fight. "What's happening?"

"The governors happen to be on site today and have been made aware of the situation. Mr Adams is on his way to see them. For now, it is best you vacate the building."

"I don't THINK so!"

Dad was set to explode, but Ms Emerald was in full teacher mode as she calmly coaxed us down the corridor. "It's better this way, Mr Rose. There are procedures to follow." But when she looked at me, her expression was blank. "Let the dust settle."

We had almost reached the main exit when something made me turn. And I saw him, Mr Adams, walking towards the office from the other direction, on his way to see the governors. I wanted to stop time right there. Stop him from turning the handle on the door. He saw me and smiled, even gave a little wave, and the blood rushed between my ears. I remembered Arthur's trusting little face looking out of the cat basket on the way to the vet's, unaware of his impending fate.

chapter nineteen

"FUCKING PAEDO," DAD MUTTERED AS WE left the building. They weren't words he would ever want to use – *swearing shows a lack of vocabulary* – but clearly they were the words he felt he *should* use. Even though there was no one but me there to hear him.

I couldn't shake off the image of Ms Emerald's stony face. I stumbled home in the wake of Dad's angry strides and tried to convince myself that she too had been playing a role, just "following procedure", but I knew she didn't believe me. Colleagues together, them against us, batten down the hatches and keep the trouble at bay. I tried to be angry – after all, she was supposed to protect me, I was a pupil – but that hardness in her eyes...

I should have taken Ms Emerald's reaction as a warning and heeded the guilt that crawled over me, making me feel clammy and disgusting to myself, but we had barely closed the front door when Dad took me by the shoulders. He pulled me close and kissed the top of my head repeatedly, punctuating each kiss with a word. "We... will... get... this... dealt... with... I... promise."

This wasn't us, we didn't show affection, but I was so drawn into the soft bubble of unaccustomed closeness that I couldn't bring myself to say anything that might change it. I wanted him to hug me tightly and tell me that everything was going to be okay, even if I had got the facts wrong. Even if I'd made a silly mistake. I wanted to be able to retract everything and put it all right but he was studying me intently and I swallowed the words back down. His frown had all but vanished and there was a strange twist to the side of his mouth like he was trying not to smile. But he couldn't be smiling. That would be absurd.

The police arrived when I was curled up on the sofa with a hot chocolate that tasted of sour milk. Dad ushered them in: a middle-aged woman in a dark suit and a young uniformed policeman with a clean, scrubbed face. I sat up and placed my knees together carefully, every bit the vulnerable schoolgirl. The policewoman said I could call her Linda. She was a little overweight with a bluntly cut fringe and I could see the outline of her bra through her white shirt when she unfastened her jacket. Her colleague, PC Coverley, didn't seem much older than Ozzy, but where Ozzy was all swagger, this man in front of me was sitting up straight and neat, his long skinny fingers poised over a notebook and pen. Keen.

Linda's voice was gentle. She spoke slowly and ended each sentence with, "Is that okay with you?" as though I might ask for something to be done differently. Dad was allowed to stay in the room with me and he sat close, a protective arm around my shoulders. I dared not move.

"Now, I'm going to ask you a few questions, is that okay with you?" Linda was leaning forwards on her plump knees whilst PC Coverley wrote a continuous stream of notes with his sharpened pencil. I wondered what on earth he could be writing as I had yet to say a word.

I nodded.

"If, at any time, you feel uncomfortable or you want to stop, we can take a break. Is that okay with you?"

I already wanted to stop. I was already uncomfortable. Dad rubbed my shoulder and said, "I'm right here, everything will be fine," but it didn't help. I thought about Mr Adams, pictured him at home with Alice. He must have told her by now. He would be pacing the floor, pleading with her to believe him. Would she hold him close, and mutter words of reassurance? I thought not. My head was fuzzy. I imagined Alice throwing her neat, dull clothes into a neat, dull suitcase and storming down the stairs with Mr Adams calling after her. A teacher groping a student – how could she ever trust him again? How could she go on to have children of her own with a man like that? That's what she would be thinking, that's what everyone would be thinking. Alice and Mo and Imogen and Taylor and Esme… and then I saw Ozzy's face and the image splintered into pieces. Something was gnawing at the inside of my stomach and it wasn't hunger. "Dad?"

I clutched at his hand and smelt the whisky on his breath. But he couldn't be blamed for having a drink today, could he? It was a stressful situation.

"It's alright, Naomi." He grasped me tightly and I could feel his hands shaking. He moved a fraction and took hold of my face between his hands; the close proximity felt alien. "You just have to tell them what happened and then that bastard won't be able to do it to anyone else, I promise."

"But he's not—"

"Shh now, be strong. I've raised you to be strong, haven't I?"

"Dad…" I whimpered.

"Tell them. Tell Linda. *Go on.*" And then he had hold of my shoulders, directing my body back round to face the front, to face Linda with her sympathetically tilted head and PC Coverley with his eagerly poised pen. He gave me a discreet nudge, as though I were a child reluctant to speak to a distant relative, and my shoulders sagged.

Linda's questions drifted through the air and hung around my head as I answered each one softly. She wanted to know about our relationship prior to the events which had brought us all here today and I told her, honestly, about my school life and my love of writing. I explained how Mr Adams had singled me out in class to read or voice my opinion.

"And did he ask the other students similar questions?"

"Sometimes. But he seemed to like my responses best."

"And how did you come to be alone in his office, Naomi?"

I looked up at this point and registered PC Coverley's tilted head, mirroring Linda's. "I would go and see him for help with my work."

"Even though it sounds like you didn't need it?"

"Mr Adams was supportive, he liked that I wrote stuff at home… asked to read it."

"I see."

I explained how I would enter the office and sit in the chair opposite his desk.

"And would the door be open or shut, Naomi?"

"Pardon?"

"The office door. Would it be open or shut when you were in Mr Adams' office?"

"Open, I think…" I pictured the office and remembered Ms Emerald poking her head around from time to time. "Yes, open." That was good, that would go in his favour. Damage limitation.

"Clever bastard," Dad said under his breath.

"What? But Dad—"

"Mr Rose, please."

Dad threw his hands up in an abortive gesture. "Well. It makes it look less suspicious, doesn't it?"

My stomach flipped over.

"And then what would happen, Naomi?"

My mouth opened and then shut again, the words missing. I studied my shoes intently.

"Okay. We're going to take a little break, is that okay with you?"

Dad's hands were back on my shoulders.

"Naomi?" Linda was leaning forwards, her bulky chest almost touching her knees.

"She doesn't need a break. Come on, Naomi, tell them."

"Mr Rose!"

"Get it over with so they can stop him. You want them to stop him, don't you? You don't want him going near other girls?"

I tensed. If Alice left him and I said nothing, what would stop him from going back to work? I imagined Mr Adams surrounded by a new class of leggy, beautiful sixth-formers all eager to please him with their neat essays and high marks. He would be lonely and sad without Alice and give them all his attention. I would quickly be forgotten.

"He touched me."

Dad jumped up and stormed over to the window. Time for another drink, surely.

"Naomi, I want you to think very carefully now. We need to know exactly what happened and in what order." Linda pointed to something in PC Coverley's notes and he underlined a word painstakingly. "Can you tell me where you were sitting first of all?"

"On the chair."

"Across the desk from Mr Adams?"

I paused. "No. My chair was next to his now."

"And why was that, Naomi?"

"Because he moved it so that we could go through my work together."

"And was the door open or shut?"

"Open. I told you."

"We just need to be absolutely sure, Naomi. I'm sorry. And can you tell me where he touched you?"

"On my leg."

"Which leg?"

"My right leg."

"And which part of your leg did Mr Adams touch?"

I paused again.

"Can you show me? Just point."

Dad turned in time to see me pointing at my thigh.

"And did he only touch you there?"

I could feel the intensity of Dad's glare. "No."

"Where else did Mr Adams touch you, Naomi?"

I lifted my hand slightly and slid it up to the top of my leg.

"Anywhere else?"

"Is that not bad enough for you?" Dad demanded from the window.

"Mr Rose, I appreciate this is very difficult but it's important we have all of the facts. Naomi?"

I removed my hand and hugged my knees.

"Naomi. Did Mr Adams—"

We were distracted by the clink of glass as the stopper was removed from the whisky decanter. *For God's sake.*

Linda was trying to catch my eye. "Naomi, do you want a break?"

Dad gulped the alcohol down in one and spluttered a loud cough. I caught Linda raising her eyebrows at PC Coverley.

"Naomi?"

The glass hit the table and another measure was poured. The patches of colour on Dad's cheekbones rose to an angry red and he caught me staring. "Don't mind me, Naomi, get on with it. Tell her. Nothing can be as bad as what I'm imagining anyway."

I narrowed my eyes and stared at him for a moment, waiting for a moment, some sort of sign that it wasn't too late. But there was nothing. I turned back to face Linda and sank lower into the sofa. Fine. I'll give them... I'll give *him*, what's needed.

The words came easily after that. I realised that it didn't really matter what I said because the damage was already done so I made myself into a character from one of my stories, answering all of Linda's questions and even embellishing points that I had already made so that it sounded like Mr Adams had orchestrated our meetings. I explained how he had called me into his office under the pretence of talking about my work but how he'd quickly sidle up next to me, even inviting me to sit on his lap at times, and how his hand would reach under my skirt and move my knickers to one side.

"Did you tell him to stop?"

"Of course."

"But he didn't?"

"No."

"Why didn't you tell somebody? A friend, another teacher?"

I was ready for this one, I knew the right answer. "Because I was scared of him, I was scared of what he would do."

It was easy to lie once I got started. I knew what they wanted and I was giving it to them, all of it. Mr Adams became someone else, a dirty, ugly old man from a newspaper article, and my feelings for him disintegrated. I gave the girl on his lap curly dark hair so that she no longer bore me any resemblance and the bright, airy office full of Shakespearian quotes became a claustrophobic prison from which I couldn't have escaped even if I'd wanted to.

"And did Ms Emery ever comment on the two of you being in the room together?"

I waived the memory of her telling me to leave Mr Adams in peace. "Oh, no, never, she saw us together and never said a word." Why not go the whole hog and make Ms Emerald complicit in the lies?

PC Coverley was writing frantically and Linda paused so that he could catch up. Dad returned to the sofa and placed a trembling hand over mine. Eventually the pencil came to a halt and Linda stood up and refastened her jacket. "I think we have enough for now. Thank you so much for your time, Naomi, you've been incredibly brave. We'll be in touch. No, don't get up, Mr Rose, we'll see ourselves out."

Dad patted my knee.

"Well done, Naomi. Well done."

chapter twenty

"COME ON THEN, TALK TO MO."

He had arrived an hour after Linda and PC Coverley had driven off. Dad had gone – needed a walk to clear his head or something – and I realised that Mo had been brought in to babysit. I hadn't seen him since my visit to his flat but he was definitely back to his usual self – sitting across from me at the kitchen table, legs stretched wide, with one of those energy drinks that Ozzy drank in his hand.

"I don't want to talk about it."

"Course you don't. That policewoman put you through it, I reckon. What was her name?"

"Linda."

Mo wasn't wearing any socks, and his skinny scuffed ankles were visible in the gap between his huge trainers and rolled up trouser legs. I thought he might tell me how sorry he was. Like people did when Mum died. Death and sexual abuse – two events of life-changing magnitude. I scratched at a blemish on my jeans and my brain lurched between self-disgust and marvel. How easily I'd convinced myself, even if just for a few hours, that the lie was a reality.

"Linda," he said again and I looked up. He was nodding.

"Yes, that's right."

He swigged from his can. "I bet she has a tough job, that Linda."

"Yeah. 'Spose."

"Must hear a lot of bad stuff… deal with a lot of messed-up people…"

I shrugged.

"… I mean, nothing compared with what the *victim* has to go through, you get me? I'm not belittling what the *victim* goes through."

"No. Course not."

"I feel for her, that's all. I feel for *everyone* involved."

Why did he keep emphasising certain words? It made me uneasy and I got up from the table, began to rummage around for a snack even though I wasn't hungry. I opened a packet of crisps and munched one loudly. It tasted of card.

"I'm real sorry you couldn't talk to someone, Mimi."

"Huh?"

"Like, when it was *actually* happening, you didn't feel you could talk to your dad?"

I stopped crunching and raised an eyebrow.

"Or me?"

I reached for another cardboard crisp.

"He loves you a lot, you know? Your dad."

"Yeah. So you keep saying."

"Well, he does. I mean, I'm not gonna lie, there are times when I thought he could have handled things better but who am I to judge? Look at Taylor… and Esme sometimes… I do my best and they still end up acting like little shits. But you gotta think… at the end of the day, it's night, you know?"

"You always say that."

"'Cos it's true, it don't matter what happens, the world keeps going, you know?"

"Right."

"Maybe you thought you wouldn't be believed?" Mo swung one gangly leg over the other so that his right ankle rested on his left knee. I finished the crisps and scrunched the empty packet into a ball. "And you know who's to blame for that?"

I sighed. "Who?"

He paused and fiddled with the ring-pull on his can, working it back and forth until it came free. And then he spoke carefully. "All those people who make stuff up, you know?" He caught my eye and quickly looked away. "And it's sad, you know? 'Cos it's not always their fault; like, they're usually crying out for something themselves, attention or something, but…" he shook his head slowly, "messing with people's lives… that ain't right. Then the real victims," and this time he held my stare, "like *you*, they get scared to come forward."

"I need to go," I said sharply, rising from my chair and stuffing the crisp packet in the overflowing bin. It popped straight out again onto the floor and I scooped it up and forced it back in, squashing down the rubbish and hearing the familiar chink of wine bottles hidden beneath potato peelings and pizza boxes. "Dad forgets to recycle," I muttered but Mo was unperturbed.

"You've not had it easy, Mimi. If you wanna talk… you know, if there's anything you wanna say… it doesn't have to be too late."

I watched the automatic bin lid as it retracted painfully, and gave it a helping hand with my fist. Could I? Could I tell Mo the truth? Would he be able to put it all right? The thought of my father coming back and hearing I was a liar was unbearable. Oh, God, oh… God! Poor Mr Adams. I had created something so ugly that he would think of me as evil, not beautiful or bright. What the hell had I been thinking?

"You okay?"

I spun round and looked Mo square in the face. "No. Actually, I'm not okay…" I shook my head rapidly.

He nodded, he simply nodded. He knew! Just like Ms Emerald… oh, *God*. Before either of us could say anything more, my phone began to vibrate on the table and Imogen's name flashed up on the screen.

"Ozzy's been arrested!" Her voice was high-pitched and urgent.

"What? Why?"

"He's done him, he's done Mr Adams, like *properly*… broken his ribs and cracked his skull. Oh, Nae, what have you done?"

I began to shake uncontrollably and sank to the floor with the phone still in my hand. How could word have spread so fast? How did Ozzy know where to find him? Where was Dad? My head swam and I gagged twice before eventually vomiting over the kitchen floor. I was vaguely aware of Mo crouching beside me and then his surprising strength as he lifted and half-carried me through to the living room where he placed me on the sofa. I groaned and clutched my stomach and then I was given a bowl and covered in a blanket and Mo was on the phone, speaking in hushed tones to whoever. I must have asked to go to the hospital or the police station because I remember Mo's gentle voice becoming firm and telling me I wouldn't be allowed to see him. Did he mean Mr Adams or Ozzy? Who had I asked to see? Maybe both. I needed to see both of them, I needed to put it right, to say sorry…

Where was Dad?

It felt like hours and hours and hours before I heard the click of the front door. I heard him talking to Mo in the hallway and then the door to the kitchen being wedged shut. I willed him to come through and see me. I needed to hear him say that he would sort it out. I needed to know how Mr Adams was. I needed to know Ozzy wasn't sweating it out in a tiny, claustrophobic cell. Oh, God, please don't let him be locked up, please! I cried out for my dad but it was Mo who came in.

"Where's Dad?" I whimpered, my nose blocked with snot and tears.

"He'll be in shortly." Mo perched on the edge of the sofa, resting a hand on my shoulder. "Listen, Mimi, I want you to be strong now, okay? I've... explained things... your dad is upset but he's just taking it all in. Just be patient, okay?"

"Did you speak to the hospital?"

"Yeah. They didn't want to tell me anything at first but I told a little white—" Mo paused and shook his head. "It doesn't matter... your friend exaggerated anyway... the teacher's been a bit roughed up but nothing's broken. Cuts and bruises... he'll be out tomorrow."

I let out a gulpy sob. Oh, *thank God*. "And... Ozzy?"

"Don't know yet. I tried, honestly, but the police are a different matter."

"Can I see him?"

"Mr Adams? Nah... not a good idea."

"No." My voice was feeble. "Ozzy."

"Come on now, Mimi, let's just sit tight and let things calm down."

Ozzy was never going to forgive me, nor was Imogen, no one would.

I was crying fresh tears of self-pity when Dad walked in and went to stand in his usual spot by the window. He looked smaller than I remembered, his shoulders hunched in the way he used to tell me off for.

"I'll leave you guys to it," Mo said, patting my arm as he got up.

My father didn't turn and I inched myself into a sitting position, wrapping the blanket tightly to cover my entire body. "Dad?"

He left the window. The sound of trickling liquid cut through the room. Then finally, he wandered over to his armchair and sat down, gazing at the drink in his hands.

When he lifted his head and looked at me, I wished with all my heart that he hadn't. His forehead was, as usual, knitted into a deep frown but it was his eyes ... there was such a look of puzzlement as he searched my face for answers; as though he was trying to figure out who this stranger was in his house.

"Dad? I'm sorry. I'm so, so sorry. I don't even know—"

"You will need to go away for a bit, Naomi," he said, cutting me off. He was talking to the wall behind my head. "Just until things settle down."

"Dad, please."

"It's for the best."

I remembered a history lesson where we'd learned about well-to-do families sending away delinquent children to avoid shame being brought upon the household. But we were not well-to-do, and this was not a history class, this was the unbearable present. These things did not happen, not now, not to me.

"You can't be serious, where would I go? What about my exams?"

"I have arranged for you to stay with Uncle Robert for the time being. As for your exams, we'll have to see what can be done. Obviously, you won't be able to return to Harper Comprehensive."

"Dad, please! *Help me* work this out, I didn't mean to cause so much trouble." I was off the sofa now, crouching by his chair and reaching for his hands. "I can put it right, I can tell the police it was all my fault. I'll help Ozzy, I'll apologise to Mr Adams…"

There was a pause in which I clung to the arm of the

chair as though it might stop me from drowning, and Dad looked over my head.

"It was me who called Ozzy and told him."

"What? "

" I knew what he would do. I was in pieces, not thinking rationally... it sounds dreadful now... but like any parent in my situation, I wanted him, Mr Adams, to hurt like I hurt... like I thought you'd been hurt."

What was he talking about? He wouldn't do that. He couldn't mean any of it. Not my dad. My dad who always did the right thing.

"Everyone has their limits," he said. "And now, I too am complicit in this mess. Look at what your lies have done; the terrible damage... to everyone."

How long had I had him for, really? The dad that I wanted... three hours? Had he enjoyed the drama? Morbidly enjoyed playing his part? He had swooped in and rescued me, just like he had with Mum, and I'd gone and thwarted the exciting plot by giving in.

"I'm so sorry." I was pleading now all pride long gone. "I'll make it right, please don't send me away."

"I'm sorry too." He drained his glass. "I don't know what else to do with you." And then he was up and gone, leaving me broken on the floor.

chapter twenty-one

I SPENT TWO DAYS HOLED UP IN VIOLET'S PASTEL bedroom, sleeping fitfully in her flowery bed and then wrapping myself in her sparkly dressing gown to venture down and be force-fed sweet potato soup or shepherd's pie or scrambled eggs on toast. "Good wholesome food, soon have you right," said Aunt Chrissy, as though I had gone wrong – *malfunctioned*. My aunt and uncle were nervous around me, forever touching my arm or forcing me into an embrace. Every time they enveloped me in love, I thought of the phrase, *Kill it with kindness*. Or was that a song?

Violet was away on a college residential, due back at the weekend. I lay in bed on the third morning and imagined her coming home, finding me in her bed and being furious, as I would have been. When had we last seen each other? I had conveniently avoided the last two family get togethers, pleading prior engagements, when really I had been unable to stomach another occasion in which Violet would be presented as a model of exceptional behaviour. I knew she had made her application for medical school – Dad had thrown that into the conversation umpteen times – but other than that, I knew nothing about her life. Looking around the room from my mound of duvet, I took in the jewellery attached neatly to a cork board, the large clock with roman numerals above the door and the framed picture of a cow with "Animals have a soul, they shouldn't be in a bowl" written in a heart around its head. The wall behind me was covered in animal rights posters and a diagram of the human skeleton with each bone labelled in Latin. I craned my head to look and recognised the word "cranium". Violet was going to be a doctor. A vegan, animal-loving, medical genius. Of course she was. I buried my head beneath the covers.

Dad phoned every day to speak with Rob or Chrissy (never to me) about how I was behaving, and I heard my aunt tell him that he was being too hard on me: "… after all, she did lose her mother terribly young". She was clearly rebuffed because then she said, "No, of course. I realise that won't help her in the real world…" and I was left at the top of the stairs, waiting for the "but" that never came.

On Saturday morning, with Violet due back later that day, I showered and changed and made the bed. I did it painstakingly, pulling the sheet taut and brushing off the little fragments of scum that must have come from my body, and flipping the duvet so that it went up in an arc and settled back with a bubble of air in the centre. I hadn't brought much with me but what I had, I scooped up and stuffed into my college bag and pulled the drawstring closed. One more look around the room. It could do with a vacuum but Aunt Chrissy would see to that. I closed the door behind me and crept down the stairs.

No one heard me go. It wasn't like I was running away, just giving them some space to welcome the prodigal daughter home without the tainted niece there to fuck things up, giving them a window of normalcy. Thoughtful. Considerate.

I waited until I was out of sight of the house before digging into my bag for my phone. I scrolled down through the contacts and pressed call before I could change my mind.

"Hey. Can I come and see you?"

We met in a park away from the school, away from Mehmet's Mezze Bar, away from anywhere and anyone that we knew. It wasn't warm, and I pulled my cuffs down to cover my hands while I waited. I half expected to be stood up and as the minutes passed, I set little targets in my head: one minute late would mean he understood, five equalled forgiveness, ten signalled anger. But what if he didn't turn up at all? How long would I wait, half an hour, a day?

I sat alone for seventeen minutes, seven more than anger. I had set no target for seventeen minutes.

He was wearing a cap, Jayden Blackwater style, but it wasn't pulled so low that I couldn't see the stoniness of his eyes as he took a seat at the end of the bench.

"Go on then." It was a demand.

I searched his face for a glimmer of *my* Ozzy but I couldn't find it. "I'm so sorry."

Ozzy bit the nail of his thumb in an open display of boredom.

"I have no excuse." I had made an effort this morning, styling my hair so that it tumbled about my shoulders in bouncy waves and it was back to its natural silky blonde. I knew it looked good but I could just as well have shaved my head. How stupid. Despite his on/off relationship with Molly, I knew that deep down Ozzy was not one to be swayed by hair. "I... there's a lot going on at home... I got caught up—"

"Don't start with that shit. Everyone has stuff going on, they don't all go around accusing innocent men of abuse."

His words were a slap because he was absolutely right. I had been over it and over it whilst festering in Violet's bed but hearing it from Ozzy, with that vicious edge to his voice, was a hundred times worse. *Abuse. Accusations.*

"What was it you needed? Attention?"

"No." Yes? *Was* that why?

"Daddy too busy to notice you?"

"No." Yes. Shit.

"I could have been kicked out of school... could have ruined my education, had a criminal record."

I grabbed at his hand but he whisked it away with a tut.

"Lucky for me, Mr Adams has got the decency of a thousand men and he's not pressing charges."

"Thank God," I said weakly. "Do you know... how he is?"

"You care?"

"Ozzy! Of course I care! Please, just tell me he's okay?"

There was a non-committal shrug and I waited out the silence between us. The anguish in the pit of my stomach was both awful and satisfying; I had known he wouldn't make it easy for me and why should he?

"As far as I know, he's alright for someone who nearly lost his career and his freedom in one go."

Ouch.

"I don't really know how to say this," I faltered, "I mean, I know it was all wrong, and I wish wholeheartedly that I could go back and change things, put everything right again..."

"Yep."

"But I also want you to know that what you did for me..."

"What, beat up an innocent man?

"... *standing up* for me, regardless of the circumstances... it meant a lot. Especially as you were only looking out for me as a favour to Mo."

Ozzy nodded slowly. "I told you, that's not true anymore."

"Doesn't matter now anyway."

I thought I witnessed some of the hardness fade away, saw his jawline soften.

"Like I said... at first, yeah, it was a favour to Mo. But then, after a while, I kinda liked you, and all your weirdness, for real."

"Yeah?" I couldn't help it, my spirits lifted and I found myself tapping his arm with my closed fist. This time he didn't move away.

"Even though you fucked it up… and cost me my fit girlfriend."

"You and Molly—"

"Broke up for good, yeah. Reckons I was too quick to defend you. Turns out she was right."

"Yes. You probably should have listened to her."

There was another silence, and we both stared forward, watching an empty crisp packet make a circle on the breeze.

"We would have broken up anyway. She wasn't…"

"What?"

And then at last, it came, the familiar smirk. "Interesting enough."

I forced myself to suppress the sudden swell of happiness because it was far, far too soon and I supposed I owed it to Mr Adams and to Ozzy to remain apologetic for just a bit longer. I felt something else though too. Relief? Perhaps. Surprise? Definitely. Surprise that it was all going to be much easier than I'd thought. Thank God, because it would have been so tiresome were everyone to drag this out even further. Luckily for me, good people like Ozzy and Mr Adams want to believe the best about everyone. We need the good people to balance out the bad.

He came with me to see Imogen and I was immensely grateful because, despite my well-rehearsed and humble spiel, it was obvious that she was only swayed into forgiveness by Ozzy's simple "C'mon, we all make mistakes" and to be honest, I wasn't sure how long my patience would last. Immy had huffed and sighed and vented about "the look on poor Mr Adams' face" and "everyone knew you'd made it up", and "how could you?" before finally relenting and telling me that she "*kind* of understood" why I might have got a bit carried away. We parted with an awkward hug, and I hoped that with a bit of time and a bit more grovelling the whole thing would be forgotten and we could move on. Immy, like Ozzy, had goodness and decency so firmly embedded within her being, she was physically incapable of bearing a grudge. It was probably a shame that I couldn't be more like them Still, we are who we are.

Uncle Rob had given me a key and I let myself in gently, holding the catch so that the door closed without a sound. They were in the kitchen. I could just about make out the hushed tones of my uncle and aunt, and then Violet's voice, louder and clipped with a newly acquired accent – her Essex "oh" now a clean "O".

"O. How long for?"

"Just a couple of weeks, love, we all need to pull together."

"I see. And does she… I mean, has she accepted that what she did was despicable?"

Despicable. I was despicable. Despicable me.

"Yes, she understands."

I imagined Aunt Chrissy hanging her head, taking my shame upon herself, wondering whether she could have done more. I waited for as long as I dared to hear if my cousin would whine about my presence, the wayward family loser invading her precious untainted space.

"Well, of course she can share my room. I'll talk to her, see if I can be of help. It sounds as though she's mentally unstable."

"Thank you, love, I knew you'd understand."

There was a scraping of chairs and I legged it up the stairs on my toes. I reached the top as the kitchen door opened then, Violet's voice. I paused, one hand on the banister.

"The thing I do find hard to understand though…"

"Yes?"

"… just that… I mean, she always had so much *potential…*"

Oh, for fuck's sake.

I removed my trainers and sank down onto Violet's bed.

Mentally unstable.

My cousin's words hung about my head like a persistent wasp. Was I? Was I mentally unstable? Maybe there were signs along the way, things I should have noticed. Maybe I ought to have been more upset about things – Molly and her incessant crap, Dad's drinking, Jayden bloody Blackwater. *My mother dying.* Perhaps a show of emotion might have made me more normal… people had always encouraged me to cry, hadn't they?

Other people did stupid things, but what I had done to Mr Adams was a whole new level. I did know that. Even Iffy, with his drink-driving, drug-taking, drug-dealing recklessness, had had enough morality to deter him from having sex with an underage schoolgirl. Did I have any morality? Mr Adams had only ever supported and encouraged me to write bigger and better. And I, to repay him, had nearly cost him his job. And, like Mo said, it was girls like me who made things harder for real victims. Girls like me. Stupid, desperate girls like me. Girls who cried wolf. Conflicting thoughts and questions fought for space in my head until I was exhausted. My last thought was how desperately I wanted my dad.

I must have fallen asleep because when I opened my eyes, a girl was in the room, rooting silently through the wardrobe.

"O, hi," the girl said, when she turned and saw me watching. "Soz, did I wake you?"

I barely recognised her. Long gone was the short dumpy body and dimply thighs, the brown buckled shoes and frizzy orange hair, and in their place, a tall, lean picture of health, like a model from *Cosmopolitan*. Violet was smiling at me, and though her mouth was closed, I just knew that her teeth would be neat and white and gleaming. Her hair had darkened to a deep auburn and had been straightened to form a glossy mane that hung down over a skimpy vest. My sleepy gaze travelled down over low-slung, tight jeans to where her flat bare feet and stubby toes, the only unsightly thing about her, protruded from beneath the denim.

"Just grabbing a clean top," she said, returning to her task, "managed to spill coffee down the one I was wearing. What am I *like*?"

I pulled myself into a sitting position and watched her flick hangers along the rail. *She thinks I'm "despicable"*. The word went over and over in my head.

"O, how about this one?" she asked, holding up a green knitted top with buttons along the cuffs.

I nodded. "Go nice with your hair," I said. *Despicable.* "Uh, thanks for letting me stay in your room… must be hard, coming home and everything… finding out you've got me to put up with."

"Nonsense!" She whipped the top off the hanger and pulled it on over her vest. I noticed she hadn't lost her freckles. Lucky.

She looked at me briefly, gave me a quick smile. "You can stay as long as you want. Cousins, aren't we?"

"I can't remember the last time we saw each other." My attempt at conversation.

Violet picked at a loose thread on her jeans. "Probably when you were trashing my Barbie house and making Ken sleep with a man."

I smiled, despite myself. "Yeah, sorry about that."

"Don't be. It was about time that Ken explored his sexuality."

"But I've seen you since then. Remember the time you came over to tell us about going on work experience at the hospital?"

Violet threw her head back and groaned. "Oh, that was *excruciating*, wasn't it? I promise you that was *not* my idea. You must have thought I was a complete bitch."

"No. Yeah."

She laughed, open-mouthed and genuine. Her teeth were indeed perfect.

"So, listen," her expression shifted and became serious, "I don't know the ins and outs of everything but if I've learned anything, it's that there are two sides to every story."

I shook my head and hugged my knees. "Not this one."

"*Every* story. I'm sure you didn't mean to cause so much harm. You wouldn't have *intended* to cause harm, would you?"

She was staring at me, trying to figure me out.

How did I look to her, bedraggled after my doze and wearing the jumper that Ozzy had given me in the park?

"So, you messed up – so what? It happens. And you didn't exactly have the easiest childhood…"

"Let's not go there."

"Why not? It's completely true. I don't know how I would have coped if I'd lost my mum. I think you can be forgiven for a little *diversion* from the track."

"Diversion? Is that what we're calling it?"

"It's what I'm calling it," she said primly, then she gave that odd little smile again, "because you didn't mean to do it." Was she trying to convince me or herself?

"And as for your father—"

"What about him?"

"Well, he hasn't always put you first, has he?"

I bristled, suddenly defensive on his behalf. "It's a cop-out to blame the parents."

"Absolutely. But don't be too hard on yourself, that's all I'm saying."

I could tell from the nervous energy in her swinging ankles that that was not "all she was saying". "What do you mean?"

The swinging stopped. "Well, apparently, he hasn't been around as much as he should. He didn't sign you up for counselling after your mum… you know… and don't get me started on the drinking!"

"Hold on, he's done his best."

She paused, then smiled sweetly. "Yes, of course he has, they're only our observations."

"Our?"

"Mum, Dad and mine."

I paused. "They tell you their opinions of my dad?"

"They only voice them out of concern."

"Voice them to you?"

"Of course! They always include me in family discussions. I'm like a soundboard from the next generation." She laughed and nudged my shoulder. I gritted my teeth.

"Anyway, what counselling?"

"Oh, something you were offered by the health service, don't you remember?"

A vague memory of a conversation between Uncle Rob and my father came to mind but it didn't really matter, I knew what Dad would have said – "all that talking and analysing does nothing but stir up grief, best to move on".

"Yeah, well, not everyone responds positively to dredging things up. Talking and going over and over the same stuff doesn't change the facts."

"Wow. You sound just like him."

She was up from the bed suddenly and rummaging in her desk drawer. Was I just like him? I was certainly nothing like Violet. She was vibrant and happy and adult, someone her parents held proper conversations with.

"Yeah, well, you only go along with all this softly-softly crap because you're going to work in the health industry."

"Yes, as a doctor, hopefully. Not a psychiatrist. Aha!" She righted herself and held a pale green book aloft, a triumphant grin on her face. "Although I do believe in the power of writing your worries down. Now, this is a clean book," she flipped the pages in front of my face to prove it. "Why don't you spend a bit of time writing in it?" And then, with what looked like a wink, she added, "I hear you're good at it."

"You seem to hear a lot of stuff," I said sullenly. But I took the book.

chapter twenty-two

I WATCHED HIM EXIT THE BUILDING AND HOLD the door for a younger man who was waiting to enter. Though some distance away, I could still make out the polite inclination of the head and I knew he would be saying, "You're *most* welcome." I switched my phone to silent and slid off the wall. I'd spent the previous evening at Imogen's, talking and drinking wine. The wine had apparently dissolved every one of my carefully constructed barriers because I'd found myself crying into her lap while she stroked my hair, an act that now, sober, I found impossible to comprehend. Now, my lethargic body caved inwards and I craved sleep to the point of more tears but Dad's voicemail had offered no leeway on timings; he would meet me during his lunch hour. So here I was.

As though forgetting I had seen the campus a million times, Dad wandered off around the grounds with me in his wake. He pointed out various posters advertising events – a production of *King Lear*, a talk on Psychogeography (whatever the hell *that* was), a protest rally against student tuition fees – and I followed, trying to ignore the swell of nausea in my abdomen. He wanted me to be impressed, or at least interested, but fatigue gnawed at my eyes and I saw nothing but dilapidated square structures linked by a series of cold, unfathomable walkways and staircases.

We paused next to the lake where I noticed the infrastructure in place for a new, flat-roofed building. I felt I should say something positive and clutched at a collection of disingenuous phrases. "It really modernises this area," I concluded.

"Too try-hard," said Dad immediately, "completely out of character with the rest of the place." He wasn't looking for me to agree, so I didn't. "This is what happens when a new CEO comes in and decides to make their mark. No thought for the feel of the place. It's monstrous... serves only as a talking point."

I recalled Harper Comprehensive was also "monstrous". I liked the word. Monstrous. Despicable. Monstrously despicable.

The sun disappeared behind a cloud and I shivered. I wanted food and stared longingly in the direction of the café but Dad was off, leaving the monstrosity behind. Wooden picnic tables were positioned intermittently at the water's edge. I looked for signs of debauchery in the form of students swigging cheap cider and smoking roll-ups but I was disappointed. The occupants were serious-looking adults equipped with plastic lunch boxes and flasks of pale-coloured tea. We continued along the path, carefully avoiding the resident mallards and coots, and came upon a skinny boy crouching by a tree trunk. The boy rose as we approached and stood back to reveal a banner that he had been securing to the tree trunk.

"Keep our grounds clean – take your litter away," I read aloud. "Catchy."

Banner Boy raised an eyebrow but Dad ignored my sarcasm completely. "A worthy message, Ryan. Good for you." His voice was firm, slapping me back in my place.

I looked Ryan up and down and took in the university-branded sweatshirt, the too-long hair and the pile of books spilling from the open bag at his feet. A dream student.

Dad strode off and I continued to follow. I studied the back of his head sulkily and saw that he had let his hair grow too long around his ears.

Hopes of lunch faded as we passed the café and headed for the library and I felt the ominous niggle of an ulterior motive. We had not seen each other for some time but today was most definitely not a social event. Dad wanted me to know something – without saying anything at all.

The library was busy but, as always, silent. We took the lift to the fourth floor as usual and headed towards the shelves at the back. A girl with bright red hair and a nose ring leaned back in a chair scrolling through her phone. She glanced up, noted Dad and coolly placed the phone screen down on the desk. Dad's silent disapproval reminded me of a time years ago when we had sat together watching *Comic Relief*. We had been emotional, watching the short film clips of barefooted children crouching over a textbook and "borrowing" the light from a nearby McDonald's in order to study, but when I'd muttered something about the injustice of the world, Dad seemed disappointed that I, personally, could just flick a switch. He would have preferred me to be the child who struggled, the child who goes on to succeed *despite* having to borrow a light.

I wanted to be that child too. I wanted to be a girl in the library who did nothing but work and learn and become wise. A romantic notion. Denise O'Brien, she was like that; she worked all the time and people ridiculed her and avoided her table and neglected to invite her to things... but she didn't care, she didn't need me or the other girls, she had something else.

One day, shortly after the awards ceremony, Denise had suddenly begun speaking in class. She didn't even put her hand up, just blurted her thoughts out right there into the middle of the room. And once she'd started, she didn't, or couldn't, stop; the lock on her lips was broken and the words tumbled out to the delight of the teachers, especially Mr Adams who no doubt took some credit for drawing Denise out of her shell. I wanted to warn her that none of the brilliance would make her popular, that it wasn't like a film where the geek girl takes off her glasses and becomes instantly beautiful – we were at a rough-ish comprehensive where 2,000 kids vying for attention and struggling to find their place in the world had to knock others down in order to raise themselves up. Darwin's survival of the fittest. And I was right; Denise continued to be ignored, tripped and ridiculed. The difference, however, was that her desire to learn and absorb was stronger than her need to give a shit. I stopped a foot away from where Dad was riffling gently through a shelf at head height and knew that he would like Denise O'Brien very much.

"You must learn to read critically," Dad was saying, "these books, these worlds. There is so much out there to be discovered, so much more than just..." he waved distractedly in my general direction.

What? I wanted to ask. More than what, me?

He pulled a thick tome containing three works by D. H. Lawrence from the shelf.

"Didn't he write *Lady Chatterley's Lover*?" I asked, not to sound clever but to annoy him.

"Amongst other, less popularised and sensationalised works." He opened the volume and let the pages fall at random. Placing a finger on a paragraph halfway down, he held the book out to me and said, "It's not just reading the words, its understanding the structure, the sense, the flow... take any page from any great novel and read it with a critical eye. Notice *everything*."

"Why?"

Was this it? Was this where he finally brought up the *monstrosity* that was my current life and instructed me on how to live a better one? His voicemail had mentioned that he had spent some time reading the piles of short stories on my desk at home but he had yet to say it to my face. When would we discuss my abhorrent behaviour or my twisted lies? When would he finally be furious or disappointed enough to pull me back and steer me in the right direction?

I knew from Imogen that Mr Adams had returned to work something of a hero for dealing with every teacher's nightmare with such "dignity"; I knew from Uncle Robert that Ms Emerald thought it best that I take early study leave and then sit my exams in isolation at another school; I knew from Mo and Ozzy that, despite my actions, they still cared about me; so what would Dad tell me?

I watched the moods cross his face, changing it from light to dark as he struggled to find the words. His lips were dry, he looked nervous.

"You must…"

"What?" I played my part, lifting my face up to his, every bit the expectant child.

"… to write well… to *continue* to write *very well indeed*… you must read well, like you used to."

I blinked. And though the protestations were already forming on my lips, I closed my mouth and waited.

"There has been a… blip," he continued, placing Lawrence back on the shelf, "but you have a talent for writing… and clearly one for storytelling…"

And there, right there, I didn't imagine it, there was a twitch to the right of his lip, a slight curve which slid upward until he was smiling fully, not his fake smile but the real, crooked, all-teeth-showing smile, and he pulled me to him and kissed the top of my head and whispered, "You just need to channel it. Forget everything that has happened and put the talent to good use."

*

The field around the track is swamped by families and the vast array of equipment deemed necessary for a simple school event – blankets, picnic hampers, parasols, tubes of sun cream, folding chairs. We have brought nothing besides takeaway coffee.

Esme and I are amongst the last to arrive and we almost collide with the line of children being brought down from the school. I search for Kat and find her waving enthusiastically, so I pull a silly face. She giggles and points; I love that she is not easily embarrassed.

Ozzy is standing at the far end to get the best view of the finishing line in the unlikely event that Kat wins, and I study him fondly as we make our way over. He has improved over the last few years; he was never unattractive, but he's stockier now and carries the extra weight well. He nods as we approach.

"Good day for it."

"For what?"

"For the win!"

"It's a bloody egg and spoon race."

"Bean bag! It's a bean bag race, get it right!" He winks and I laugh, leaning in to kiss his cheek. Darling Ozzy. Esme says I'm mad to pass him up but he's Kat's dependable, reliable, generous and wonderful father. Nothing more. Even Ozzy has accepted that now.

The announcement of my pregnancy, after the initial shock, had been a source of general delight – to Ozzy because he assumed it would make me settle (I swiftly put *him straight), to me because it was a convenient time (I had a little money from the first book and a small window before I needed to make inroads on the second), and to Ozzy's family (who have still, particularly Uncle Ahmet, yet to comprehend that I will not be marrying into them). Dad saw the whole event as a chance to redeem himself. He found the strength to follow through with rehab and for that, I'm grateful, as it's one less thing to concern myself with. He found the whole "Mr Adams situation" unbearable, mostly due to the embarrassment of it all for himself – appearance is everything – but going off the rails with the drink only served as ammunition ("dead mother, alcoholic father – no wonder the poor girl craved a little attention") and he eventually realised that I had moved on, was no longer seeking forgiveness and was fast losing patience with him. It's not personal, I lose patience with everyone.*

Molly Smith had hung around for a long time, as bad smells do, aware that Ozzy was a "good catch". She was reluctant to let go but she hadn't wanted him, not really, and my pregnancy was the final straw. Everything worked out perfectly – Katerina arrived and Molly left.

I won.

We are sitting on the grass now, taking a break between races. Ozzy lies on his side and flicks through his phone. He rests awkwardly on his weak arm and will soon have to adjust his position because it will become too painful. His injury, the only physical reminder of what happened to Saxon House, is now as much a part of him as his facial hair and we've all grown used to his twinges and aches. The mental scars are naturally much worse, and not just for Ozzy but for Esme who, though thankful to be alive, had to watch from across the street as her home, with her family and many of her neighbours still inside, burned away to a blackened shell.

It was the first and only time that I've ever felt at one with any sort of community. It was nothing to do with me, what I was seeing, and yet I, along with the rest of the country, felt angry and heartbroken and overwhelmingly, sickeningly helpless. I was at home with newly born Kat when I saw the horror unfold on television – the flames sweeping up the side of the building, the faces at the windows, the flashing lights from mobile phones, the knotted sheets flung out as desperate makeshift ropes (I wasn't surprised to learn one such rope was the brainchild of Ozzy – it was exactly what I would expect from him) – and I had felt a great sickness in my stomach. As the final embers died away hours and hours and hours later and distress turned to anger, I felt something gnaw away at my insides; I too wanted answers. I needed reason and cause and blame just like the rest of them, just like everyone always does. I wanted people to be held to account. We're all still waiting.

I went with Dad and Ozzy to one of the many vigils and when we discovered Esme quivering under the arm of the stranger who had taken her in, there was no question that she would come back with us. It's what Mo would have wanted.

To begin with, we went back every week to pay our respects to Mo and to his wife who I never even got to meet and to little Taylor who had no longer been so little yet still far, far too young, and to everyone else who lost their lives that night. Then we began going only when Esme needed to and now, we tend to remember in our own ways: a toast at dinner, a mickey-take of Mo's sayings, a scroll through old photos, a dedication in my second novel.

By the time Dad went into rehab for the second time, Esme was already helping me with Katerina while I worked but she had long since become more than a childminder. She began reading drafts and offering opinions; she set up a website for me and forced me to update it, and most of all, she made sure that I was on top of everything concerning Kat. There was no danger of me failing to attend so much as a play-date.

The fire continues to haunt us all but naturally it affected Esme the most and I'm careful with her. There was no mention of anyone named Daniel on the list of the dead and we all secretly hope that Druggie Dan survived the fire, unlikely though that is. Esme, in particular, needs to believe he's okay.

They say the not knowing is harder than the truth.

Poor Alice. She could never know for sure, could she? She did try but she never got over the allegation. My allegation. I got it; I understood perfectly. I saw how she thought their lives would play out – the doubt lying dormant for a while until eventually, perhaps when they had children of their own, inevitably, surfacing. Rumours spreading no matter how hard they tried to conceal them. Even years later, it wouldn't sit well with their friends. They would all have tried at first, they would show solidarity and support: "Really? He was accused of abusing a pupil? I've never heard anything so ridiculous…" But it would soon become too much of an effort. The invitations would dry up, the social circle would tighten, and Mr Adams would be pushed out, forcing Alice to leave with him. You couldn't exactly invite a paedophile, albeit an alleged one, to a christening or a wedding or a child's birthday party, could you? Mud sticks.

But no matter. Alice moved on quickly enough, eager to forget the whole sorry saga, leaving the man she'd professed to love to slowly disintegrate.

For a while, Mr Adams had been fine. He carried on teaching at Harper Comprehensive (there was even talk of promotion to Head of English) where he had the sympathy of his colleagues and the older pupils who had known him for years. But despite the official name-clearing, it didn't take long for the rumours to start again and inevitably the promotion came to nothing. If I was one to attribute blame, which of course I'm not, I'd have to blame Alice for the way things turned out. I was way out of the picture by then (fulfilling all that potential), but when she left him, the gossips stepped in; no one could understand why such a perfect couple would split up unless there had been some truth in the rumours. Her departure added fuel to the fire.

The party line was that Mr Adams had left teaching to pursue a career in scriptwriting. I was pleased because it was what he had always aspired to do, but then I discovered – via Ozzy's slightly questionable detective skills – that he was in fact taking on TV extra work to make ends meet. It was a bizarre thought, Mr Adams on TV, and I waited patiently to catch a glimpse of him in something but never did. Would he have been any good as an actor? Who knows. Probably not as good as me. And then, a few years later, that grainy CCTV image in the paper. Mr Adams, reduced *to shoplifting. Finally, I had a second chance. Finally, he needed me. And I wouldn't abandon him like Alice had.*

"How's she doing?"

I hadn't seen Dad arrive, but suddenly he is there behind me, shielding his eyes from the sun and looking hopelessly amongst the throngs of children for Kat.

"She's over there, Dad, by the teacher. Where are your glasses?" It's becoming an irritating habit of his, leaving things behind.

"Left them on the kitchen table. It's fine, I can see perfectly fine."

I roll my eyes, and Esme hits me on the shoulder.

"Hey, Oliver," she gets to her feet and gives him a kiss on the cheek, "good to see you."

Dad breaks into a grateful smile and then Ozzy gets to his feet and shakes his hand and the smile widens further. Dad is like that now that he's sober: impossibly grateful for everything, even an invitation to a sports day. The clinic worked wonders for him. It took a long time, and several attempts, but this is the longest stretch of sobriety that Dad has managed. And, of course, when I required the services of the clinic again more recently, it was useful that I already knew the vast majority of staff on a first-name basis. My request that I remain an anonymous fee-payer was met with initial suspicion but after some gentle persuasion, policies and guidelines were subtly adapted. After all, "Could it really do any harm?" said an email from the board of trustees. Amazing what the smell of money can achieve when seeking the cooperation of private enterprise.

"Has she won anything?" Dad asks, pushing back what's left of his hair and blinking.

"Not yet, but there's still the hoop-jumping relay." Ozzy actually rubs his hands together and I can't help but laugh.

"If she wins the relay, it will be down to the other members of her team," I say fondly, narrowly avoiding another swipe from Esme.

I wait for Dad to pipe up with something about showing more loyalty, but he no longer speaks against me. He merely pats me on the shoulder and laughs. "Well, she's like her mum, isn't she? Academic rather than sporty."

"Ignore her, Oliver," says Esme, "she's just being a grouch."

It was explained to me once, when Dad was first in rehab, that alcohol had been his best friend, that he was likely to be lonely without it, that I would need to find more time for him and give him support other than in the financial sense. Naturally his loneliness had been exacerbated by losing Mo, and to some degree I do understand the grief that accompanies the loss of a friendship. Imogen took a job in Cardiff after she graduated. She wrote to me a couple of times (not an email but a bona fide paper and pen job) but something had altered between us and I couldn't rectify it. Her last letter had ended with the disclosure that she "loved me but no longer understood me", whatever that meant. I've yet to reply to that one.

"What time's your session, Dad?"

"Not until six. Plenty of time yet."

I understand that he has turned up on the off chance that I might still accompany him and I sigh, knowing I'll *have to let him down gently and try to avoid noticing his disappointment. I've been to a million meetings with him but I have plans for tonight and I don't like to alter plans.*

Esme and I leave a mildly subdued Kat in the care of a far more disappointed Ozzy ("She was robbed! The lanky girl had an unfair advantage!") and rush back to the office to accept delivery of the first print run of the new book. We stand by the window, holding separate copies.

"Great cover!" she says, nodding keenly.

"I need you to take one over to the Wellbridge Clinic on your way home."

"What, the clinic over there?" She gestures at the window and looks puzzled. "Why?"

"Someone I know works there and I want him to have the first copy."

"Oh. Okay. You never said you knew anyone in there?"

I ignore her. "Wait while I pop something inside."

When I'm done, she snatches the cheque from my hand and whistles. "Woah, that's a lot of money!"

"Not really," I reply, taking the cheque back, "just a summer bonus. I don't expect a gardener's salary is too good."

She is flicking through the first few pages of another copy while I carefully tuck the cheque inside the book and close it tight.

"So... I need to take this over the road and tell them it's a present for the gardener from a friend?"

"Yes, please."

"This is ridiculous, why not just take it yourself?"

I find a roll of tape in the drawer of my desk and package the book and the cheque in stripy gift wrap.

"*Because I've asked you to do it.*"

"*But don't you want to see your friend?*"

I sigh. I love Esme to bits but she still hasn't learned when to stop asking questions. "*I do. But not yet.*"

She leans on the edge of the desk and I brace myself. But, thinking better of whatever she was about to say, she laughs instead. "*You're so weird.*"

I smile. Like I've not heard that before.

Esme is still thumbing through pages, playing for time. I saunter breezily across the room, making a show of gathering papers and pens and stuffing them into my bag. She's seen the dedication page as I knew she would eventually. I right myself, drop my bag on the desk and wander back to the window. He's raking the leaves again. So many leaves… such a never-ending, thankless task. He rests on the rake and looks up into the trees. A squirrel has caught his eye. How different things could have been. How different they might still be. But easy does it, I don't want to scare him off. Not that he should be scared, he should be grateful and he will be… once he knows everything I've done to save him.

"*Naomi…*"

Here it comes.

"*… this dedication…*"

He will be grateful.

"*Who the hell is Mr Adams?*"

Acknowledgements

The journey of Naomi Rose from my head to the page has been somewhat precarious. Having the will to write is so often at odds with having the time – children, jobs and other bits of life all too often take over – and I want to thank the following people for ensuring that Naomi worked her way back up the list of priorities rather than remaining on a dusty memory stick for all eternity:

To the production team at Troubador, who have held my hand through what would otherwise have been too daunting a process.

To Lynn Curtis, for editing the first real draft and (gently) shoving me out of my comfort zone and into the realms of possibility.

A huge thank you to my family, especially to Tim, who not only read and re-read every section, but somehow believed in me before I had written a single word. To my parents, for always finding the time to make doing what I love, feel so important. And to Liam, Carys and Nathaniel who, with the wonderful and unshakeable faith of young people, kept me from giving up with a simple 'But why would you?'

To Michelle, for the constant supply of coffee and encouragement and allowing me to 'wamp on' about writing for hours without ever telling me to shut up.

To James, for proofreading the final edit, and to my other wonderful, wonderful friends who have read or asked questions or simply pushed me to get it finished, you know who you are - thank you x

About the Author

Kirsten Esden grew up in East London and moved out to Essex to study English and Sociology in 1999. After graduating, she trained to become a teacher and took a full-time post in a primary school. Upon leaving the profession in 2015, she completed a master's degree in Creative Writing. She currently divides her time between writing fiction and working for a charity which aims to reduce isolation for migrant and refugee women living in the East of England.